THIS LITTLE PIGGY

ALLURE OF WALL STREET
SHATTERS A PERFECT LIFE

M.G.CRISCI

BASED ON A TRUE STORY

Cover Art: M.G. Crisci
Cover Design: Good World Media
Edited by Holly Scudero

Published by Orca Publishing Company USA

ISBN-13: 978-1-4566-3259-5 (Amazon KDP)
ISBN-13: 978-1-4566-3064-5 (hardcover)
ISBN-13: 978-1-4566-3063-8 (paperback)

Third Edition

Also by M.G. Crisci

7 Days in Russia
Call Sign, White Lily
Donny and Vladdy
Ergonia, Land of Giant Ants
Indiscretion
Mary Jackson Peale
Only in New York Volume I
Only in New York Volume II
Papa Cado
Project Zebra
Salad Oil King
Save the Last Dance
She Said. He Said.
Still Standing
The King of Violins
This Little Piggy

Learn more at

mgcrisci.com
twitter.com/worldofmgcrisci
YouTube.com/worldofmgcrisci
facebook.com/worldofmgcrisci

Table of Contents

1.

The $20 Bet

NEW ROCHELLE, NY, 1992

It was Victor's first college mixer, and he was a bit intimidated.

As the son of two middle-class Italian-American immigrants—one a butcher, the other a telephone operator—his social calendar consisted primarily of dates with local *guidettes*—noisy girls who simultaneously chewed gum and spoke with a heavy New York accent.

Victor's parents wanted a better life for their son, which meant getting a good education. When Victor's best friend and next-door neighbor, Jim Badino, decided to attend Iona, a small commuter college less than 20 miles from home, Victor followed suit.

~

"It's time for us to step outside our comfort circle," said Badino. "There's a mixer at Good Counsel College this Friday evening. Let's crash the party."

"That's a pretty snooty, upscale kind of place," said the insecure Victor. "Can't we start with something where the girls are a little easier?"

"Don't you want to see how the other half lives?" laughed Badino, who was a year older than Victor and the seasoned veteran of three prior college mixers. "I guarantee they won't bite unless you bite them first!"

~

Soon, the two boys, dressed in sportscoats and ties, were sipping punch in the Good Counsel student lounge. They were surrounded by a chatty group of polished young women, who were subtly eyeing the available inventory of young men.

The D.J. began to play *Just the Way You Are* by Billy Joel. Badino headed for a tall, slim girl in a simple, elegant black satin dress. Moments later, they were dancing cheek-to-cheek.

Badino pointed at a girl standing alone. Victor stared at the floor self-consciously. When the music stopped, Badino waved Victor over. "Victor, say hello to Lois, and this is her best friend Sandra."

Sandra's Mediterranean complexion, dark eyes with a touch of yellow, and long black hair looked like something out of the pages of *Vogue* magazine. As Victor stared, she smiled shyly. Bryan Adams started to sing *Everything I Do, I Do for You*. Badino and Lois returned to the dance floor. Victor thought, *What the hell.* "Sandra, may I have this dance?" She paused. There was a certain sparkle in her eyes.

"No, thanks," she said.

Her rejection made Victor more determined—he decided he wouldn't take no for an answer. "I'll make you a deal," he smiled. "I promise I won't ask you to marry me until the second dance."

Sandra remained aloof, but Victor sensed he was wearing her down. "Trust me, I understand your reluctance. But I assure you, I'm not who you think I am."

"And who is that?"

"The dreaded Joker that Batman has been chasing around Gotham City for years."

"That's was lame," she said with a smirk. "Is that the best you can do?"

"How about I get down on my knees and beg?"

She smiled. "Now that's more like it. But where are my roses?"

~

Michael Bolton started singing *To Love Somebody*. Victor opened his arms and Sandra entered. She gently placed her head on his shoulder. At that moment, Victor knew he was one and done—*he had found his soulmate*. They spent every minute together for the rest of the evening.

As the mixer came to a close, Sandra wrote down her phone number. Badino said goodbye to Lois with a big kiss. Victor looked at Sandra, but she shook her head no. "Girls like me never kiss boys like you the first time they meet them."

On the drive home, Badino started to laugh. "Now that was one sensational pair of chicks. I see you *almost* got to first base."

~

"Did Sandra tell you about her little agreement with Lois?" asked Badino later.

"What agreement?"

"Sandra didn't want to come. She told Lois the only way she'd go to the mixer was if Lois dressed in a black negligee and wore heels as a disguise."

"Looks like the nuns who chaperoned don't own slinky evening attire," laughed Victor.

"Lois and I agreed that the next time we get together," boasted Badino, "she'd wear the same nightgown but ditch the heels—*and* Sandra. Speaking of Sandra, it looks like you did okay."

"That's one way to put it," Victor replied.

"Is there another way?"

"Yeah, I've decided I'm going to marry her."

"Just like that. Does she know?" asked Badino.

"No, not yet. Turns out Sandra is only a high school senior. She crashed the party because Lois is a Good Counsel freshman."

"So, let me get this straight," smiled Badino, "you just met a pretty high school senior and have decided—at some point in the future— you're going to marry her."

"Yup, and sooner rather than later," replied Victor matter-of-factly.

Badino laughed hysterically. "Sport, you've been watching too many Cinderella movies. I'll bet you ten dollars that it doesn't happen at all. Not sooner. Not later."

"Make it twenty," Victor replied. "And I want the bet to be paid in full at the wedding—no IOUs."

~

During the next two years, Victor wore down Sandra's resistance, despite her protestations that she was too young. The couple married a few days after Sandra's 20th birthday, and had two kids and tons of responsibilities before they were 23.

2.

A Girl Named Sydney

LONG BEACH, NY, 2007

Driving forty-five miles in a torrential downpour from Greenwich, Connecticut, to Long Beach, Long Island, was not Sandra's idea of a dream evening.

"If I didn't love you so much, I'd make *Fatal Attraction* look like a fairytale," said Sandra. "Tell me again, why are we going to a birthday party in a driving rainstorm with a $250 bottle of wine for a woman named Sydney?"

"Johnny says his wife is good people; we'll like her."

"You're telling me that pothead who works for you is married to a woman named Sydney? Why on earth would someone name their daughter Sydney?"

"Babe," Victor shrugged, "I know you think Johnny Katz is a bit of a free thinker."

"A *bit*?" interrupted Sandra. "Are we talking about the same person? The guy who decides when *he* wants to work, takes amphetamines before client meetings, and sings Gregorian chants in the bathroom?"

"Honey, you've got to trust me on this one. Johnny has a knack for growing businesses by putting seemingly unrelated pieces together."

"If you say so," glared Sandra sarcastically.

In fairness to Sandra, Johnny and Victor were strange bedfellows. When Victor was promoted to a senior vice president at stodgy Arthur and James (A&J) Advertising on Madison Avenue, he needed an account supervisor to replace himself. After interviewing the available internal candidates, he decided he didn't want a corporate yes-man.

Katz's initial interview was memorable; he had done his homework. After exchanging pleasantries, Katz pulled Victor's favorite sandwich out of his attaché case—lean pastrami and imported Swiss cheese on German pumpernickel, neatly wrapped in aluminum foil.

"I know this is hoity-toity A&J, but it's lunchtime. How about we eat and talk? I've even brought a couple of Dr. Brown's celery sodas [an old-time New York deli staple]." Thirty minutes later, Katz's insightful business observations and self-effacing sense of humor got him the job.

For the next three years, Victor and Katz were envied and despised by their career-climbing peers. But nobody openly challenged their string of successes, which were measured in increased billings and new clients.

~

"What does Sydney do?" asked Sandra.

"Johnny tells me she's a creative advisor to the rock community."

"What does that mean?"

"I don't know." Victor replied with a shrug.

"Let's try a real simple one," said Sandra. "Where did the happy couple meet?"

"At a rock and roll festival."

~

As their new BMW 750 hydroplaned down the poorly drained Cross-County Parkway, a loud ping interrupted the Johnny-Sydney conversation. The windshield wiper motor died and the blades lay motionless. Victor pulled to the side of the road. "Now what?!" cried Sandra.

Victor smiled, trying to make the best of an already tense situation. "Relax; we'll switch to manual mode."

"Manual mode?" replied Sandra incredulously. "Do you make this stuff up?"

"That's why you love me. There's never a dull moment!" Victor explained as Sandra nodded reluctantly. "I'll attach my tie to the driver's side blade and your scarf to the passenger side, then we'll open the front windows enough so you can pull your wiper blade to the right, and I can pull to the left. Once we get to Johnny's, I'll call AAA."

The plan *almost* worked. The couple was able to see just enough to drive, but the heavy rain poured through the slits in the windows. By the time they arrived at the Katz apartment, Sandra and Victor were soaked to the bone.

~

Lido Shores was an upscale maze of tinted glass towers sitting right on the beach at the eastern end of Long Beach. The door to the Katz apartment on the 27th floor opened. A man with thick, bushy black eyebrows, wearing a colorful, floor-length kaftan and a trippy, drug-induced smile looked at his soaking wet guests and smiled. "What the hell happened to you, my man?"

"Long story."

"Sydney, come here. You've got guests. They came by boat across the Atlantic Ocean."

A tall, slender woman with long black hair to her waist stumbled to the doorway. She, too, wore a kaftan. Her eyelids were heavy from the weight of substance abuse. "I bet this is boss Victor and his lovely wife, the nurse. Forgive me, but what was your name? No matter; welcome to Chez Katz. Our home is your home."

Sandra couldn't believe her eyes. In front of her was a large room covered with floor-to-ceiling printed fabric dotted with Persian figures, ancient allegories, and a few electric guitars. Hammered tin candelabras dangled from a brown burlap ceiling, and the air was thick from the scent of hashish. The tent's residents included several partially nude bodies sucking on colored bongs and little clay pipes.

"Let's get you into some dry clothes before you party." Sydney handed Sandra a colorful kaftan. Katz did likewise with Victor. No sooner had they changed than Sydney handed Sandra a clay pipe. "How about a hit or two? It's good stuff from Morocco."

Sandra politely declined, then whispered in Victor's ear, "I want to leave right now!" But Victor reminded Sandra that she would have to grin and bear it until the AAA service truck showed up.

Sandra nodded and handed the wine to Sydney. "Happy birthday. Victor thought you might like a Chateau Margaux. It's a 1982."

Sydney began to giggle and stumble. "Johnny, isn't this sweet? A bottle of wine that's older than your little wife. Why don't you have our guests put the wine on the dinner table next to the other condiments?"

Katz laughed and put the wine on a table filled with pills and powders: some recognizable, some exotic, all undoubtedly illegal.

~

Two weeks later, Katz was accused of selling drugs to senior A&J executives during business hours. Victor tried to be supportive, but the evidence was overwhelming. He had no choice but to fire Katz.

After Katz was escorted out of the building, Victor found a handwritten note in his drawer. "Thanks for your support. I plan to return the favor when next we meet. Till then, your pal, Johnny."

3.

Into the Darkness

MALIBU, CALIFORNIA, 2009.

Wall Street wunderkind Franklyn Ryman's 50th birthday party was miles different from Johnny Katz's.

His 12,000 square-foot pile of reflective glass with bare white walls, trendy white pickled floors, and oversized white-on-white furniture sat majestically on Malibu's northern tip, overlooking the Pacific Ocean.

The male revelers looked and acted like a collection of sleazy 1980s Richard Gere clones, and the statuesque, heavily perfumed women suggested the presence of $2,000-a-night call girls. Booze and drugs littered tables, chairs, and ledges. Van Morrison's *Brown Eyed Girl* pounded over the speakers while guests performed imaginative feats of sex in every nook and cranny of the $20 million-plus pad.

Party host Ryman—heavily-bearded and morbidly obese—wandered among his guests in a hooded, Middle Eastern Jalapa with sandals. The weight of 24/7 excess was written all over his weathered face and hunched body. He was a poster child for the depraved, idle rich.

Suddenly, Ryman paused and looked around, then stumbled down a long flight of stairs toward the blackness of Malibu Beach. Nobody seemed to notice the host was in absentia.

~

As he stumbled along the beach, foamy waves slammed violently on the shore, punctuating the madness of the moment. Ryman was not *in* darkness; he was darkness personified. A milky slime of a white powdery substance dribbled from the corner of his mouth.

His feet slipped, and he tumbled headfirst into the sand along the water's edge. The shifting tides swirled around his bloated frame; a strong undertow beckoned. His body slid toward the pounding abyss. His will, now tattered and spent, subconsciously wished to be carried away by the forces of nature.

At that moment of ultimate surrender, a large horseshoe crab with a ruddy brown shell washed ashore, far from its natural spawning habitat in the Yucatan. The usually mild-mannered crustacean did the unthinkable: it stabbed Ryman's lifeless mass of humanity back to reality with its long, pointed tail. Ryman's gruesome howl created a macabre backdrop to the thundering waves. His time had not yet come.

A few days later, a waterlogged cell phone washed ashore. There were no search and rescue missions, no internet stories, no funeral notices; it was like Ryman never existed.

The prevailing wisdom of friends and enemies alike? Ryman

had drowned after an assumed overdose, and eventually his body would wash ashore somewhere.

~

NORFOLK, CONNECTICUT, 2010.

The front door of the upscale, discreet Silver Hill Detox Center in the sleepy rural town of Litchfield, Connecticut, slowly opened.

Ryman had been a *guest* at the inn for quite some time. It was a bright sunny June day as he headed back to his Sutton Place penthouse. His five senses, clearer than they had been in years, touched, smelled, and felt the world around him. Birds chirped, flowers bloomed, and warm, gentle breezes feathered his neatly combed, long black hair.

Once inside his Manhattan sanctuary, he quickly discovered a depressing reality: his business empire was in shambles and his net worth had been severely diminished.

Several of his privately-held businesses—including his crown jewel, the Chicago Clearing Exchange—had closed their doors for lack of leadership, vision, and cash flow. The assets and control of his remaining businesses—primarily public enterprises, created, built, and structured by him—had been legally transferred to former partners and investors looking to grab the whole pie with no additional capital investment.

Ryman sat quietly, reflecting upon the insanity of the past decade, the observations of his latest shrink, and the urging of his Silver Hill support group. Ryman rationalized that a business do-over was the only sane option. He was confident his "Midas touch" would again lead him to unconscionable wealth; he just needed to identify the right business and the right players.

But first things first. There was a damaged ego to restore to its former glory! The business community needed to realize Franklyn Ryman was alive and well and back in the saddle. He likened his plight to that of Mark Twain: "Rumors of my death are greatly exaggerated." In his prime, Ryman was a master self-promoter with a sixth sense about mœurs du jour.

Three months later, a soulful first-person mea culpa about drug abuse in the executive suite was published in the prestigious *Gotham Business Magazine*. The author? An articulate and anonymous international business entrepreneur gone astray. A man determined to give something back! "I've held nothing back," said the author, "so that others might learn from my mistakes. A man's self-worth should not be measured by the intoxication of business excess."

Ryman roared his approval when the article was quoted all over the internet. He was confident that the article's subliminal message was being heard—Ryman's back, and he wants his pound of flesh.

4.

The Ryman is Back!

MANHATTAN, 2011.

During Victor's 12 years at Arthur & James Advertising, he had become the poster child for what was right and wrong with corporate ladder-climbing in America.

A&J supporters called Victor's rise from the mailroom to executive vice president in so short a time a testament to innovation, grit, determination, and hard work. His detractors said he was a modern-day Sammy Glick: a master at deception, betrayal, and self-promotion fixated on securing a top management corner suite, leaving his more educated Ivy League peers to suck wind.

At 37, nothing appeared out of reach to Victor, including an improbable run at the top. Rumors abounded that A&J's visionary president, Gordon Naye, planned to retire in five years. Victor felt he had the inside track because he was one of only five direct reports, was the company's top rainmaker, and was, not unimportantly, the resident master at blowing smoke. As one of the agency's Fortune 500 clients explained, "When Victor talks to you, he makes you feel like the most important client in the world —at that moment."

~

It was the annual budget meeting for one of the agency's biggest clients, Kraft Foods Company, which customarily spent $200 million in advertising on their various brands. Victor knew the fastest way to increase his year-end bonus was to present new insights that demanded marketplace urgency and a substantial increase in the advertising budget. He likened the client budget meeting to a poker game, where you do whatever you need to do to win, including bluff like hell.

As always, Victor's assistant, a cherubic former hash-slinging waitress from the landmark Square Diner in Tribecca, Janet Waters, booked the cherry-wood paneled conference room on the executive floor. It made the clients feel important and told Chairman Naye that Victor, as he had been for the last three years in a row, was hard at work trying to increase Kraft's billings and income for the next fiscal year by 15 percent or more.

Victor decided this year's urgency message should be based on the agency's new market research study, "The Eating Behavior of Upper Socio-Economic Households."

One of the senior executives, Lofton Key III, a graduate of Harvard business school, offered a doom-and-gloom scenario for the coming year. "Interesting reading. I see consumers are becoming increasingly interested in value-driven, quality food choices. Unfortunately, most of the Piedmont division products are prepared food in a box."

Victor stepped on the gas. "Agreed, the study does make that point. But it also screams that our primary target, moms with kids, want family-pleasing, convenient recipes to fulfill their role as a mother. That's why we've come up with a strategy to offer our bread mix and some of our other basic products as a mandatory ingredient for any everyday meal occasion. And, to maintain frequency of use, we'll offer her more recipe suggestions than all of our competitors combined."

Key frowned. "I like the idea, but not at the risk of eliminating our brand advertising."

"Again, great minds think alike," said Victor. "We both know that the Piedmont division represents more than 30 percent of Kraft profits. So, the idea is to add this *supplemental* ingredient strategy to our ongoing advertising activities."

"How much are we talking about?" asked Key.

"My financial guys did some preliminary spreadsheets. They figure a budget increase of $20 million should pay out pretty easily," replied Victor.

Another client, the more conservative Tom Brown, tried to toss a curveball. "Victor, that's a hell of an increase! Does that include social media activities?"

Victor had no idea, so he bluffed. "Tom, we just ran out of time getting the research findings together. I assumed that was today's priority."

Victor then looked at creative director Anthony Osgood, who had a history of dealing with his impromptu responses. "Tom," said Osgood, "the good news is your creative team is also working on an interactive recipe template that can either stand alone or be incorporated into Piedmont's current website."

Victor went for the close. "Why don't we review the details of the incremental media proposal and get some signatures?"

As Victor passed the contracts around, Janet unexpectedly entered the room and slid a note with a message from Johnny Katz in front of Victor. He waved her off; he hadn't talked to Katz in two years. Janet stood fast, hands-on-hips. "Boss," she said in her distinctly New York accent, 'your *nanny* was begging. You know she's not one of my favorite people, but my instinct tells me you should take this one."

~

"Ladies and gentlemen," Victor said. "I've got a little family emergency. Do you mind if we take a short break?"

"I understand," said Brown, himself a father of three. "These teenagers, just full of surprises."

Victor slipped into the nearby executive bathroom, cell phone in hand. "Johnny, this better be goddamn good; I'm in the middle of increasing my goddamn Christmas bonus!"

"Buddy," replied Katz, "remember how we used to fantasize about being rich beyond our wildest dreams and bagging the corporate bullshit?"

"Ah," smirked Victor. "The stupidity of youth."

"Like Yogi [Berra] said," chuckled Katz, "it's not over till it's over. Your pot of gold has just arrived—THE Franklyn Ryman is back!"

"You pull me from a room full of important clients to tell me Ryman is back." Victor paused, frowning. "Who the hell is Franklyn Ryman?"

"The one and only. Mr. Super Rich, Mr. Mover 'n Shaker, Mr. Wall Street. I've convinced him you're THE perfect poster child for his new IPO [initial public offering]. He wants to meet you ASAP."

"Johnny, give me a goddamn break. How could you even get Ryman's ear, much less convince him that…"

"Long story. Let's just say Ryman and I have taken a few trips together."

"Great, so Mr. Wall Street is a drug addict."

"No, you've got it all wrong," pleaded Katz. "Ryman's clean now, and he took the time to clean me up too. It's all good. Honest."

Despite Katz's past erratic behavior, he had never lied to Victor.

"Okay, let's assume what you've said is true; what the hell do you and I know about public offerings?"

"All you have to do is follow the leader. Ryman's taught me the Wall Street game—it's not exactly rocket science."

"Johnny, I have to get back to my day job; otherwise, I could be selling pencils on Wall Street." He sighed. "Where and when?"

"Epstein's Coffee Shop, Fifty-Second and First, Friday morning at 8:30. You and the Great Ryman, alone."

"You've gotta be kidding. I'm meeting this Wall Street genius at one of the busiest coffee shops in Manhattan?"

"Hey, what can I tell you? He likes the multi-grain bagels and smoked whitefish. Besides, it's around the corner from his apartment."

~

The remainder of the Piedmont meeting went even better than Victor imagined. Piedmont agreed to a $25 million budget increase, $5 million more than initially recommended. "Victor," chuckled another senior Piedmont Foods client and close friend, Steve Thompson. "Consider the extra $5 million a *personal performance* kicker. Christ, you could sell ice to the Eskimos in the middle of winter."

After the clients left, Victor returned to his office. "Boss," said Janet, who was waiting in the doorway. "Mr. Naye called. He wants to see ya on Thursday morning, his office."

Insecurity runs rampant in corporate America. Victor thought to himself, *Am I being fired?* Janet read Victor's body language and rushed to reassure him. "Boss, relax; da man said it was all good. He even asked if I knew how the meeting went."

"What did you say?"

"I told him from the smile on our clients' faces, you did good. Real good."

"Where do you get the chutzpah to tell the chairman that?"

"Boss, was I right?" He smiled and nodded. Janet grinned. "So what's to stress?"

5.

Fairytale Family with Two Careers

NORTH GREENWICH, CONNECTICUT.

As Victor rose through the ranks at A&J, Sandra did likewise at Greenwich Hospital, where she started as a nurse and eventually was appointed director of surgical services at age 35. As the hospital's director of surgery said at Sandra's promotion dinner, "cream always rises to the top."

They lived a step or two beyond their means—their elegant five-acre estate in North Greenwich was a testament to the couple's climb up their respective corporate ladders.

On the personal side, friends called theirs "the fairytale marriage that only happens in the movies."

Quietly, they worked hard at their marriage; both adopted the attitude that 90 percent of everything was not significant, so when one of them expressed a preference, there was rarely a disagreement.

They also made it a point to share—their life was filled with loving families, good friends, happy times, country clubs, private schools, and two sons—Matt and Mark—whom they spoiled to death.

~

It was Matt's sixteenth birthday. Sandra was tending to the final details. The couple had been persuaded by Matt and Mark to open their five-acre estate and 200-year-old, 12,000 sq. ft. colonial home to a "by invitation only" celebration. The kids transformed the tennis court into a disco, surrounded with twinkling lights and strobes. The rap sounds of Ice Cube, Tupac Shakur, and Easy E blasted into the surrounding woods from local disc jockey Mario Vitrella's spanking new Yamaha Stagepas 500 portable PA system. Fortunately, the closest neighbor on their isolated country road was tens of acres away. Sandra thought the arrangements seemed a little lavish for 50 or 60 kids but elected to say nothing, particularly since neither she of Victor had not been asked to contribute a dime to the festivities.

~

"How was Prince Charming's week?" asked Sandra.

"Just your typical run-of-the-mill activity. I convinced some clients from Harvard to spend an extra $25 million, and the chairman invited me to have a continental breakfast in his office on Thursday."

Sandra smiled. "Is that all?"

"Actually, no. Our old friend Johnny Katz rang to tell me one of the kings of Wall Street wants to buy me breakfast on Friday morning and tell me how he's going to make us filthy rich."

Sandra frowned. "The druggie with the wife named Sydney? I thought we'd seen the last of them; I thought they went up in smoke, literally and figuratively."

Victor tried to put his spin on Johnny. "That was then. He's cleaned up and made a name for himself on Wall Street."

"That's one of the things I love about you; you can justify anything or anybody."

Seventeen years of marriage had taught Sandra that this was not the time or place to say more. "Why don't we chaperone tonight's party with a bottle of good wine and talk more about Johnny tomorrow?"

~

Matt's party was not exactly as billed. The invitation had been photocopied and "accidentally" passed around school. A line of 200+ kids stood at an entrance table. Victor pulled Matt aside. "Young man, what the hell is going on? I thought this was a party for your close friends."

Matt grinned. "Dad," he said in his best Madison Avenue-speak, "I'm as surprised as you."

Victor knew his son was blowing smoke. "Yeah? Then who are those two guys collecting money at the entrance table?"

"Dad," Matt smiled winningly. "You should be happy; I'm an evolving entrepreneur. Word got around that we were having a party with live music. I just decided to capitalize on the opportunity. My research suggested that kids would pay ten bucks a head to get in. Look at it this way: I should make enough after expenses to pay for schoolbooks and gas when you lease me a car."

Victor held firm for a moment, then cracked up. "Just keep this damn party under control, alright? The last thing we need is a neighbor calling the cops and your mother getting all over my case."

"Dad, no sweat. Matt's got your back." As Victor headed back to the main house, he saw Matt wave to a black pick-up truck filled with beer kegs sitting in the darkness. Matt pointed to the service road that led to the pool area.

~

Three hours later, two armed policemen approached the patio, clubs in tow. "Who the hell is running this shindig?"

"I am, Officer," responded Victor sheepishly.

"We were patrolling the area and noticed cars parked everywhere."

What could Victor say? In addition to the cars, there was the open presence of a dozen beer kegs with taps and the outstretched arms of countless screaming kids holding cups. Underage party drinking was a real no-no in Connecticut. Victor was sure he was about to meet the citation pad and have the party shut down. Maybe worse.

"Sir, do you know there are cars parked up and down your block?"

"Officer, I didn't realize the party would be…."

"Sir," interrupted the officer. "My partner and I have called for assistance. We're going to place roadblocks at both ends of the street so that no else enters unless they live on the street or are coming to the party. Our captain will give us hell if we don't keep some order. North Greenwich is supposed to be a pretty ritzy neighborhood."

6.

Naye's Unexpected Decision

MADISON AVENUE, NYC.

"Victor," said A&J Chairman Gordon Naye graciously, as they shared a cup of freshly brewed Kona coffee in Naye's private library. "Thanks for stopping by."

"When the king summons, his loyal subject responds."

Naye smiled playfully. "Victor, where do you get this stuff?" He didn't realize Victor was damn serious. "My wife says the same sort of thing."

The silver-haired, nattily attired Naye looked like something out of central casting: witty, articulate, slender, athletic, and in possession of a raspy voice that was authoritative yet warmly engaging.

"By now, you must know how fond I am of you and your wonderful Sandra. Personally *and* professionally." Naye leaned back in his flame-stitched wingback. "You're a smart guy. I'm sure you realize I'm not planning to run this company forever; time waits for no man."

Victor thought to himself that this was a little earlier than expected, but what the hell; he could grow into the role. "Gordon, you're still a young man," replied Victor, blowing a little extra smoke in the boss's ear.

"It's not up for discussion," said Naye. "I've decided to retire in three years at age sixty. Elizabeth [Naye's wife of thirty years] and I have already begun making plans. But I want to lead A&J through this dreadful economy first. It doesn't seem fair to leave the new management team with an albatross around their neck."

"Well, I guess congratulations are in order," replied Victor.

"And congratulations to you too," smiled Naye. "I've decided you've earned a promotion to Executive Vice President and Chairman of the A&J Steering Committee. It comes with a handsome raise and some additional perks. Matt McLain will talk to you about them." McLain was A&J's Director of Senior Management Resources.

Victor was shocked, but pleased. "From now on," continued Naye, "you'll report directly to Rhoda Barbuto."

"I don't understand. Why Rhoda?" asked Victor, confused by the direction this conversation was going.

"I plan to name her my heir apparent. I want you to work closely over the next few years so that you can anticipate her every move. Carry out her vision. You'll be her sounding board. Her backstop. Her confidant. I've convinced her that, as a team, you'll take A&J to the next level."

At that moment, a devastated Victor had only one thought: *I don't believe it; fucking Rhoda Barbuto, fucking Rhoda Barbuto!*

~

There was a knock on the door. Naye pressed a button on the side of his chair. In walked Ms. Barbuto, a drop-dead gorgeous blonde with dark brown eyebrows and just the right number of streaked brunette highlights to top off her New York power broker look.

She had joined the agency about four years before from Richardson, Dobbins, & Kline, one of the world's leading direct response agencies. Using her charm, guile, and good looks, she had convinced Naye and other top managers that the future of brand building depended upon accountability. A&J's roster of sophisticated clients would no longer spend millions on branding without tangible metric responses. Cleverly, she positioned herself as uniquely qualified to lead the agency into the next generation.

Naye had bought her act lock, stock, and barrel.

Rhoda and Victor had bumped heads on a few internal strategic boards. To say Victor was not a fan would be an understatement. He saw Barbuto as a contradiction of everything Sandra was, and everything she stood for as a woman and a professional.

Barbuto didn't miss a beat. She smiled and extended her hand, "I look forward to working with you, partner." Victor returned the accolade; Naye beamed.

~

Minutes later, the two were walking down the hall to their respective offices. Barbuto stopped. "There is one thing," she said, not losing any time. "I heard you walked out of the Piedmont pitch meeting the other day to take a phone call."

"Who said that?" asked a surprised Victor.

"That's none of your goddamn business. You work for me now; don't ever forget that!"

"No disrespect, but my wife had a genuine emergency."

Barbuto brought new meaning to the phrase "if looks could kill."

"Don't give me that bullshit. No man jumps like that for a woman!"

Victor wanted to smack the bitch in the mouth because of her condescending demeanor. But, as Naye said, they were a team, destined to be best buddies. As he had done so many times climbing the ladder, he stuffed his dignity in his pocket and played the game. After all, there were private school tuitions, country club fees, mortgages, and mega real estate taxes to pay, and all the other mandatory trappings of living beyond one's means.

~

Victor toyed with the idea of saying nothing further to Sandra about the Katz call, or even mentioning the upcoming Ryman breakfast and the Naye decision. But they had shared everything for seventeen years. Why stop now? He prepared his pitch like a client meeting. He reviewed the potential objections and rehearsed his responses.

Sandra expressed doubt, concern, and distrust of Katz and his quest for a quick buck—it was simply not the way she was raised. But she also knew that the Ryman opportunity was something Victor was hell-bent on exploring, given the Barbuto decision. So, she feigned support.

"Babe, I'll make you a deal," said Victor, sensing her reluctance.

"If things don't go according to plan, I'll bail. *Promise*." There was nothing else to say. Sandra loved Victor without reservation.

7.

Butter-Stained Hermès Ties

SUTTON PLACE, MANHATTAN.

Epstein's Coffee Shop on Fifty-Second and First Avenue was a madhouse in the mornings.

Take-out customers stood impatiently in line while a little Latino guy named Samosa screamed their orders into a steamy kitchen, which was cluttered with waitresses wrestling for pick-ups. The regulars held court at one of thirty tables, situated so close you could hear farts, curses, and whispers from those nearby.

Franklyn Ryman, wearing a pinstriped suit with pointed lapels, sat quietly in a corner reading the *Wall Street Journal*. Not a big man and certainly no longer young, his jet-black wavy hair and dark eyes gave him an aristocratic presence.

"Good morning, Mr. Ryman," said Victor with a firm handshake.

"Franklyn, please," said Ryman. "Victor, I've heard nothing but good things about you."

Two high-protein, high-fat, high sodium muenster cheese omelets, accompanied by grease-laden sausages and onion-and-garlic bagels generously covered in cream cheese, suddenly appeared. "Eat, eat," Ryman directed, sounding like Victor's Sicilian mother-in-law. "You know, I've traveled the world, but the only place you can get a good muenster cheese omelet is in Manhattan."

Ryman took a bite, then lite up a twelve-inch Cuban Macanudo. "Gotta love these suckers." For the next twenty minutes, he puffed like a locomotive, devoured his omelet and sausages, and told *his* version of his life story.

Victor watched the butter drip off Ryman's bagel onto a very expensive Hermès yellow silk tie, which was resting on a bold burgundy striped shirt with a heavily starched white collar.

"I'm just a kid from a middle-class Jewish family from Malvern, Long Island," said Ryman. "Dad was a mid-level accountant in the financial department at Long Island Gas and Electric Company. He taught me the finer points of Wall Street statistical analysis."

Victor tried to establish a personal rapport. "What a coincidence! As a kid, I used to spend the summers as a vendor on the beaches at nearby Rockville Center. My dad was a butcher who scraped up a little cash to buy a summer bungalow."

Ryman didn't give a shit. He just continued with his own story. "I graduated with honors from high school at sixteen and was accepted into the Wharton School of Business. I think I'm the youngest person to ever graduate magna cum laude from Wharton."

Ryman continued, believing everybody craved the minute details of his life. "My first job was a junior analyst on Wall Street with Smith Barney, developing the company's buy-side research reports."

"That's impressive," said Victor, meaning it.

Ryman leaned back on the wooden chair's rear legs as more butter dripped off his bagel, this time to the floor. "That's when I realized many of America's so-called public growth companies generated increasing profits through mergers, acquisitions, and the elimination of duplicate operating costs, rather than real internal growth. And their shareholders only cared about one thing: increased stock prices. So, in my spare time, I began searching for an undervalued business segment that had not been picked over."

Victor glanced at his watch. They had been at the coffee shop an hour already and he still didn't have a clue about the business Ryman expected to grow.

"Franklyn, this is interesting background but…"

"I know, I know," roared Ryman. "Where is all this going? First, you've got to know the rules. The key to building a major business is never using your own money—use Wall Street. It's cheaper and it carries no personal risk. The second rule is to have a sexy business strategy that investors can easily understand and get excited about."

"That's sounds good in theory, but do you know any success cases?" asked Victor.

"The healthcare industry."

"That's not exactly an unknown industry." Victor was doubtful.

"It was 20 years ago when I concluded that aggregating doctor-owned, private hospitals into a single health care provider brand could have serious Wall Street appeal."

"You mean brands like Kaiser Permanente and Oxford Health?"

"You young guys," laughed Ryman, "those brands didn't exist in the sixties and seventies—I invented them. I was the guy who completed the first health management IPO—$125 million—to buy private hospitals and integrate them into one healthcare brand while eliminating costly operational duplication. The deal was oversubscribed before it hit the market. I named the company United Medical Systems."

"I'm not familiar with…"

"Of course, you're not. It's long since been renamed Yuma Medical."

"Yuma Medical, the $15 billion hospital management colossus?"

"One and the same."

"With that kind of track record, why go back to work?"

"An obvious question," crowed Ryman. "My hospital acquisition scheme was so successful that it wasn't long before competitive hospital networks sprang up. Wall Street's pea-brain analysts thought competition would be a problem—you know, cut market share and stuff. But I saw it as another $10 billion opportunity. I created a venture capital fund that lent money to my competitors."

"Why the hell do that?" Victor asked, now chomping on his own butter-covered sesame-garlic bagel.

"DAAAA!" Ryman screamed. "Would you rather have 60 percent of a $10 billion market or 30 percent of a $50 billion market? Within two years, United Medical was listed on the New York Stock Exchange and my capital fund, Seminal Investors, was listed on the American Stock Exchange. I wasn't even thirty and I had more money than I knew what to do with." Everybody in the place was now staring at their table, but Ryman remained oblivious.

"Then I had another stroke of pure genius! Why not execute my private hospital acquisition strategy in Europe? If McDonald's could export fast food to Europe, why couldn't I export a successful financial model? So, I created Crystal Bond Medical. But I quickly learned hospitals there were inextricably linked to their government's socialized medicine. So, I decided to improvise and consolidate the medical instrument industry instead."

"How did that go?"

"Like taking candy from a baby!" replied Ryman smugly. "We were listed on the London Exchange in less than fourteen months. The money just kept pouring in—I even had two kick-ass 737s: one for me, one for my best friends, my prize Newfoundlands Buzz and Wilfred. The three of us made the rounds at hot parties and cool drug binges. I had more women than I could accommodate—Brits, Scandinavians, whatever."

Suddenly there was silence as Ryman stared, emotionless.

"Franklyn, are you alright?"

"Leave it to me. I fell madly in love with Samantha Brighton, the femme fatale of Knightsbridge in London," said Ryman wistfully. "I chased her all over Europe. Not only did she refuse to marry me, but she unceremoniously dumped me for a Scandinavian jetsetter, Inga Ahlborn! Imagine the blow to my ego

—one of the world's most eligible bachelors, publicly humiliated. I couldn't handle it.

"The ego-driven merry-go-round came to an abrupt halt at my Malibu beach house," said Ryman with surprising humility. "I just fell off the edge of the earth for what seemed like an eternity. Nobody knew where the hell I was, including me. My financial empire crumbled. Some of my assets were stolen by my associates, the rest foreclosed on by the banks. When I regained my sanity, everything and everybody was gone. I've spent the last twelve months getting fit and regaining my mental edge. No alcohol, no drugs."

"Does that mean you're broke?" I asked bluntly.

"Let's just say that the rumors of my demise are greatly exaggerated. But I want to get it all back, plus some."

~

While Ryman was a bit of a pompous ass, Victor sensed he had a certain *dark side* charisma. "I see reservation written all over your face," said Ryman. "You're wondering, why the hell would I need you?"

Victor nodded.

"I'm looking for someone with a polished corporate veneer who craves being filthy rich. The question is, are you that kind of hungry?"

Victor answered the question with another question. "Hard to say; I still don't know what your sexy business concept is."

"Concept! We're substantially beyond the concept stage. I've invested a half-million in researching and developing my new business," declared Ryman, flicking his cigar. "I've also spent serious time with a number of my Wall Street advisors. The unanimous consensus? This scheme can't miss."

"How can I be sure this isn't some business fairy tale?"

"Victor, let's not dick around with all that corporate psychology mumbo-jumbo. Let me be perfectly blunt. I need someone with the right corporate pedigree and who's the right age to promote the project, raise the capital, help close the acquisitions, and then run the companies. Most importantly, I need that person now, right now! Are you interested?"

Victor pushed back. "And the business is…"

"Jesus, I'm sorry; I assumed Johnny filled you in on some of the details since he completed all the research. My new business is simplicity itself. We're going to consolidate the barter trading industry through a series of public financings and high-profile acquisitions."

"But I don't know anything about barter."

"What's there to know?" retorted Ryman enthusiastically. "People have been trading goods for centuries, but it's never evolved into an organized corporate enterprise. My company will be the first to consolidate all the critical functions of re-marketing excess inventory under one roof, thereby becoming the market leader overnight.

"And here's our strategic twist. We are going to concentrate on remarketing consumer products that manufacturers have left for dead. Katz's research indicates billions of dollars' worth of toys, clothing, electronics, and other stuff become passé every year. Most of the manufacturers are geared towards selling new lines, rather than focusing on getting rid of the old stuff."

"That's… sexy?" asked Victor.

"You are quite the in-the-box thinker," replied Ryman smugly. "Wall Street is begging for innovative growth companies that can generate stable revenues and real profits. They've had it with smoke and mirror tech opportunities and accounting gimmicks. I plan to acquire and consolidate historically successful private barter companies with attractive operating histories, and get the public to pay for them."

"Are there enough of these companies to consolidate?"

"Enough! My research says that barter is a highly fragmented $40 billion industry populated by *hundreds* of street-savvy mom-and-pop entrepreneurs who specialize in one type of inventory, or one channel of distribution. Some buy excess inventories for cash. Some buy under a barter arrangement, and some buy for a little of both. But nobody does it all. We will be the first public company of its kind."

"Isn't the government forcing the investment banking industry to batten down the hatches on speculative public financings?" asked Victor.

"I'm not talking about traditional a Wall Street IPO. Been there, done that. I'm talking about raising the initial capital through the more entrepreneurial Penny Stock Market."

"Isn't that segment disavowed by mainstream Wall Street?"

"Who cares? Despite all the SEC saber-rattling, government investigations, and corporate bluebloods making like the penny stock world doesn't exist, tens of millions of dollars are raised in that niche every day by smart, savvy entrepreneurs. Best of all, the rules are fungible; it's like the wild, wild west of investment capital."

Ryman kept pouring it on, partially out of ego, partly out of need. "That's where you come in. All *you* need to do is make the business sound sexy. As you well know, marketing is all in the packaging. With your blueblood pedigree, we'll become America's great whisper stock—mainstream investors will line up at the door."

~

"Do you have a business plan?" asked Victor.

"Here's how I see it. First, we launch the company concept as a $6 million IPO on the penny stock market. That will give us working capital to identify and create 'subject-to' acquisition contracts with three or four of the most successful private barter companies we can identify."

"What's a 'subject-to' acquisition?" asked Victor.

"Best way to describe it is, we use some of the IPO capital to place deposits on those companies we want to buy. Then we restate their historical earnings and eliminate redundant functions to add additional income."

"What criteria do we use to identify core barter companies?"

"Jesus, Victor, please; let's not get bogged down in bullshit details.

Business is not about business; it's about money. If you can't get filthy rich on someone else's money, why bother?"

Ryman flicked some cigar ashes on the floor as he kept rolling. "All you need to do is follow my lead. The stock price will skyrocket and, before long, the traditional investment bankers will be begging to manage our public financing."

"How much do you think I can make?" asked Victor.

"Let me put it this way," said Ryman, who now knew he had Victor hooked. "After two or three additional financings, we'll both be wealthy beyond our wildest dreams. Me for the second time, you for the first."

"But how much is that in dollars?" pressed Victor.

"Fifty, maybe a hundred million dollars in three years. Depends."

"That sounds too good to be true. I need some time to talk to my wife—she's not a big fan of change. Besides, I've had a great career these past 12 years with a first-class organization. I can't just…"

"Oh, I get it," interrupted Ryman. "You want to check me out. Fine. You'll see everything I told you is true. How much time do you need?"

"A few days," said Victor.

Ryman went for the close. "That's fine, but no bullshit stringing me along; I've got to get on with my plan. If not with you, then somebody else. Do we understand each other?" Ryman was good. Very good.

Victor remained unflappable. "By the way, Franklyn, does your new venture have a name?"

"Yeah. International Trading International, Incorporated. The stock symbol is ITI. It's easy to remember and sounds like a subsidiary of AT&T."

The men shook hands, promising to meet again soon. Victor noticed a large butter stain on Ryman's silk tie. "Sorry about that Victor; I have a bad habit of talking and eating at the same time. I wind up tossing away a ton of butter-stained $125 Hermès ties."

Then Ryman noticed Victor's own butter-stained tie and smiled. "Looks like we might be business *and* etiquette partners. Might I suggest a new tie for our next meeting?"

8.

Convincing Sandra to Change

GREENWICH LIBRARY, DAYS LATER.

Victor was determined to figure out how much of Ryman's pitch was fact versus fiction.

After a thorough internet search at home, he decided to rummage through old newspapers and magazines at the Greenwich Library. To his amazement, everything Ryman had said was true, right down to the torrid romance with Brit Samantha Brighton, who turned out to be a cousin of Prince Andrew.

As Victor was learning, Ryman did leave out a few tasty morsels. Inga was Ingmar Ahlborn before her sex-change operation eight years ago. And the British and Scandinavian tabloids had had a field day for weeks following the girls' exploits, making Ryman the laughingstock of corporate Europe.

The humiliating experience changed Ryman's point of view concerning women. Never again would he allow himself to become victimized by something as silly as true love. To restore his persona, he publicly dated only gorgeous, high-profile women. A typical date meant dinner in Paris, followed by dancing the night away at Harry's Bar in London, compliments of his private jet.

~

Victor's research also suggested Ryman's business record was a love-hate relationship with the investment community. Friends said he had a knack for identifying unique niches, raising capital, and making associates wealthy. His foes implied he had absolutely no conscience and did whatever was necessary to achieve his corporate, financial, and personal objectives.

Ironically, in virtually every media interview, Ryman pontificated about the importance of personal integrity. As one of his former business associates pointed out, "Ryman believes his bullshit, despite reveling in a world of murky gray."

As Victor sat in front of the fireplace at home that night, he wondered which Ryman had he met at the coffee shop.

~

The following Monday at A&J, Victor was reviewing his weekly schedule with Janet when the phone rang. Janet picked it up, put a hand on her hip, and shoved the phone in Victor's face, "Boss, it's for you."

"What the hell did you do?" shouted Katz.

"About what?"

"Ryman claims you blew him off," said Katz.

"I told him I needed a little time to think about this opportunity in the context of my A&J career."

Katz went ballistic. "Get real, man! I heard about the Rhoda thing. You can work your ass off for another ten years in your snooty A&J tower, revel in your big fancy office, and walk away with nickels and dimes. And then what? Before you know it, you're forty-nine, out on your ass, saddled with a humongous mortgage and a mountain of college tuition debt. My suggestion? Man up *now*; not many people get this kind of opportunity!"

Victor knew there was merit to Katz's assessment. "Assuming I want to go forward—and I'm not committing, mind you—what's the next step?"

"Ryman said you agreed to meet his attorney, Allyn Tishman, and his financial advisors, Johnathan and Louisa Dothan."

"Fine," said Victor, knowing full well the subject had never even come up. "Set it up for Thursday afternoon."

"What was that about with Katz?" asked Janet after Victor hung up.

"He has this guy who wants to make me the prince of Wall Street world."

"Boss, do you trust me?"

"With my life; why?"

"I have it on good sources that your creative buddy Phil Osgood was talking with Rhoda Barbuto after the Piedmont meeting. She made some cracks about the need to 'make some major personnel changes on the Piedmont account.'" Janet paused. "Are we in trouble?"

"Relax. Gordon could not have been more complimentary when we spoke."

As Victor rode home on the Metro-North train, he began to wonder if Katz's warning about "someday" had arrived early.

By the time he reached Greenwich, Victor had convinced himself that ITI was that perfect surfer's wave. The trick was to get Sandra equally stoked. The last thing he needed was a familial albatross.

~

Sandra was not fond of abrupt change, so Victor had to set the stage carefully. "Hey, honey," said Victor sweetly over the phone as he pulled out of the commuter lot. "Do we have any health care crises at the hospital on this beautiful summer evening?"

"No, all's quiet on the western front," Sandra responded. "I just got in the car. I'll be home in about twenty minutes."

"How about we have a sunset dinner at the Paradise Grill? I'll go home, round up the kids, and meet you there. We can sip a few Bloody Marys, have a piece of fresh fish, and I can watch the sunset in your eyes."

"Sounds wonderful. I'll freshen up a bit and be on my way." Sandra, like her mother before, made sure she was always well-groomed and well-dressed in public. She lived by her mother's axiom: "It's one thing to catch the man of your dreams, and it's another to keep his attention for as long as you both shall live!"

~

Thirty minutes later, the kids were pounding down cherry cokes while Sandra felt no pain due to her third Bloody Mary.

"What a surprise, huh Ma?" remarked the precocious thirteen-year-old Mark, sporting his spanking new $40 Afro filled with dark brown curls. "So, Pops, what's the occasion? Home early enough to have dinner with your wife and kids. Get fired?"

Mark's comment made Victor feel guilty about the time he spent building a career that provided a good life for his spoiled but loving children.

"No, Mark, but Dad did get offered a big job on Wall Street."

Sandra's body stiffened. "Oh, really," murmured Sandra.

"Will you make more money?" asked Mark matter-of-factly.

"Considerably more," said Victor.

"Is that considerably more as in a new dirt bike?" asked Mark. "Didn't we just get an expensive hairdo?" Victor replied.

"What's a new dirt bike got to do with a haircut?"

challenged Mark.

"Boys, why don't we let Mom and Dad talk about this after dinner? If everything turns out as Dad thinks it might, I'm sure you clever young men will be able to extract plenty from Mr. Soft Touch."

The sunset was spectacular, but Sandra hardly noticed. She sat quietly, waiting to hear about *any* potential disruption to her nice, neat world—she wanted the whole story.

"Kids, Mom and Dad need to talk alone in the study; why not play a few video games in the family room?"

"Heads up, Dad," smiled Mark deviously. "Mom never tells us to go play video games!"

~

In full Madison Avenue flower, Victor presented *most* of Ryman's business background to his life partner and best friend. However, like Ryman, he avoided a few details, like Ryman's past relationships with women, his drug abuse, his fungible business ethics, and the seedy side of the penny stock market.

Nevertheless, Sandra was still horrified. "God, this guy's life sounds like a roller coaster ride."

"I think Ryman's a standup guy. He owned up to his business mistakes," replied Victor. "Hell, he was even honest enough to admit he had a marijuana habit."

Sandra remained skeptical. "Maybe it's the fact that Katz made the introductions. I'm not ready to trust him with something as important as your career. I don't get all this acquisition and financing stuff."

There was no way Victor could change her opinion about Katz. "Sandra, Wall Street is not my strength either. But Ryman says raising capital for emerging concept companies happens every day. And he's willing to teach me the fine points while I get paid handsomely."

"Doesn't that strike you as desperate? Somebody promises he's going to make you rich *and* pay you while you learn?" said Sandra.

"Honey, like Ryman said, there is an entirely entrepreneurial side to Wall Street that people like us don't know. He knows firsthand about the pitfalls and roadblocks."

"What do you expect me to say?" said Sandra, sweetly but firmly. "You buy me dinner, feed me a few drinks, and then tell me you want to disrupt a lifestyle that has taken us seventeen years to build. And for what? To take a chance on the possibility of becoming filthy rich based on a business concept that you don't fully understand with somebody you hardly know."

"Look, honey, you're coming at it from the wrong perspective! You've always been a little resistant to change. It's in your DNA. Your dad was a serviceman for General Electric for thirty-seven years. He told me he never even applied for a supervisory position. How many years did he work for that measly pension? I mean, your parents still plan vacations to a precise budget. Is that any way to live?"

"It was a great way to live," responded Sandra, offended. "We had love; we had fun. We never wanted for anything. My mom and dad don't owe anyone a penny. Their daughter went to nursing school and graduated with no student debt. Plus, they've got great friends and good health. What more can you want out of life?"

"What about my reality?" replied Victor. "I have to suck up to every boss I work for because they are either insecure, dumb, or politically wired at the top. At A&J, I'm nothing more than a well-paid hired gun. When I'm used up, I'll be discarded like the legions of forty-somethings before me."

"I'm confused; weren't we just thinking president once Gordon retires?"

"That's a dead issue. The other day Gordon told me he decided to anoint Rhoda Barbuto his heir apparent."

"Rhoda Barbuto? As a woman, that's a great thing to see. But that vicious tart? I thought A&J was the blueblood of bluebloods."

"As you said yourself," smiled Victor, "guys do stupid things."

"That's not what I was referring to," said Sandra, standing face-to-face.

"Let's forget all that. Meeting Ryman was fate. It's made me rethink who I am; I'm not meant to be a by-the-books organization man. Down deep, I'm an entrepreneur, just like my dad."

"Entrepreneur? Wasn't your dad a butcher who had trouble making ends meet?" glared Sandra. "As I recall, it was *my* father who helped us pay for most of the wedding."

"I know my dad was embarrassed till the day he died that he contributed so little. But things were not always that way. In his late thirties, Dad took our family's life savings and went into business with a childhood buddy, Nino Marucci, who had made big money on the black-market during America's World War II meat rationing.

"My dad knew Nino's expansion capital was tainted," continued Victor. "But he saw the partnership as the chance to leverage his expertise and industry reputation to make a small fortune quickly. Unfortunately, Nino had other plans. Thanks to Dad's retail experience and a lot of hard work, by the end of the second year, the operation turned a profit. Three years later, the venture owned sixteen stores and was generating significant cash. But while my dad worked in the stores, Nino worked the books! Dad never knew what hit him. Nino's crew professionally and efficiently embezzled millions, bankrupted the business, and left Dad with virtually all the tax liabilities."

Sandra sat still, quickly sipping her drink.

"Eventually, the FBI caught up with Nino's illegal activities, but he only served a minor prison term because he was smart enough to hide the vast majority of his profits in a labyrinth of overseas financial institutions.

"By the time you and I met, my dad had been forced to go back to work as a part-time butcher, and Mom, after spending thirty years as a stay-at-home mom, was forced to go to work with no apparent skills. That's how she wound up being a telephone operator at the age of 52."

"Finally, after seventeen years, I get the whole story," said Sandra sweetly.

"There's more. Remember when my dad died of a sudden heart attack just twelve months after we married? He left Mom with a real mess. The IRS slapped Mom with an additional claim for $249,547 in back taxes, plus twice that in penalties and interest. They even put a lien on her paycheck."

"She never said a word."

"Personal pride; Mom was a tough old bird. The IRS harassed her for years, believing she hid money in Switzerland. Eventually, they gave up, returned what they had deducted, and let her keep her small AT&T pension."

"I'm so sorry."

~

Victor knew he had Sandra on the ropes; he moved in for the close.

"I never want something like that to happen to us. Ryman's been around the block. He wants to teach me what he knows about Wall Street. It's like getting a new lease on life, with no downside."

Sandra protested weakly. "I'm still a little confused. When did you develop this infatuation with Wall Street? Other than A&J options, what stock do we even own?"

Victor dodged her question with another question. "What would you say if I told you that in less than five years, we'd have enough to never be concerned about money again?"

"Suppose Ryman's brilliant plan doesn't work?" countered Sandra. "What happens to all the monthly bills, the kids' private-school tuition, the country-club dues, and our spanking new $1.9 million mortgage? Just thinking about the size of it sends chills up and down my spine." She paused for a moment.

"Don't we lose the unvested A&J stock options and those other deferred plans you keep raving about?" she continued.

"Honey, those deferred corporate perks are merely paper assets.

Virtually all our cash is locked up in this house and illiquid A&J shadow stock programs. I, for one, would like some breathing room. Ryman is making me a founding stockholder. That means I will own ten percent of the company with no adverse tax consequences. As the company grows, that stock will be worth significantly more than any A&J stock program. We're talking $50 million, maybe more within a few years."

Sandra wasn't convinced, but was willing to give Victor the benefit of the doubt; she could feel his passion. Besides, she was starting to like the sound of $50 million.

~

"So," sighed Sandra, "you *really* want to do this?"

"I really want *us* to do this."

"How does all this happen?"

"First things first. Ryman has invited us to dinner at his place. He's heard so much about you."

Sandra smiled. "I love it when you butter me up."

9.

Things Are Not Always What They Seem

There were estates in King Point, the exclusive waterfront enclave 30 minutes from Manhattan, where cottages started at $5 million. And then there was Franklyn Ryman's humble abode.

The place had twenty-three rooms with eight baths, all garishly furnished like Donald Trump's Fifth Avenue apartment. On top of all that, it had a private beach on Long Island Sound, a five-room cabana, a dock, tennis courts, a spectacular rose garden, a garage full of antique cars, and a barbecue area that comfortably sat five hundred.

Ryman's pride and joy was the state-of-the-art kennel where he kept his two 150-pound Newfoundlands, Buzz and Winfred. The boys had a grooming salon, dining area, and bathing room.

As Ryman, Sandra, and Victor sipped appletinis on the beach, she was uncharacteristically blunt. "Frankly, why does a successful businessman with all of this need to work at all?"

Ryman's uncanny sense of purposeful theater went on display. He knew Sandra had to come along willingly. "I don't *need* to work. It's not about the money; it's about personal growth. Deep down, I'm just a New York City kid who needs the stimulation, the challenge; otherwise, my brain will turn to mush. I also learned a long time ago that making lots of money allows you to give back."

Victor thought to himself, *What a crock!* But Sandra took the bait. Ryman sounded credible with just the proper hint of embarrassment generated by the filthy rich display of opulence that surrounded him.

Of course, nothing was ever quite as it appeared with Ryman. In reality, Ryman was damn close to broke, by his own standards: down to his last $20 million, most of which was tied up in a glitzy Aspen, Colorado, sports club he owned and couldn't sell. Because of his cash crunch and enormous overheads, the King's Point house was being discretely offered for sale through Sotheby's, as were the furnishings, cars, and even Buzz and Wilfred.

~

As the three of them sat around an enormous antique mahogany dinner table with claw feet, the first course arrived, served by a friendly middle-aged lady in a casual uniform. "My goodness, this soup is fabulous," said Sandra.

"Glad you like it. It's a fresh zucchini soup. Family recipe with vegetables straight from my gardens," smiled Ryman. He noticed Victor quizzically staring at the white mound floating in the middle of the soup. "Victor, trust me; the crème Fraiche doesn't bite! Just place a bit on the spoon when you scoop the soup. The tastes complement each other perfectly, as does the sensation of hot and cold." Ryman's description relieved Sandra, who thought the white substance might have been curdled milk.

Subsequent courses were more recognizable. Dining with Ryman was like eating at an intimate five-star French restaurant—with none of the awkward condescension. The baby dandelion and radicchio, the braised trout in rice parchment paper, even the crêpes with beluga caviar were a feast for the eyes and the stomach. Three hours later, Ryman decided to suck up to Sandra with a final toast.

"Victor and Sandra, how about a port for the road? I believe there's a bit of Fonseca '49 left in the wine cellar. Give me a few minutes," Victor and Sandra nodded, although neither had ever tasted vintage port wine. Minutes later, Ryman returned with a dark, dusty bottle.

"Ta-da," said Ryman, bowing and making like a sommelier with a treasure. "Madame, a sweet for the sweet." He carefully removed the cork and poured the deep blue-brown liquid through a cheesecloth filter into a crystal decanter, and ultimately into three antique Baccarat glasses.

Sandra sipped. "Ryman, the port is delicious, and these crystal glasses are fabulous."

"The glasses are pretty," said Ryman toasting Sandra, "but you, my dear, are exquisite."

~

You could hear a pin drop in the car on the ride back. Sandra knew something was bothering Victor. "Victor, why so quiet? It was a wonderful evening; Franklyn was such a gracious host."

"Gracious host! My future partner was hitting on my wife, right in front of my eyes." Victor began to mimic Ryman. "*The glasses are beautiful, but you, my dear, are exquisite.* Christ, I thought I was watching a Spencer Tracy/Katherine Hepburn movie."

Sandra reached over and gave Victor a tender kiss on the cheek. "Jealously becomes you. But never forget: you're the love of my life, and you always will be."

~

An impatient Ryman was confident he had secured Sandra at dinner, but he hadn't heard from Victor in 24 hours. As far as he was concerned, it was closing time.

"Victor," said Ryman on the phone, "you have got one classy wife. What the hell does she see in you?"

Victor was starting to get the hang of Ryman's poker game. He played the Sandra card. "Franklyn, everything sounds great, but Sandra's still a little reluctant. We've been living way over our heads for years; she's worried about taking a short-term cash flow hit for a promising future."

How amusing, thought Ryman, *the organizational virgin trying to best the master.* He decided to let Victor win this hand. "Ahhh, that's an easy fix," said Ryman. "Let's bribe her! How about I give you a sign-on loan? Say $150,000 out of my pocket to cover your family's incidental day-to-day expenses; take her to Grand Exuma and bathe her in the sunshine.

"When you meet my attorney, Allyn Tishman, he'll create an addendum to your founder stock agreement and the employment contract. I'll also tell him to make the side loan non-interest-bearing until you sell a few shares of your stock after it vests."

Victor sensed that another bluff might add to the pot. "Christ, that's unbelievably generous of you, but I think it's about more than about money with her."

"Aww, bullshit, it's always about the money! Let's make it $250,000—that should help with the private schools."

"I'm leaning," replied Victor. "I'll outline the whole deal tonight to her."

"Leaning," growled Ryman. "What the fuck does that mean?

Maybe I've got the wrong guy. ITT is the opportunity of a lifetime for somebody with big balls. It isn't for the faint of heart. I thought you were a savvy New York street kid?"

Ryman had pressed Victor's hot button. "I'm in. I'm in. Just let me break it to Sandra in my way. But no public announcements, okay? Intil the IPO is completed, and I give formal notice at A&J."

10.
Selling Used Parts To Rocketman

"Let's grab a little dinner, just you and me."

Victor could see it in Sandra's eye—she knew something was brewing.

Minutes later, they were in front of a crackling fire at Giovanni's Steakhouse, a homey, local restaurant where the staff knew most of the patrons by name.

"Franklyn called again today," said Victor, sipping a glass of red wine.

"Oh?" said Sandra coyly.

"Ryman upped his already generous equity offer, and he threw in a $250,000 tax-free signing bonus."

Sandra's eyes nearly popped out of her head.

"I'd be the first to admit I don't know the guy very well, but you have to agree it does sound exciting. That sign-on bonus would allow us to get our expenses current, and leave a few bucks for that all-weather putting green I've been dreaming about."

"Why do you get a putting green?" she smiled.

"Well, baby, what's on your wish list? You've probably earned it after all these years of being married to me."

"I agree," smiled Sandra, her resistance weakening by the moment. "I was thinking of a new clay tennis court; that would cut our country club expenses in half."

"That's my girl: the opulent pragmatist."

"Speaking of pragmatism," Sandra said, "how about you run the proposition by Jim Badino one last time before we take the plunge?"

"Why Jim?"

"He's a respected CPA and your closest friend in the whole world, isn't he?"

Badino's business career was ultra-conservative. During summer breaks during college, Badino had interned at the prestigious big-five accounting firm Arthur Andersen & Company. After graduating as an accounting major, he was offered an entry-level position at AAC, married Sandra's girlfriend Lois, and became one of his firm's youngest managing partners. Badino's primary area of expertise was auditing and providing advice to the firm's larger public company clients. He was considered an expert in SEC (Security Exchange Commission) rules and regulations.

~

Badino listened without interruption as Victor painted a rose-colored picture of the Ryman opportunity over an aged New York strip steak and a glass of zinfandel at Peter Luger's Steakhouse.

"So, what do you think, oh wise one?" smiled Victor.

"Like always, the steak is perfect," teased Badino.

"I'm picking up this outrageously expensive lunch because Sandra trusts you more than me. Sometimes I wonder if we got the wives mixed up. You know, part of Sandra loves boring!"

Badino smiled and rubbed his chin, wondering if Victor wanted his advice. "Victor, I can't comment on the validity of the business concept; I have to assume there is a barter trading business that could potentially be consolidated. But the idea of funding a major corporate enterprise through the penny stock market sounds suspect."

"Why?" asked Victor.

"I did a little research on Ryman. His specialty seems to be operating on the lunatic fringe of Wall Street. He's made and pissed away fortunes and left a lot of destruction in his wake. You might want to tread cautiously; the SEC is looking hard at Ponzi schemes post the Bernie Ebbers fiasco."

"ITT isn't a Ponzi scheme."

"No and yes," said sanguine Badino. "You're not planning on using other people's money to pay early investors, but you *are* projecting future earnings based on restated historical performance, absent the costs of reducing operational duplication."

"Translation?" Victor asked.

"You may mislead investors by significantly overstating future performance."

"That's not possible," Victor replied with conviction.

"Let me tell you something, my friend," warned Badino. "You may be a good corporate pitchman, but Ryman is in another league. He could sell used parts at a premium to that crazy North Korean Rocketman."

"Thank you, Pope Badino. Any other words of wisdom?"

"As a matter of fact, yes. Why do you have to rely exclusively on acquisitions?"

"Ryman says it's the fastest way to build earnings, and that's what Wall Street is buying these days."

"I'm guessing your partner isn't trying to build an enduring business," replied Badino. "Given his history, I'm guessing he plans to create a sexy earnings story, then cash out as unsuspecting mainstream investors place their bets."

"Jim, with all due respect, you're making a value judgment without ever meeting the guy in person."

"Fair comment," responded Badino.

"I think the guy can take Sandra and me where we want to go."

"But at what cost?" said Badino. "Just ask yourself that."

~

That evening, Victor gave his version of the lunch to Sandra. "Jim says we're good to go. By the way, Franklyn has invited us to brunch at his apartment on Sunday."

"Another chapter in the lifestyles of the rich and famous?" laughed Sandra.

"No. Franklyn said it would just be you, me, him, and his girlfriend."

"That sounds surprisingly normal," smiled Sandra.

11.
Sutton Place Penthouse

The lobby of Ryman's apartment at 45 Sutton Place looked like the lobby of the Bellagio Hotel in Vegas, with bubbling fountains, ornate statues, and elaborate artwork.

"We're here to see Mr. Ryman," Victor announced to the concierge, who pointed to the elevator and pressed the button to the 27th floor.

"And the apartment number?" Victor asked.

"I'm sorry, sir," said the concierge with a toothy smile. "Mr. Ryman *is* the 27th floor!"

Sandra gulped.

When the elevator doors opened, Ryman welcomed Sandra with a warm smile and a hug. "I've been looking forward to seeing you again."

What an act! Rhett Butler on the comeback. Sandra was charmed. Ryman offered glasses of Dom Perignon 1993 to top off the delivery.

As the three toasted their future together, a gorgeous woman with a sensational figure and long black hair strode out of the master suite and smiled erotically at Ryman. Without missing a beat, he returned a grin and then turned to his guests.

"Sandra and Victor, I'd like you to meet my girlfriend, Aruba Lucka."

"Lucka is a very unusual last name," commented Victor. "I've only run into it once before. As a junior executive, I worked with a talented German photographer by the name of Gerhardt Lucka.

We developed an award-winning advertising campaign for Chiquita Bananas."

"I know the work well," said Aruba, "some of the artwork hangs in our gallery at home."

"What a wonderful coincidence," bubbled Sandra. "How did you acquire them?"

"Quite easily," replied Aruba. "I'm Gerhardt's wife."

Brunch went downhill from there. Victor got the silent treatment from Sandra during the trip home, through the family's Sunday dinner, and into the Monday morning commute. Not until the next evening, after the kids were in bed, did Sandra break her silence.

"Honey, you know I want to say yes. The money is a real carrot. But it's also about character; you and Ryman are from different planets. What makes you think your partner, who is screwing another man's wife, will deliver on his promises to you?"

"Baby, give me a little credit, will you?" Victor replied. "Remember, I'm a street kid from the South Bronx. I've had family in THE family. I know bad actors and how to work around them."

"I've heard you use that tough-guy stuff for almost 20 years," Sandra replied. You and I both know you're really just a baby teddy bear who cries when he hears a romantic ballad on his cell phone."

"I'm growing up. Everything will be in writing, and to my satisfaction. Even then, I'm not on board until the funds and shares are transferred."

"Suppose the business plan doesn't work?" asked Sandra.

"That's another non-issue. Even if ITT failed, at worst case, I can always get a top tier job at one of the international agencies. The current recession will be over and the agencies will be clamoring for my *real-world* business experience."

Sandra was wearing down from the pressure of it all. "Tell you what," Victor suggested. "Let's give it one more shot. Invite Franklyn to our place for a Sunday afternoon barbecue. Check him out on our turf, and we'll see if he can pass the Sandra smell test."

"Fair enough."

"Besides, if we stage this right, I can lay the groundwork to renegotiate for more equity and a higher base salary."

"I thought you already had a deal."

"It's only a *verbal deal*. It never hurts to squeeze a little more just before the ink dries. When my new venture goes public, I want everybody at A&J green with envy, especially that bitch Rhoda Barbuto!"

~

"Franklyn, you know we've had a few false starts with Sandra, so think of Sunday as a final audition."

Ryman interrupted incredulously. "You can't be for real. I've never met a guy so concerned about his wife."

"The solution is simple," continued Victor. "Just suck up to my kids big-time and assume Sandra will be watching."

Ryman showed up at Victor's Greenwich estate with another beauty—a rare black 1962 Morgan convertible in mint condition.

"What a sweet little car," smiled Sandra as Ryman pulled into the driveway.

"Sandra, that's the first time I've ever heard a $250,000 car called sweet!" chuckled the casually dressed Ryman in his most charming tone.

Sandra gulped and then took Ryman on a house tour.

It was now Ryman's turn to gulp. He was pleasantly surprised at the 45-foot living room, the 70-foot kidney-shaped pool with a trickling waterfall, the five-room cabana with a fully equipped kitchen, and the indoor hot tub. But what impressed him most was the wine cellar, carved out of solid granite in the basement of the 240-year-old section of the house.

As the two men walked down to the pool area, Mark and Matt were playing one-on-one on the basketball court at the far end of the tennis court. Victor waved. "Hey kids, come over here. I want you to meet somebody,"

Ryman picked up signal. "Looks like you guys enjoy basketball?"

"Are you that rich guy?" asked Mark innocently.

Sandra was horrified. "Mark!"

"What's the matter? What did I say?"

"Enough," said Sandra. "Say hello to dad's friend, Mr. Ryman."

"Mark, I'm not only rich," smiled Ryman, "I used to play basketball."

"Really? How about a little two-on-two?" suggested Mark with a confident smile. "You and my dad against Matt and me?"

"Victor, you up for the challenge?" asked Ryman.

Victor nodded. Moments later, Ryman returned from his car with a small yellow canvas athletic bag. He slipped on two giant blue kneepads like he intended to dive after balls all over the court. The boys laughed. They should have known better. "Victor, let your sons take the ball out first." He said with a wink. "I'll guard Mark, and you take Matt."

"Got it," Victor replied.

Mark inbounded to his brother. Victor guarded Matt as he drove to the basket. Ryman did a good job of fronting him, but Matt casually passed behind his back to Mark, who dribbled ten feet from the basket and waited until Ryman lumbered over. Mark then passed up an open shot, dribbled under the basket past an outstretched Ryman, and flicked in a reverse lay-up.

"Winners out," laughed Mark. Ryman had been stuffed by a thirteen-year-old kid!

The boys ran the same play again. Burned once, a determined Ryman turned up his game. Mark couldn't dribble around him. When he tried to shoot a jumper, Ryman blocked the ball with a vengeance. Matt waved Mark into a brief huddle. "I'll pass you the ball, then go back door on Dad. If Mr. Ryman tries to double back, you should have an open shot."

Sure enough, Matt's strategy worked, keeping the young boys competitive with men twice their size and three times their age. In the end, Ryman and Victor ultimately lost by a basket, but Ryman scored points with the kids, as planned. More importantly, he scored big with Sandra. Her apprehensiveness about Ryman's womanizing began to dissipate as she watched the display of courtside machismo unfold and her sons' evident respect for Ryman's competitiveness. He had passed the smell test.

After the game, the four sweaty bodies jumped into the pool to cool down while Sandra prepared the barbecue with steaks and burgers, along with wine and beer.

"Great family, great food, great home," said Ryman. Sandra beamed.

"Who takes care of this place?" asked Ryman.

"Originally, I thought I could," replied Victor. "But after spending an entire weekend cutting the lawn, common sense took over. Now, we have a part-time staff of three. The fact of the matter is, we could use them full time. The main house is 200 years old and always needs something, plus the grounds and adult toys are high maintenance."

"Victor," said Ryman looking straight at Sandra, "I guarantee you've worried about stuff like that for the last time."

Sandra was cooked and done!

12.

Negotiating in Bad Faith

As agreed, Victor cabbed it to the offices of attorney Allyn Tishman on Forty-Fourth, off Fifth Avenue, to review the SEC filing document and finalize his equity agreement, loan note, and employment contract.

Tishman was nothing like Victor imagined—he was a small, almost frail figure with a warm smile, wavy salt-and-pepper hair, and tiny reading glasses hanging from his nose. It was like meeting Mr. Rogers, complete with a light blue sweater vest, away from his PBS neighborhood. "Victor, so nice to meet you. Franklyn has told me so much about you. Why don't you come into the conference room, and we'll chat."

Tishman sounded friendly enough, but his reflective stare suggested a calculating, analytical mind. The depressing conference room consisted of a big table with just enough space to sit down and get up. At the far end of the table sat a jar of peanut butter, a dish of thin, unsalted cracker squares, and a pitcher of iced tea.

"I gather you and Franklyn go back to the hospital days," Victor said in a cheery voice.

"It been quite an exciting ride, *both ways*," smiled Tishman. "I was just about to have some lunch. Perhaps you want to share? I've made high-protein peanut butter part of my lunchtime regimen. Interestingly, the baked whole-grain crackers and their unrefined complex carbohydrates are a natural complement to the peanut butter. I wash it down with a refreshing cinnamon-apple herbal tea. Like all of us, I'm trying to fight the ravages of age."

Victor didn't know what to say. Was this some kind of test? Tishman continued. "Franklyn tells me that your knowledge about raising capital in the public marketplace is a bit limited. Mmmmm."

"That's true," Victor admitted. "That's why I told Franklyn I might be the wrong candidate for the project. My real business expertise is working with major corporations, developing and implementing marketing programs that increase product sales. I'm part-management consultant, part-salesman. Given the recession and all the market turmoil, am I really what Wall Street wants?"

Tishman was certain Victor's humility was a pitch for more of something; he just didn't know what. "Not an issue," said Tishman, daring to wonder if Ryman had made a gigantic blunder. "There's nothing complex about the Wall Street financing process, particularly in the penny stock sector. I'll be advising you over the coming months as we develop the red herring. You'll be quite knowledgeable by the time you begin to meet potential investors."

"What's a red herring?" asked Victor.

"My, my, we *are* starting from scratch," chuckled Tishman in a friendly but condescending tone. "A red herring is another name for a prospectus, which is the document we will be submitting to the Securities and Exchange Commission to obtain the necessary federal approvals to market our common stock directly to the public. A portion of the document is printed in red to reinforce the speculative nature of a given offering to prospective investors. Hence the name."

~

"Victor," said Tishman, sounding like consigliere Tom Hagen in a scene from *The Godfather*, "I've spent most of my day working on the language of the equity agreements and the employment contracts that get incorporated into the SEC red herring. Ryman has signed off, but we need to make sure you're satisfied. As you know, all these documents become part of our filing with the SEC.

"Let's review your employment contract first, shall we?" continued Tishman. "A five-year deal with a Year One base of

$200,000 increasing to $400,000 in Years Two and Three, and $550,000 in Years Four and Five."

Victor hesitated to communicate concern. "Allyn, I've been thinking about the proposed Year One base. If it were just me, I could live with it; I understand the long-term rewards. But, as Franklyn may have mentioned, we've got a bit of a complication. It's called my wife, Sandra. Franklyn saw how we live, what she expects. I think she'd insist I pass on the deal rather than take such a salary cut."

"I understand," said Tishman, annoyed but pleasant. "But you do realize you're also being granted twenty million founder shares?" At that moment, Victor had no idea that Ryman had five times that amount, plus an equal number of stock options. "Do you have any idea what your position could be worth?" asked Tishman. "Do the math; assume the stock rises to fifty dollars a share within five years, like Franklyn's other public deals. That's a hundred million dollars, maybe more."

"Allyn, I agree the number could be staggering," said Victor, "but as Sandra will tell you, that's only the company's projection."

"I can appreciate Sandra's position," said Tishman, putting on his sincere face. "I've been married twice myself." Victor didn't know that Tishman had come out as gay after his second wife left with a 23-year old male stud.

"I might also point out you have a generous performance-based annual bonus provision, which should amount to hundreds of thousands per annum."

"I appreciate that," Victor replied, "but I've been around the block a few times. We all know bonuses are always discretionary."

"Let's not cause Sandra to fret; I'm sure I can convince Franklyn to increase your Year One base to $250,000, and increase the Years Two through Five proportionately."

~

That settled, Tishman pressed forward. "Let's move on to the earn-out provision of the contract. Per our previous conversations, your annual bonus will be equal to three percent of the company's after-tax profits during the duration of your five-year employment contract. The bonus will be payable in ITT stock, pegged at the then market price."

"Understood," Victor replied. "But can you explain why Franklyn's bonus formula is significantly different?"

"I beg your pardon?" said Tishman, realizing he had underestimated Victor's financial prowess.

"Franklyn gets a five percent bonus, which seems like an appropriate spread between the number-one and number-two guys," said Victor. "But why is his five percent *before-tax* and my three percent *after-tax?*"

Tishman got the message. "I must have misunderstood the deal. I'll revise that section."

"And what about the loan documents?" asked Victor. Tishman glared. "What loan papers?"

Ryman appeared at that moment. "Sorry I'm late, fellows; where are we?"

Tishman summarized.

"Victor, it never occurred to me we needed papers for our loan," commented Ryman. "My word is my bond."

"I know that Ryman, but this is about providing *our* mutual friend Sandra with the comfort she needs."

"Gentlemen, will you please explain what's going on," said Tishman, flabbergasted at Ryman's largess, since this new tax-free loan, if audited, would never pass the IRS smell test as a business deduction.

He also wondered how the cash-strapped Ryman would come up with a quarter of a million dollars in the next thirty to sixty days.

"Would you fellows mind if we take a break?" said Ryman. "Nature calls." Tishman got the signal and followed Ryman into the bathroom.

"Franklyn, where is this $250,000 pre-offering loan coming from?"

"You."

"Me? Hardly."

"Allyn, this is not a discussion. I've made you millions. I covered your ass during those SEC inquiries. You owe me."

"And if I refuse?"

"Your ITI founder stock goes back to the treasury, and I blow the whistle and take you down."

"You wouldn't."

"Try me, motherfucker."

~

"Boys, now that we've wrapped up the nickel-and-dime haggling," said Ryman upon returning, "I've got some important news on the financing front. The Penny Boys love our *subject-to* acquisition strategy."

"Our what?" asked Victor.

"O ye of short memory," smiled Ryman. "We discussed this in our first meeting at the coffee shop. Step one is to create a sexy concept IPO to raise the first $10 million in the penny stock market, and then use that cash to place down payments on those acquisitions, allowing us to raise larger capital trunches with a mainstream investment banking firm."

Victor remembered no such conversation but chose to give Ryman another pass. "Sounds like we're buying houses with no money down," joked Victor. Nobody laughed.

13.

Ryman Takes Care of Number One

Victor's details now complete, Ryman wanted to establish his ego as the undisputed heavyweight champions of all things Wall Street. Tishman watched the show.

"After talking to a number of my former investment bankers, I was surprised at Norwest's bandwidth," said Ryman, acting like Dick Tracy. "I discovered they are the penny stock market's leading underwriters with a long track record track in completing IPOs and performing post-IPO market-maker functions." Ryman conveniently overlooked the fact that *The Wall Street Journal* had branded Norwest "a charlatan to be watched."

"Franklyn, like I said to Allyn, some of these terms are new to me. What's a market-maker?"

Ryman huffed and puffed. Tishman took over. "Victor, think about it this way. Selling the IPO is the beginning of the journey, not the end. There needs to be continued interest in the stock, so as our share price increases, it in turn lowers the price of future acquisitions we buy for cash and stock, or all stock."

"Got it; we capitalize on Norwest hyping the stock," said Victor matter-of-factly.

Tishman glared. "I wouldn't use that term. Wall Street has rules. Do we understand ourselves, Victor?"

Ryman continued to summarize his findings. "Norwest's underwriting fees are half that of Merrill Lynch and Goldman Sachs, and they own the kind of investor database that's accustomed to taking a little more risk to make 50 and 100 times their investment. Everybody is looking for the next Microsoft."

Victor mused out loud, "Microsoft."

"Yeah," said Ryman. "Most people don't realize Microsoft began as a penny stock. Look what Gates and Ballmer are worth now."

"And, thanks to ITI's rapid growth acquisition strategy, our advisory group suggests we issue six hundred million shares, set an opening share price of 50 cents, and make available 400 hundred million shares to the public."

"What happens to the other 200 million shares?"

"They are held by management and the advisory group. That's where your 20 million shares originate from."

"Who comprises the advisory group?" asked Victor.

"They are a group of people I've worked closely with over the years," said Ryman dismissively. "Other than Allyn, their names won't mean anything to you, but you'll get to meet everybody in due course. The only other financing matter I believe we need to address is Norwest's request for a pre-launch meeting with their brokers, so we can tell them the ITI story first-hand and light a fire before they hit the phones."

"I don't see any problem with that," said Tishman, confident Victor knew nothing about SEC *quiet periods* when managements are required to remain silent until their prospectus is approved. "Do you, Victor?"

"No!" said Victor, dazzled by what millions of shares meant to Sandra and him.

"So, do I have a motion to approve Norwest Securities as our underwriter?" said Ryman.

"I so move," said Tishman.

"I second," said Ryman. "The motion is so passed."

"Good. I'll call Norwest and tell them to get the word out that they are the exclusive underwriter for one smoking hot IPO. Ryman, perhaps it's appropriate to explain the details of the financing to Victor, since they are quite favorable to him and his family."

"I'm good," Victor said. "I'm a multi-millionaire."

Ryman winked at Tishman. "I guess our new Chief Operating Officer is starting to understand the fine print!"

~

Two hours after the meeting, Victor burst through the front door of their home, smiling like a Cheshire cat. "Our comp deal is done. I took the boys to the cleaners, thanks to my Sandra guilt-complex strategy."

"What in the world does that mean?"

"Every time they wanted to shut me down, I said I needed more money because of the style to which you had become accustomed!"

"You didn't!" said Sandra, horrified.

"Aww, don't worry about it. On Wall Street, everybody employs *some version of the truth* to gain advantage. But cash flow is only one part of the game. The real increase in our net worth is based on the company's valuation."

Sandra smiled. "I have absolutely no idea what you are talking about."

Victor took out a pad of paper and started to scribble the numbers he had been given. "Based on conservative projections, the company valuation should grow tenfold over the next five years. In plain English, that means we will be worth $10 million when we go public in a few months, and worth over $100 million in the not-too-distant future."

"I have so many questions; I don't know where to start."

"Try me."

"What does ITI make?"

"Nothing. We just take old products nobody wants anymore and sell them to people who want to buy them."

"Why would they do that?"

"Because they are dirt cheap."

"If you sell products dirt cheap, how can the company grow so fast?"

"There an entire wholesale market chain that…" Victor paused. "Let's do 20 questions some other time. Right now, I feel like celebrating my newfound wealth over a glass of wine with my best friend."

Sandra wanted to support her husband's newfound passion for Wall Street unconditionally and loved the idea of never having to worry about money, but she felt conflicted.

"Are you sure about all this?" she asked sweetly.

"Honey, I saw it for myself. You and the boys had a great time getting to know Ryman at our house. He's got a few warts, but then, don't we all? Trust me, as you have these past 20 years."

"When is all this supposed to happen?"

"The final papers have to be approved by the government before we can commence operations," said Victor. "The boys estimate the process could take six weeks, more or less. So, remember that until then, it's business as usual at A&J, and at your hospital."

~

Victor failed to realize that Ryman had taken care of *Number One*. He granted himself 80 percent of the 160 million founder shares and another 160 million warrants to purchase an equal number of shares at the opening price of fifty cents. Tishman designed the option to have a five-year life and could be exercised via a non-interest-bearing, 10-year loan from the company.

14.

Marino's Cuban Cigars

A long black limo with tinted windows pulled up in front of Ryman's Sutton Place apartment.

In the back seat sat an expressionless, heavy-set man with slick, straight black hair, wearing a black suit, a black shirt, a white tie, and black sunglasses. "Franklyn," said the man, "I'm Marino, President of Norwest Securities; we spoke on the phone."

With introductions made, Marino broke out his favorite Cuban cigars. Moments later, the rear of the limo resembled a gas chamber. "What bullshit is this Cuban embargo thing, eh?" said Marino. "Makes these fucking cigars about the same price as an ounce of gold. It's just not right. The damn government should do something about it." Ryman nodded agreement.

"Our mutual acquaintance tells me you're one hell of a stock promoter," Marino looked at Ryman through the haze. "I think your skill and my backroom should make this an easy deal."

"Any concerns you can't do it?" asked Ryman. "It's a lot bigger than the typical penny IPO."

Marino laughed. "Not to worry. Assume the deal is done."

"And the aftermarket?"

"So long as you do *your* part," said Marino. "My rooms are built to handle the churn. Capische? Our early prime investors prefer to make most of their money at the opening bell. And then they spread the word so the suckers come to play, and my guys make a ton on the back end."

"It might be useful if I explained my hospital management experience," said Ryman. "I built a major enterprise by financing and merging private hospitals into a large corporate enterprise. I plan to do the same thing with ITI, creating a major trading company built through acquisitions and mergers."

"What the fuck has that got to do with the price of tea in China?" asked Marino impatiently.

"This deal is just the first phase of our financing plans." Ryman took the cigar out of his mouth for only a moment. "There will be several other rounds. When I'm finished, ITI will be on the New York Stock Exchange. I plan to grow the company dramatically, make the stock so valuable that acquisition prospects line up to be acquired, and we…"

"I don't give a shit about the New York Stock Exchange or your business strategy. That's your business!" interrupted Marino. "It's really simple—you ain't doing jack unless the initial stock price takes a ride. And that requires Marino and Company leaking some juicy insider stuff nobody else has."

Ryman felt compelled to show Marino that he was dealing with the big boys. "I'm not sure you get it. There'll be new information around every turn. I guarantee ITI stock will be an attractive investment, current and future."

"Let's be real clear," said Marino coldly. "I'll do the deal, but don't fuck with me about future leaks. It's dangerous to con a con man."

The two men got out of the smoky limo looking like two stooges in a fire drill and headed into the Four Seasons, New York's most sophisticated, most elegant, and most expensive restaurant. The maître d' scanned the pair and escorted them to the restaurant's less prestigious area, the Bar Room. "I believe we reserved a table in the Pool Room," said Ryman angrily. "The Bar Room is for peons."

"I beg your pardon, sir. We do not refer to Four Seasons' patrons as 'peons.' Furthermore, there are no tables in the Pool Room. We are fully booked this evening."

"I think if you look at your reservation book again," said Ryman, slipping the maître d' a sawbuck, "You'll notice we specified the Pool Room."

"Ahhh, yes, here it is!" came the smiling reply. "You're right. You did confirm the Pool Room. Sorry about the misunderstanding. Let me show you to your table."

At a different Pool Room table, out of sight, sat an old friend and business associate of Allyn Tishman's, Irwin Friedway. Friedway was an independent investment banker who looked like a seedy Jack Nicholson, only shorter. A Harvard MBA cum laude, Irwin wore a dark linen suit, a white tie, and a white-on-white shirt with a $1000 pair of green Italian alligator shoes—the Godfather meets Liberace. A Four Seasons regular, Irwin's prime business strategy was looking for investment deals and finder's fees by eavesdropping. Tonight, he'd get an earful.

"I thought your lawyer guy, Tishman whatever, was going to join us," said Marino. Friedway perked at hearing his friend's name. Marino and Ryman talked louder to overcome the occasional roar of airline traffic to and from La Guardia.

For the next two hours, Ryman laid out the details as Friedway listened intently. "Marino, are you sure you can put this IPO away?" asked Ryman as he signaled for the check.

Marino removed his dark sunglasses. His eyes were like two black daggers. "What do you want me to do? Sign in blood? It's done," he exclaimed, grabbing the edge of the table with both hands as if to keep himself from jumping across the table. "All you gotta do is keep your part of the damn bargain! Keep filling the bucket with acquisition prospects, real or otherwise. Capische?"

"Consider the bucket filled," replied Ryman. "Capische?"

"Now that's what I like," smiled Marino, "a CEO with balls. My guys are gonna love you. Why don't you bring along that slick Madison Avenue sidekick when you come over?"

Friedway heard enough to know there could be a fat finder's fee in his future if he presented the right acquisition candidate.

15.

Winning Over the Boiler Room

Ryman called Victor the next morning after his Marino lovefest.

"We've got a meeting tomorrow night with the principals of Norwest Securities. They want to kick the tires."

Victor, concerned word might leak back to A&J, tried his standard excuse—humility. "I'm happy to go, but with my limited knowledge of the stock market, I may be more of a liability than an asset."

Ryman's ego would not permit him to say Marino specifically asked for his presence. "No sweat. The Norwest boys are not the brightest crayons in the box. They're street people, and I don't mean Wall Street. Just be careful; Marino and his buddies aren't interested in finding America's next great growth company. They got into the penny stock market to make a lot of money fast. Conscience is not their middle name."

"I get that, but..."

Ryman interrupted, "Trust me; they'll love your mainstream corporate pedigree. Norwest brokers rarely see a startup IPO with a management team with a proven record on Wall Street *and* Madison Avenue. Besides, if you get in trouble, I've got your back."

Ryman's enormous ego again reared its head. "Of course, when we get to the larger financings on the more traditional side of Wall Street, it will be all about *my* track record. Successful corporate guys are a dime a dozen in that venue."

"So, how do you see my role for this meeting?"

"Just keep your mouth shut until I feed you a question. Then let your resume do the talking, but keep the Madison Avenue bullshit to a minimum. And for Christ's sake, none of that 'Sandra and the kids' crap. These guys are not big on family values."

~

As the rain fell in buckets, a long black limo pulled up in front of A&J. The front door opened, and the driver held up an oversized golf umbrella as he walked Victor over to the spacious rear cabin to join Ryman and Tishman.

Twenty minutes later, the limo exited the Lincoln Tunnel in Hoboken, New Jersey. In a new, three-story red brick building in the heart of the refurbished waterfront area, the Norwest offices were alive with fresh flowers, and the unpretentious lobby had postcard-like views of Manhattan.

Marino appeared, wearing his signature black sunglasses, shiny black sharkskin suit, and business smile. "Glad you guys could make it. Sorry about the rain," he said cordially. "You must be Victor. Heard a lot about you." Victor thought to himself that Martino was a dead ringer for his family's only *officially declared* Mafioso cousin, Antnee (Anthony) Palermo. Warm and friendly on the surface, but a nasty, violent greaseball under the hood.

Marino noticed Victor staring at his suit. "Like the threads, kid? It's Italian silk from around Lake Como. Special order."

"Sorry about the staring. I have a cousin who wears something very similar."

"Not possible," said Marino indignantly. "You've gotta know somebody who knows somebody. What's your cousin's name?"

"Antnee Palermo."

"*The Antnee Palermo*, like in Mr. Genovese's capo?"

Victor smiled. It wasn't something many people knew.

"What a bum rap—eight years for taking out that Russian cheat. Next time you see him, tell him 'M' was asking for him."

~

84

"I thought we'd start with a little tour of the trading floor, meet a few of my top producers," suggested Marino. "They've got questions. Then my key management people will meet us in the main conference room so that we can wrap up any outstanding details."

Marino slowly opened two large wooden doors behind the reception area. To Victor's surprise, the boiler room was a sprawling, well-furnished space with huge windows, high ceilings, and rows of neatly organized desks, telephones, and computers. A stock-quote LED screen hung in each corner, while a giant four-sided screen, like the scoreboard at Madison Square Garden, dangled from the ceiling in the center of the room.

"This place is a zoo during trading hours," said Marino. "Right now, though, there's just a few traders: my top producers, massaging clients for tomorrow's opening bell. With all the CNBC-TV shit, the financial Internet sites, and the after-hours trading, even the little prick with five grand thinks he's Mr. Fucking Know-It-All. So, my best guys know they gotta work the crowd a little harder."

~

In the corner of the trading room, two dozen twenty-something young men—each well-groomed, wearing a freshly starched shirt and a silk tie—were talking quietly. "Of our 220 traders, these gentlemen represent the crème de la crème of Norwest. I imagine they'll put away about eighty percent of the ITI deal, and be go-to-guys post the IPO," boasted Marino.

Wasting no time with getting-to-know-you chatter, the young traders started hurling questions. "Mr. Ryman, the business concept sounds great," said the first. "But have you got any real acquisitions identified?"

"Fellas, you know SEC quiet period rules precludes me from naming names," replied Ryman, cleverly slipping through a loophole. "But read the tea leaves; I made almost 240 hospital acquisitions within the first three years of operation at United Medical Systems."

"Does that mean you're going to be that aggressive again?" came a second question.

"Let me put it this way. The ITI opportunity to build via acquisition may be two or three times larger than my private hospital consolidation."

The traders began whispering among themselves. Tishman was horrified. He whispered, "Franklyn, please be careful."

"Trust me. What did I say?" replied Ryman in an uncharacteristic whisper. "Did I even mention one name?"

A third trader spoke up. "Any chance you guys are going to let us in on what the hell you're talking about up there?"

Ryman and Tishman hesitated, uncertain of their reply. Victor stepped to the front of the room. "Allyn and Ryman are just debating who gets the blonde and who gets the brunette waiting in our limo." He smirked. "Ryman wants them both. He doesn't think Allyn can handle either," quipped Victor. "What do you guys think? Wanna take a vote?"

~

Ryman and Tishman stood in stunned silence. Had Victor just blown it? Ten seconds passed. Then Marino started laughing out loud, and his choir of traders followed suit. "And who the hell are you?" yelled one of the traders in the rear of the room.

"I'm Victor Martini, one of the ITI principals. My job is to ensure you get the right news to pass on to your clients. You with me?"

They were. Suddenly, Victor owned the room. "So, what's the real scoop?" boomed another.

"Simple. Like Franklyn was saying, he'll reel in the acquisitions. I'll crank up the synergies between the companies, and in no time, one plus one will equal three," beamed Victor. "We also realize you've got to stay a step ahead of the internet, so there will always be an exclusive Norwest stream of goodies from unnamed sources."

"Talk's cheap," one of the traders shouted. "We'll see."

Marino stepped in. "Victor's like family. He's Antnee Palermo's cousin."

The traders applauded, happy as pigs in shit which, in a sense, they were.

Marino leaned over to Ryman. "Victor's smoking hot; this deal has *huge* written all over it!"

Ryman was furious, yet pleased. He'd lost the spotlight, but Victor had saved the day with his unexpected street-savviness and family connections.

~

Ryman sent mixed messages to Victor on the return trip. "Jesus, Victor. You almost crossed the line in there. I told you to let me handle the dialogue."

"With all due respect, Ryman, you were losing control of the meeting. All I tried to do was…" Unknowingly, Victor had challenged Ryman's ego in front of Tishman.

"Let's get something straight right now. You may know your stuff in corporate America, but you're an amateur on my turf. You don't know shit about the Street. Not after one goddamn meeting," glared Ryman. "Comprende?"

Tishman tried to mediate. "Franklyn, you're obviously correct about your experience, but Victor seems to know how to read his audience quite well. And he's quite adept on his feet."

Ryman got Tishman's point. "Hey, Victor, don't get me wrong. I'm not pissed. We just need to have ground rules between us."

Victor got Tishman's point—the best way to deal with Ryman's massive ego was to stroke and jab. Stroke and jab.

~

Speeding toward the Park Avenue tunnel at Ninety-Sixth Street, Victor wondered who was taking whom for a ride. He was certainly not the engineer, but he was more than a passenger. Where was the train going? How much control did he really have?

He had boarded this dark-side Wall Street money train to gain absolute financial independence from everyone and everything. But suppose the train jumped the tracks; where would that leave him? And what about the growing number of half-truths? Had he crossed a line?

Certainly, there was something rotten about Ryman, Tishman, Marino, et al, but were they fundamentally any different than Rhoda Barbuto and her version of corporate hopscotch?

Then there was Sandra. Born solidly middle-class, she enjoyed the status of being the boss's spouse: the client socializing and the first-class trappings. The A&J experience had been like gaining entrance to an exclusive, upscale college fraternity. Was this the right time to graduate?

16.

The King and Queen of Penny Stocks

For more than two decades, Johnathan and Louisa Dothan had generally been considered the King and Queen of Penny Stocks by seedy market-makers like Norwest Securities.

Louisa, five feet two inches without heels, wasn't much of a looker but had a commanding presence. Her nerdy-looking, bespectacled, blueblood husband identified fledgling companies with a sexy futures story and no earnings history, then wrote glowing research reports about their potential for a fee—and pre-launch founder shares. Supplemental services included the distribution of these reports to anonymous high-net-worth individuals seeking publicity in exchange for more company shares, warrants, and options at or near the opening price. Using that business model, Johnathan had managed to earn over $100 million over the past five years without ever being investigated, deposed, or even accused of wrongdoing.

Like her husband, Louisa had also been financially successful, earning millions in sales commissions by hyping companies as diamonds-in-the-rough to unsophisticated, middle-class instant-gratification investors. Her support was snippets of information she had gather from her unnamed sources.

Unlike the squeaky-clean Johnathan, the brash Louisa was a walking lawsuit. She'd been charged with securities fraud on numerous occasions, but had always managed to avoid conviction. As her Mafia cousins proudly explained, "Her rap sheet is clean."

Their employment records prior to their stock-hype careers were equally undistinguished. Johnathan and Louisa, who met at Wharton, had been fired as stockbrokers from Merrill Lynch and HSBC for misleading sales practices.

~

Ryman and Johnathan were puffing on Montecristo Cuban cigars at Ryman's penthouse as Louisa studied a handwritten list of names.

"Jesus, boys," complained Louisa, "this place looks and smells like a three-alarm fire. Open the damn window before one of your snooty neighbors calls the fire department."

Ryman did as he was told.

"So, Ryman, who have you contacted so far?" asked Louisa.

"Nobody," replied Ryman. "That was the purpose of today—to review our complete friends and family list to avoid duplication of effort."

"You giving me bullshit?" snapped Louisa.

"Louisa, please," advised her husband with a gentle touch. "If Ryman says he hasn't, then he hasn't."

"So who the hell are they?" pressed Louisa, ignoring Johnathan.

"Don't get so goddamn mad. Maybe I spoke to a few people," said Ryman. He took the list from Louisa and circled four names.

"Is that everybody?"

"Jesus, don't you believe me?"

"No, Paul Revere, I don't." she responded sarcastically. "How much?"

"They each said they'd take $500,000."

"Is that firm?"

"As your ass. They'll postdate their check," replied Ryman, who had a love-hate affair with Louisa and her gruff manner.

"Franklyn, that's a good boy, very good." Louisa leaned back and smiled. "So, we've already got twenty percent placed. I assume the rest of us can get at least half of the deal pre-sold, or maybe more, right?"

"Let's not get too aggressive," advised Ryman. "We've got to leave some crumbs on the table for Marino and his boys. Otherwise, we won't get the aftermarket surge."

"Fuck Marino!" shot back Louisa. "We take care of our own first. That's the way it works. That's the way it's always worked."

"I understand your point," said Johnathan, staring over the rims of his glasses. "But remember: we're *not* dealing with the Boy Scouts here."

"I agree with Johnathan," said Ryman. "I've just learned Marino's got some pretty unsavory connections."

"Marino's an uncouth gorilla that's all bite and no back." Louisa waved her hand dismissively. "Just give him a box of those testosterone-filled Cuban telephone poles you guys smoke," she commented.

~

"What about your new operator?" asked Louisa. "How much of the opening flip did you give him?"

"Zippo," said Ryman. "The less Victor knows, the better. I told Tishman to issue and deliver his founder stock certificates, keeping him and his wife quiet while we close the financing. The guy's never seen, much less touched, a certificate for ten million shares of stock."

"But Ryman," commented Johnathan, "does Victor realize that the 144 legend means his stock is illiquid for the next 24 months, regardless of the stock price?"

"Like I said." Ryman took a big puff. "Who cares? The less Victor knows about how the SEC works, the better."

"Tell you what," said Johnathan, "why don't Louisa and I take them out to dinner and make nice? Never know when we might need him."

"Fine," said Ryman. "But how about investing a few bucks in a new dress for Louisa first? Sandra's pretty classy."

"Fuck you, Franklyn!" replied Louisa.

~

"Honey," said Sandra sweetly, "I just talked to the wife of one of your senior advisors, Louisa Dothan. She sounded very friendly; we've been invited to dinner at Barolo Restaurant in Tribecca. She said Johnathan swears they serve the best veal Milanese in town."

Outside their inner circle of amoral, greedy friends, the Dothans were quite charming. "We're really excited that your husband joined the team," smiled Johnathan. "We all plan to earn some nice money in Ryman's latest venture. I was with him during the hospital years; I think ITI has the potential to be even bigger."

"Victor's really excited too," said Sandra. "Personally, I think the money and all that is great, but I'm hoping to have some fun. This should be quite the adventure."

Louisa stared at Johnathan as if to say, *Is this Mary Poppins for real? Nobody gives a shit about fun on The Street, it's* only *about the money.*

"A girl after my own heart," Louisa offered her friendliest smile. "I've been telling the boys their deals could use a little bit of a woman's touch. But you know men and their fragile egos."

17.
Time to Say Goodbye

The ITI offering sold out in a matter of minutes, thanks to Marino's trading room, Louisa's VIP customer drive, and Ryman's unnamed group of big-hitters.

All that remained was for Victor to say goodbye to A&J. He ignored the usual chain-of-command. He was going to tell Gordon Naye about his resignation directly; Rhoda Barbuto could learn secondhand. It no longer mattered.

Gordon was on the phone as Victor walked into his office.

"Please start," said Gordon, cupping his hand over the phone and waving toward a continental breakfast full of goodies. "I'll only be another minute."

"Joe, I appreciate your point about wanting to open two additional offices in Australia," continued Gordon into the receiver, "but why don't we make Sydney a model operation first before we expand in Australia? It's remarkable what you've done so far. You young bucks need to slow down a little. The opportunity isn't going to evaporate." Another pause. "Say hello to Essie. Ellen and I look forward to having dinner the next time you're up from Down Under."

Gordon hung up and pressed a little button on the side of his chair. Eerily, the door to his office closed automatically. He and Victor were alone together for what Victor knew would be the last time. "Good to see you," smiled Gordon warmly. "Can I offer you something?" Victor pointed to his plate of croissants and jam. He was intimidated by Gordon's s graciousness.

"What a coincidence you should call," said Gordon. "We've just put the final touches on an event I know that beautiful wife of yours will love. We've rented the rotunda at the Museum of

Modern Art for the evening to have a private showing of the Cezanne Exhibition, followed by a catered dinner in the newly renovated Gardens. Our clients should love it. I wanted you to be one of the first to know because I think our wives should run this one, and I'd like Sandra to be on the planning committee."

~

"Victor squirmed in his chair. Naye noticed.

"What's the matter? You were going to put the touch on me for another raise, were you?" chuckled Gordon.

"I don't know if you realize," Victor began self-consciously, "my Dad died about ten years ago. Since that time, I've thought of you as a father figure, somebody I really would like to emulate. That's what makes this so difficult."

Gordon raised an eyebrow.

"An opportunity has come my way that can change my life forever." Victor kept talking, concerned that if he stopped, he'd crumble from the emotion of the moment. "I've been asked to become the co-founder of a public startup company."

"Oh," said a surprised Naye. "It doesn't sound like you're heading to another advertising agency."

"No, I'm entering the world of Wall Street."

"I didn't know you were a student of The Street."

"I wasn't until this offer came along."

"Tell me a little about it."

"The plan is to remarket excess consumer inventories and grow the company through strategic mergers and acquisitions."

"Now that's one I would never have imagined for you," replied Gordon.

"I was really proud of the promotion you gave me the day I met with you and Rhoda, but I had already given my word. All the details of the IPO are now in place, so I wanted you to be the first to know."

"Wall Street can be a rough place," advised Gordon.

"So can the advertising business."

"It's different. My brother, James, was an investment banker before he crashed and burned at forty-one. The pressure, the money, the shortcuts, and his divorce all contributed to him committing suicide."

"Gordon, you know Sandra and I well enough to know we have a strong, unbreakable bond."

"Agree, but you are giving up a stable long-term career at A&J for the *possibility* of untold wealth."

"With all due respect, I think our new startup is quite a bit more than a possibility. The IPO is already fully funded."

"How does Sandra feel?" smiled Naye. "She's a wonderful lady."

"She's a little nervous, but supportive."

"Then your mind is made up?"

Victor nodded.

~

"Would you mind a little advice from an old friend?" asked Gordon.

"I'm honored that you care," responded Victor.

"I've sensed your desire for the good life for quite some time. There is no crime in wanting to be rich. I'd be a hypocrite if I said otherwise. I know firsthand that wealth brings pleasures otherwise unachievable. But as somebody a few years older, and perhaps a little wiser, let me give you a bit of wisdom as you begin your new journey."

Victor absorbed every phrase, every intonation. His subconscious imagined a dreamy, wholesome Sandra sitting next to Gordon. Was she an A&J surrogate? Was she Gordon's surrogate? Or was she Victor's support system?

"How you accumulate wealth can be as important as the wealth itself," said Gordon, sounding older than he had in years. "I'm confident you'll achieve all your dreams. You're that kind of person. But your road will be filled with forks. Go down a wrong one, and it will be difficult to find your way back."

"I understand and appreciate what you are saying," replied

Victor. "And no one could have said it better."

"I wish you and Sandra only the best." Gordon hugged Victor as if he were saying goodbye to the son who both knew would never be quite like his father.

~

As Victor left the A&J lobby, he turned one last time to look at the home where he grew up. The moment was filled contradictions. Bittersweet recollections blended seamlessly with the excitement of unlimited possibilities. He wiped the tears from his eye

18.

Leslie's $3 Million Lease

TISHMAN'S OFFICE, DAYS LATER.

"Gentlemen, for the last three weeks, one of Cushman & Carpenter's top commercial real estate specialists, Leslie Haller, and I have worked closely together, looking at nearly two dozen availabilities," said Johnny Katz, who had added real estate to his boy Friday job responsibilities. "We've narrowed it down to three locations: two in Midtown; and a third on Park Avenue South, around Twenty-Eighth Street."

He showed them a profile of Leslie, who looked like something out of trendy *Bazaar Magazine*: impeccably groomed with shoulder-length brown hair, perfectly augmented by form-fitting slacks and a Donna Karan silk blouse suit with just the proper hint of cleavage.

"I figure we'll need about 5,000 square feet for the next two years for our corporate headquarters," offered Katz. "Offices for each of us, space for some administrative assistants and a financial group, and a few conference rooms. I assumed all the acquisitions would remain in their existing space during this period."

"Sounds about right," responded Ryman.

"What's your recommendation?" asked Victor, watching Ryman salivate as he scanned Haller's photo.

"Well, the Park Avenue South location is a renovated bank building. Lots of high ceilings, a very avant-garde space. Unusual big old brass windows, figures painted on the ceiling. Hip location, East Twenty-Eighth Street."

"How much?" asked Victor.

"Pretty reasonable: $28 a square foot, triple net, plus they are willing to negotiate concessions on build-outs and caring. We also get three free months rental concession," replied Katz.

"And Midtown?"

"Our best options are the Lipstick and the Seagram Buildings," Katz replied.

"I love the Seagram Building; that's one of the classiest buildings in New York," smiled Ryman. "But what's the Lipstick Building?" he asked.

"It's that new oval-shaped red granite building on Third Avenue and Fifty-First," said Victor, who knew all about nicknames and word games.

"I'll bite. Why the hell is it called the Lipstick Building?"

Katz shrugged his shoulders, laughing. "I haven't got a clue. I asked Leslie the same question. She had no idea either."

"How much?"

"Forty-eight dollars a square foot, two months rent-free. Plus some carpet and painting concessions."

"And the Seagram Building?"

"The space is gorgeous," said Katz. "All floor-to-ceiling windows, two beautiful wood-paneled conference rooms, brand new carpeting, and the offices are perfectly configured for our needs. And it's available for immediate occupancy."

"Love that cafeteria!" mused Ryman. "'What cafeteria'?" asked Victor.

"The Four Seasons," smiled Ryman. "We can have our employee meetings every day in the Pool Room." He turned back to Katz. "What floor is the space?"

"Fifty-fourth. Spectacular city views."

"Sounds perfect. Let's take it," said Ryman.

Sounding like the group nerd, Victor asked, "Don't we want to know the cost per square to analyze versus other options?"

"Oh," said Ryman dismissively, who couldn't care less.

"Admittedly, it's a bit pricier," said Katz. "All in all, about $94 a square foot."

"What concessions are they willing to negotiate?" asked Victor.

"None," replied Katz. "It's the Seagram Building. Take it or leave it."

"Look, if we ran the numbers, by the time we finished with the construction upgrades, etc., the rents would be roughly comparable," rationalized Ryman.

Victor kept prodding. "With all due respect, Ryman, I believe there's a glut of space on the market. The financial industry is hurting. People are losing jobs. We can negotiate down."

"Christ, Victor, this in not A&J; we don't need to waste time doing analysis," exploded Ryman. "The location is goddamn perfect. It will make a great statement to acquisition candidates, investors, and the financial community. Trust me: I've done this stuff before. I know what we need."

"But…"

"Let's take a vote," insisted Ryman. "Johnny?"

"The Seagram Building."

I looked at Tishman, who had yet to open his mouth. "Well?"

"Allyn has no vote on operational matters," responded Ryman. "So, there we have it, Victor: two to one. Johnny, call Leslie and tell her to get the lease drawn."

~

A few days later, Leslie stopped by with the Seagram's lease. "It's pure boilerplate," she said, flirting with Ryman. "No special clauses, no curveballs. I've even included a sixty-day out provision, so you can easily upgrade to a larger space in the building. The landlord had no problems with the clause because they feel the space is so desirable. They can re-rent it in a matter of days."

"What about a sublease clause, in case we want to keep the space for one of our acquisitions?" asked Ryman.

"I thought about that, but the landlord wanted a $7-per-foot increase for the right to include a sublease clause. It didn't seem to make good economic sense, given your aggressive acquisition and financing plans. However, if you wish, I'd be happy to revisit the issue."

Victor again acted as if he was the only businessperson in the room. "Are we sure about this? It's a huge commitment for a start-up."

"As you know, this is not my prime project," said Leslie with a look in her eyes that made Ryman hard. She kept her eyes trained on him as she continued. "Guys, in the broad scheme of things, this is a nickel-dime transaction. I agreed to invest my time because my intuition tells me ITI is on a fast track and will need serious space quickly. That's when I'll make *my* money."

Leslie sat down and slowly crossed her shapely legs. "You know, Jewish girls in Manhattan don't live on bread alone." Ryman signed the lease with a flourish.

"I also need the countersignature of your COO. Would that be Johnny?" she asked.

"Johnny?" laughed Ryman, pushing the lease across the desk to Victor. "Congratulations. You are about to execute your first act as Chief Operating Officer."

Victor followed Ryman's lead and signed without looking at a single clause. "Hallelujah! We're moving on up to the East Side, to a deee-luxe office in the sky," chuckled Ryman, doing his best impersonation of George Jefferson from the 80s TV sitcom *The Jeffersons*.

"See you about eight?" asked Katz as Leslie packed her bag. "Don't be late," she smiled back over her shoulder. "It's not often I cook at home."

~

"So, how goes it at ITI?" said Sandra sweetly that evening in front of a crackling fire.

"It's certainly different than A&J." Victor read concern in Sandra's body language. "Relax, baby. It's nothing like that. Decision-making is just a lot less formal."

"Translation, please."

"Today, we signed on the dotted line for our first corporate space. I think we committed about three million dollars on the spot. No committee meetings, no financial reviews, no detailed analysis."

"Holy crap, three million dollars! What did you guys lease?"

"Five thousand square feet for five years."

"You've got to be kidding." Sandra couldn't believe her ears. "If I made a recommendation like that at the hospital, they'd think I was crazy! We can build a whole wing for that kind of money."

"Honey, I appreciate what you do. Healthcare is a noble profession," said Victor with a hint of condescension. "But the way you guys think nothing of spending twenty dollars for one titanium orthopedic screw for some spoiled doctor, well, that's not exactly how real business works."

"Oh really," said Sandra, now mildly annoyed. "Then tell Mommy, what's your rationale for such a shameless display of opulence with the public's money?"

"Franklyn loves the Four Seasons restaurant for lunch."

"Well, that makes a lot more sense," said Sandra.

19.

Astrid's Complicated Past

Ten days later, Katz, Ryman, Tishman, and Victor held ITI's first official meeting in their new corporate headquarters to discuss the status of potential acquisition candidates.

"We have a firm appointment with Morton Alexander & Associates, a relatively new barter company on Forty-Fifth Street that specializes in excess sporting goods," said Katz, standing in front of a presentation board with the Manhattan skyline as a backdrop. "We'll also be meeting with Ryman Jenkins, Inc., a twenty-five-year-old re-marketer of prime quality excess retail office space, and, compliments of Allyn, the Treadwell Corporation, a company that specializes in trading media for branded food products with marketing giants like Unilever and Proctor & Gamble."

"Sounds like an excellent start," commented Victor.

"Naah," roared Ryman. "By this time, my hospital management team had twice as many acquisitions lined up. These sound like a nice little bunch of private, dull companies."

Tishman nodded. "Ryman, on a related matter, what are Marino and his boys doing?"

"What makes you ask?" responded Ryman innocently.

"Our stock is already over two dollars; that's four times the initial offering price, and we haven't announced a single company signing yet!"

"You haven't been talking to him?" Tishman peered over his granny glasses.

"Absolutely not. But I wouldn't be surprised if the leaks are coming from the Dothans. You know Louisa's a real bulldog."

Victor had suspicions. Ryman noticed and quickly changed the subject. "The details and the phone calls are starting to pile up. This is no way to run a business. We need a few administrative assistants, pronto."

"I've been working on that," said Katz. "Franklyn, I've located an ideal candidate for you. She is on your calendar tomorrow at 10:00 a.m."

~

"Ryman, I'd like to introduce Astrid Fundland," said Katz, escorting a young woman into the office of Ryman, who immediately felt his private parts grow larger.

"As you can see from her resume, Astrid is quite computer literate. She speaks three languages—English, Swedish, and French —and does word processing at seventy words a minute."

Ryman could see just fine. Astrid was a slim blonde with the legs of a supermodel. The rest of her looked like a Las Vegas showgirl with a touch of TV soap opera star.

"Astrid's also been living in Aspen for the last year, so I suspect you will have some common interests," concluded Katz with a twinkle in his eye.

Ryman looked her over like a hungry man admiring a fresh steak with all the trimmings. She handed him her resume. He didn't even glance at it.

Astrid knew what time it was. She slowly tilted her head. Her shiny blond hair glided to the side of her face. Then she ran her tongue around her large, sensuous lips. "Thanks for seeing me. These are beautiful offices, Mr. Ryman. The view is quite stunning."

"Call me Franklyn," insisted Ryman, who relished sexy, hip, smart women that were more than willing to compromise to stay in the fast lane.

"Well, Franklyn, I think my professional skills speak for themselves. I am available to begin work immediately."

"How long did you live in Aspen?"

"About five years."

"Surprised that I never ran into you there. You know, I'm one of the owners of the Aspen Club. Do we have people in common?"

"Yes, but I'm not sure we want to go there."

Ryman gave her his patented look. "Let's do. My partner was Dick Donovan." The Aspen Club had been one of Ryman's most expensive *faux pas*. He first met Dick Donovan at a private party of the rich and powerful in Short Hills, New Jersey. They quickly discovered they had much in common: fast cars, the accumulation of obscene wealth, beautiful women, and the glittery lifestyle of Aspen.

Two weeks later, they were on Dick's private jet, examining potential sites for what was to become a pre-eminent celebrity hideaway in Aspen.

Two years later, the club was opened to incredible fanfare with the jet-set circle around the world. The place was jammed with celebrities, who wanted to be anonymous, and quasi-celebrities, who came to be seen.

From opening day, the club lost a ton because neither Ryman nor Dick knew anything about operating such a property, and their egos would not let either suggest hiring professional management. When he was about $30 million in the hole personally, Ryman discovered Dick was flat broke. His wealth came from his wife Allison's side of the family. Rumor had it that she caught him cheating and cut off his play money.

"So, you're the one," said a wide-eyed Ryman. "He never volunteered your name. Didn't you just disappear or something?"

"Ryman, I'm uncomfortable discussing this any further. I'm just here for a job."

"Astrid, the job is yours. You start at $50,000, on Monday," said Ryman, who then laid it out in the open. "Dick dragged his dick around the club for months. Pardon the pun," he added with a chuckle. "What the hell happened?"

"Allison found us in bed one night in an Aspen Club suite," said Astrid reluctantly. "The next morning, she had the banks shut down all of his short-term credit lines. Then she told her loving husband he could have his freedom, but she would make sure Daddy also cut him out of her trust fund. Since Dick didn't have a dime, he decided it was more important to maintain his financial status than have a great lay, and he blew me off. I got into a funk—drugs and stuff, messed up my head—shamelessly tried to woo Dick back. Allison eventually gave me a ticket to get out of town and twenty thousand dollars. I'm just about tapped out, but at least I'm clean now, and here we are."

20.

Ten Greedy Black Beards

"Ryman," said Johnathan Dothan the next morning, "I'd like you to present your corporate spiel to a sure thing."

"Who?"

"A group of lower East Side Hasidic Jews in the electronics business. These guys are major investors," continued Dothan. "Marino put them in the stock at ten cents. About three million shares. After we drove the price to thirty cents, they made a nice little profit. And now they're waiting for us to tell them when to get back in. Plus, they have a regular supply of excess product inventory, an excellent source for the company."

"Can they keep their mouths shut?" asked Ryman.

"Would I bring the wrong people?" replied Dothan.

"Okay. Friday morning. I'll give them an *informal* update."

"Informal? These guys want the whole nine yards," Dothan instructed. "Get that blonde of yours to order the bagels and lox, maybe some smoked whitefish."

"ITI is not a fucking delicatessen. That's not what I hired her to do."

~

Ten bearded Hasidic stockbrokers, dressed entirely in black and led by one Otis Weinstein, arrived on site for the latest ITT business update.

Bald, ugly, and pushy, Otis didn't have a bone of finesse in his short, fat body. Astrid thought he could use a shower, or at least a strong deodorant.

"Dothan told me you are going to make us rich," commanded Otis. "Explain."

"Well, I don't know about that," said Ryman, exuding a phony modesty. "But we do have an interesting story. My chief operating officer here, Victor Martini, will take you through a little presentation to show you where we are. Between the COO and I, and our senior advisor, Johnathan, we should be able to answer most of your questions."

"We'll see. Start talking," said Otis as the other black beards nodded.

"How about Victor gives you a quick ten-minute overview of the business?" suggested Ryman. "Then Johnathan and I will try to answer your investment questions."

"Make it five. That'll eliminate the bullshit," replied Otis gruffly.

"Jesus, Otis," said Ryman, "I don't think that's possible."

"I'm good," Victor replied, having dealt with impatient clients during his A&J days.

"Franklyn, Victor says it's okay," echoed Weinstein.

Victor began his spiel. It was a near-direct repeat of Ryman's spiel at the Sutton Place Coffee Shop, only better.

"Re-marketing excess consumer goods is a highly-fragmented ten-billion-dollar business in the U.S. comprised of hundreds of private companies that specialize in one type of inventory, or one channel of distribution," Victor began, winging it all the way.

"Some are strong at buying at a good price. Others are stronger at selling. Some buy for cash; some buy under a barter arrangement. Some buy for a little of both. ITI will be the first company to combine all these functions and product categories under one roof." As he spoke, he worked in various facts and figures, which he scribbled on the whiteboard for emphasis. "We should become the de facto market leader overnight. The key will be acquisitions and financing."

Ryman smiled. He realized he was listening to one hell of a pitchman. The audience was eating out of Victor's hand.

"How big do you expect to be?" asked Weinstein.

"About 500 million dollars," said Victor with Madison Avenue aplomb. "Give or take 100 million within three years."

The whiteboard behind Victor was now filled with colored boxes and arrows. Otis & company were salivating. Victor checked his watch. "That's my five minutes."

"C'mon, Victor. We were only trying to break your balls," said Otis, begging now like a hungry hound. "Nothing personal. We do it to everybody who wants our money. ITI sounds like an interesting proposition. We don't know squat about the barter business. Take whatever time you want."

"Then let's start with acquisitions," continued Victor, throwing them a bone. "We're interested in three broad categories: trading companies whose primary skill base is finding deals; distribution companies who know how to get rid of products discreetly and profitably; and supply companies who will create the inventory of goods and services—like media, printing, and transportation services—that we'll use as trading currency for our purchases."

"Give us an example of the kinds of companies you are looking to acquire," pushed Otis.

"Well, let's take the trading area. There are great little companies like Morton Alexander & Associates, which specializes in buying and re-marketing sporting goods, or like Treadwell, which moves food products, and so on. We currently have about fifty companies in some stage of negotiation."

"Fifty!" said Otis. The greedy little brokers mumbled while they scribbled notes. "If you project 500 million in five years," Otis kept probing, "what do the year one and two pro formas look like?"

Victor stared at Ryman; he had no idea what the hell a pro forma was. Ryman jumped in. "Otis, Otis," he said, holding out his hands as if to stop a truck. "You know the rules. Victor's done an admirable job of giving you an idea of where we are going, but we can't go any further with the details."

"I assure you we're off-the-record," pleaded Weinstein.

~

"Otis, Franklyn's right," replied Victor, knowing they had Otis moments away from a significant investment. "It's too early in the process. For example, we have only arranged a preliminary meeting with SFM Media. How would we even be able to include them in a pro forma, much less estimate their earning potential?"

"SFM, the media giant?" asked Weinstein, his bubble-like eyes ready to burst.

"Let's leave it at that," said Ryman, as if on cue. "My accomplishments at United Medical are part of the public record. You did the research. You know how big the company was at the end of two years of acquisition activity. Assuming the availability of capital, ITI, conservatively, should be twice the size of United Medical over a comparable period."

By the time Otis and his bunch left, they were on the verge of mass orgasm.

"Jesus Christ," Ryman looked at Victor. "Where the hell did you get all that stuff?"

"From my executive imagination," said Victor with a grin. "Thanks for bailing me out on the pro forma stuff."

Ryman smiled proudly. His junior partner was a young Ryman in disguise.

~

As Victor went back to his office, Ryman and Dothan met behind closed doors.

"Ryman, after listening to Weinstein," said Johnathan, "I think we need my brother to create one of his impartial *Market Insights* reports on the ITI prospects."

"How much?" said Ryman.

"Our treat. Louisa says it's your birthday present."

"When will Steve's report be ready for distribution?"

"Depends. He's a respected market analyst; we've got to give him some meat to work with—acquisition candidates, pro forma projections, anticipated growth rates. Today is different than the old hospital management days—you can't get by on fluff alone. The dotcom babies burst that bubble."

"Anything else?"

"H needs to segment his database so that the report winds up in the right hands. I'm guessing Victor can help there."

"Forget Victor. Our report is strictly a private matter; I know I can trust Johnny Katz to keep his mouth. Just make sure you print an extra 2,000 copies for Marino and his boys. And for Christ's sake, tell Steve to use a printer in the boonies like Cedar Rapids, Kankakee, or Sioux City. Make it impossible for anybody to link me to the report."

21.
World's Greatest Liquidator

Based on what he had overheard at the Four Seasons restaurant and the publication of Market Insights report, Irwin Friedway saw a double-dip opportunity—a finder's fee for a qualified introduction and an early stock ride.

"Franklyn, I may have the acquisition that'll put ITI on the map," teased Friedway on the phone. "A brand name plus substantial historical earnings. But they won't come cheap."

"Who are we talking about?" asked Ryman impatiently.

"Franklyn, you and I have done a lot of business over the years. Despite that, we've managed to stay friends, right? So, let's cut the bullshit," demanded Irwin. "Get me a signed remuneration agreement, so my fees in this transaction are clear, and then we'll talk. If you want to save time, I can draw up the standard Lehman formula finder's fee agreement and my partner can bring it over."

"Partner? Since when?"

"Since this deal. Julie Jakowitz has been a close friend and advisor to the acquisition candidate for years. He'll provide you with valuable insights into the company and what they're looking for."

"Julie?"

"It's Julius, but he prefers Julie. Julius sounds too ethnic. I'm not going to argue."

"Is she a he?" chuckled Ryman.

"*He's* a CPA. I'd keep the bad taste jokes to yourself when you meet Julie and the acquisition."

~

Ryman arrived at Irwin's office on Park Avenue and Forty-First Street fifteen minutes late to meet the middleman and sign the papers. Floor-to-ceiling bookcases filled with legal volumes dominated the conference room, implying Irwin's mastery of the law. Like so many things in Irwin's life, the books were a prop designed to give him an edge in negotiations. His entire life was a negotiation, from buying a new suit to selling a company to trying to pick up a woman at a bar. But he wasn't a lawyer. Everything he knew about the law he'd learned from a correspondence course, television shows, and John Grisham novels.

Jakowitz was not what Ryman expected. In his late sixties, he was an older man with a full head of wavy gray hair, lots of friendly wrinkles, and a rich, dark suntan. Wearing an open-collar sports shirt and a checkered sports jacket, Jakowitz could pass for a grandfather on the Family Channel. "Pleasure to meet you, Franklyn," Julie reached across the table and vigorously shook his hand. "I've heard a lot about you."

Ryman bet he had. That's why he'd kept Victor out of the loop.

"Irwin has been most discreet about your partnership with him," Ryman began, the picture of confidence in his trademark pinstriped suit. "Maybe I should give you some background on ITI: what we've accomplished to date, and where we are planning to go."

"Let's not worry about that," said Julie. "Your reputation as a promoter precedes you—you're a man who gets it done. It's Sam and his family that you have to sell on the idea. What we need to do first is get *our* deal done. Irwin…"

"As we discussed, in standard Lehman terms," noted Irwin, handing Ryman the three-page document.

"As you know, I have a fiduciary responsibility to have Allyn review all agreements of this nature," said Ryman mildly, wanting to hear more about the acquisition before he signed anything. If Allyn's research had already identified the buyers, then he could negotiate a reduced fee. "Why don't we talk a bit about the potential acquisition? Allyn will get right back to us."

"Fine, if that's the way you want to handle it," said Jakowitz smoothly. "Irwin and I will have lunch while you and Allyn modify the agreement any way you want. Then Irwin and I will review it, provide our comments. Allyn can then make another round of revisions. Ultimately, we'll sign a mutually acceptable agreement."

Translation: *Fuck you, Ryman! No agreement, no information* was the message, loud and clear.

Ryman wanted to scream, but he was desperate for acquisition agreements—the bigger, the better—given the marketplace anticipation he had created. Marino had it right: "My boys need something 'off the record' to talk about."

"Julie, I know you've traveled in from California, so I won't waste your time. Let's do the agreement right now and get it signed," said Ryman, skimming the document. "It's boilerplate all right, except for one small matter—the fee schedule is about thirty-five percent higher than the usual five — four — three — two — one."

"This is an unusual transaction," responded Julie. "We have a pretty substantial company with a long operating history and clean books. Your accounting and due diligence costs will be zilch, and Sam and the family are willing to wait until you get your next financing executed. But hey, if it's too rich for you, it's okay. These guys can continue operating just fine without you."

Money grubbing pigs! Ryman thought. He felt like amputating their hands. Friedway and Jakowitz were going to split the fee and wanted a full share each.

"Christ, you guys are killing me," protested Ryman meekly.

"The Board is going to have my ass."

"Franklyn, I heard that's never been a problem for you."

Franklyn took the bait like a mouse to cheese. He signed the document.

"Now that we've got the housekeeping out of the way, let me tell you a little about the principals, Sam and Dave," said Jakowitz before Ryman's signature was dry. "The Sam Nachman Company is fifteen years old and generally assumed to be…"

"You don't mean THE Sam Nachman, who does those huge retail liquidations?"

"One and the same. We're not horsing around here. I'm too old to bother with small time. Sam is getting on in years, and his younger partner Dave Herman wants to cash out before he's too old to spend it. Sam Nachman built his business by starting with the mammoth $800 million WT Grant liquidation," explained Jakowitz.

"Sam rolled the dice, put everything he owned into the deal, got some of his billionaire retailing buddies—Jerry Sugarstein, Sol Frank, and Mel Simki—to back him. Sam's idea was simple but radical for its time: run a retail liquidation like a conventional retail sales event, hence the birth of the giant going-out-of-business sale.

"But instead of returning the usual fifteen to twenty cents on the dollar to creditors, Nachman and his partners were willing to guarantee creditors thirty-two cents on the dollar. On 800 million bucks, that is one shit pile of money. The other bidders bailed out —

too much risk. Sam's super sale yielded forty-four cents on the dollar. The creditors jumped for joy, and Nachman made a killing. Since then, there have been several imitators, but there is still only one Sam Nachman."

"Why does he want out?" asked Ryman.

"Sam doesn't think his partner, Dave, or his son, Albert, a UCLA lawyer, have the determination to keep his brainchild thriving. He'd also like to see the Nachman name on a legitimate corporate entity."

"What do you mean by 'legitimate'?"

"Liquidation has a dirty reputation—the deals, the payoffs. Sam wants a legacy beyond 'The World's Greatest Liquidator.' That is why he bought the Indiana Pacers NBA franchise. That deal, plus acquisition by a public company, would be like making a three-point shot."

Jakowitz looked at Ryman critically. "You got balls enough to play with him?"

Ryman sat back in his chair. ITI was about to travel to the other side.

~

Jakowitz called his buddy Nachman about the arriving gravy train called ITI.

"Sam, I'm in New York with Irwin Friedway. He introduced me to a new public company called Integrated Trading International and its visionary founder, Franklyn Ryman. They are looking to build a public barter company. This may be a great way to cash out."

"We've been together a long time," said Sam, his raspy voice making him sound like Marlon Brando. "If you think it's something we should look at, then do it. Remember, I really want to eliminate those personal bank guarantees every time we buy a big deal. I'm getting too old to have to worry about tying up my estates every time I buy an inventory of over ten million."

"I understand," replied Jakowitz.

"Everybody thinks of me as the ultimate poker player. But between you and me, I'm losing my stomach for the all-or-nothing roll. It's no big deal to lose fifty grand in a stud game, but losing thirty or forty million is a different matter."

He paused a moment. "Julie. What do you know about this Ryman?"

"He's definitely been successful in raising big bucks in the public markets. No criminal record, or even violations. But he's been into drugs and lost millions on a clearinghouse venture in Chicago. He's a promoter. Doesn't know jack shit about operating companies. He's hired some corporate blueblood named Victor

Martini to run the acquisitions, but I haven't found out much about him."

"Ryman is hungry. Gives us a big edge. What's the next step?" asked Sam. "I'd suggest a face-to-face meeting at my hotel suite in Las Vegas, just in case he's full of shit. I don't want to disrupt my poker schedule."

Jakowitz called Ryman. "Sam is happy to meet with you in Las Vegas. He's in the middle of a two-week round robin poker tournament."

"I'm talking about buying his business," protested Ryman. "It's one thing visiting his operation, but a card game? Christ, I've got three acquisition meetings next week here in New York."

"I can appreciate your busy schedule, but Sam's passionate about his hobby. Let's try to find a date in the future."

"Screw it," harumphed Ryman. "Let's meet in Vegas."

"Good," replied Jakowitz smugly. "Meet you at the MGM Grand registration counter about 11:00 p.m., Thursday. And bring Victor; Sam and I would like to meet him."

~

"Franklyn, getting Nachman in the fold could be the key to creating a flood of acquisition deals," said Tishman over lunch later that day.

"They know about Victor," said Ryman. "They want me to bring him along."

"Consider it a learning experience for him. I gather Victor has handled himself very well at your broker meetings. Katz tells me Victor's a politically correct version of you," smiled Tishman.

"But be careful," he warned the next moment. "I doubt Victor has ever dealt with sharks like this."

~

Sandra was none too happy about Victor's first ITI business trip. "You're going where?"

"Las Vegas."

"And the meeting is what time?"

"11:00 p.m."

"Now how stupid do you think I am?"

Victor knew what Sandra was thinking. "If I was going to cheat on you after all these years, would I make up something that farfetched?"

"So who is this Sam guy?"

"You know those crazy going-out-of-business sales you and your girlfriends shop from time to time, looking for bargains? That's his area of specialty. He buys the merchandise, advertises it, and sells it, all in the same location. Ryman thinks his experience would be a perfect distribution channel for the excess inventory that we would buy from other manufacturers. We'd just display the merchandise at one of his going-out-of-business sales."

"The idea actually makes sense," said Sandra thoughtfully. "Just don't pick up any of those professional Las Vegas shoppers between meetings."

22.

Victor Gets a Makeover

Ryman's life regimen included staying fit and dressing impeccably in the most delicate English fabrics. By contrast, Victor, while not overweight, was woefully out of shape with little to no muscle tone, and with a closet full of baggy, shapeless dark blue Brooks Brothers suits.

Without irreparably bruising his young partner's ego, Ryman decided Victor needed a drastic makeover—and sooner rather than later.

~

"How about joining me for a workout at the Vertical Club before we head to Vegas? It's the hippest singles scene in town," said Ryman, crashing into Victor's office. "And then a light lunch."

Victor tried to make an excuse. "I'd love to, but I don't have any workout clothes or shoes here. Let's do it another day." The truth was, Victor hadn't worked out in years, other than an infrequent morning walk on the weekends.

"No problem. Paragon Sports is just a few blocks from the club, and they carry everything. My treat; consider it an advance on your Christmas bonus."

Two hours later, Ryman and Victor were standing on a half-mile indoor jogging track suspended above the club's expansive Nautilus room, which was equipped with two hundred sleek machines and a plethora of weight-lifting gizmos. About fifty men with bulging pecs and seventy taut, shapely women in one-piece tights were grunting, groaning, and sweating, each lustily inspecting the others around them.

"I've got a slow-build routine," boasted Ryman. "About ten laps in all. The first three at a warm-up jog, the next four at a medium pace, and the last four are balls-out aerobic."

During the first three laps, Victor huffed and puffed as the two men talked about business. At the beginning of lap four, Ryman stepped up the pace. Victor kept up for about half a lap but then stopped short, gasping for air as he grabbed the railing to steady his wobbly legs.

"Christ, you gotta get in better shape. You are going to need some real stamina for what lies ahead—the traveling, the stress, the bullshit," admonished Ryman. "I'd suggest we get you a personal trainer. At company expense. Gotta keep our key executives in tip-top shape."

Ryman waved at a black lady with zero body fat in red and black striped exercise tights. She and Ryman spoke, then they both walked towards Victor. "Victor, meet your new trainer," smiled Ryman. "This is Gisella Johansson."

"I will help you in any way I can," smiled Gisella. "Just let me know when we can begin your sessions." Victor thought to himself, *This is one corporate perk I probably won't disclose to Sandra.*

~

Ryman and Victor went downstairs to the café, where they each had a mango and papaya fruit cup—a Vertical Club specialty —and a vegetable salad comprised of Ryman's favorites: raw beansprouts, soybeans, lemon wheatgrass, and water chestnuts. Victor pretended he was eating cheeseburgers. Between courses, Ryman talked about Nachman and his crew. "Be careful in Vegas; Weinstein's black beards are pussycats compared to these piranhas."

~

"Been meaning to ask," said Ryman in a cab on the way back to the office. "Where do you get your suits?"

"Brooks Brothers."

"Thought so. You look like a stuffy old man."

Victor shrugged. "Nobody ever complained at A&J."

"Trust me; they won't go over as well in Vegas," said Ryman. "Fortunately, Edward Sexton of Seville Row is in town."

"Who's Edward Sexton?"

"My custom couturier for almost a decade. I was referred to him by Prince Charles when I lived in London."

"Sounds expensive," Victor said doubtfully.

"This is your lucky day," said Ryman, ignoring Victor's concern. "Edward's agreed to stop by my penthouse to do an emergency fitting so we can get you properly attired."

"What the hell; I guess there's a first time for everything," replied Victor.

About an hour later, the men were greeted as they entered Ryman's Sutton Place spread by a smartly dressed Brit with slickly matted, curly black hair. "So good to see you again, Mr. Ryman," said the Brit. He gave Victor the once-over. "My, my, Mr. Ryman, I see what you meant. We do have some work ahead of us."

"Edward, be nice. Let's start him off with a few single-breasted, pointed-lapel suits."

"Are we sure they may not be a little too extreme for the gentleman?" Translation: The style is too sophisticated for his type!

Victor looked at a group of oversized swatches layered at the end of Ryman's ten-foot-long Louis XIV dining room table. "The fabrics are lovely."

"Aren't they? The material is called Scotch V100. It has the feel of cashmere and the durability and breathability of the world's finest wools." Translation: This material is damn expensive!

"What do you think of this color?" asked Victor, picking up a red Glen plaid.

"Simply not you." Translation: It will make you look fatter than you are. "I believe this patterned herringbone in a midnight blue will look fabulous. Midnight is a special order, but worth the wait." Translation: This material will cost you even more.

"Let the process begin," Edward smiled, relishing the idea of measuring Victor from his crotch to the top of his shoes.

About twenty uncomfortable minutes later, Edward was finished measuring, but not selling.

"Mr. Martini, since you've been kind enough to purchase two magnificent suits, I would be remiss if I didn't suggest a gray mohair topcoat as an accompaniment. You will be a fashion statement." Translation: Let's spend some more while I've got you here.

"Maybe next time."

"Tell you what; because you're an associate of Mr. Ryman's, I'd like to offer you twenty-five percent off. Does that sound fair for a handmade, double-breasted topcoat that will last forever?"

Victor hesitated. Edward glanced at Ryman, who nodded.

"I just happen to have made a stunning camelhair topcoat for a customer who is about your size. Just try this on and see what you think." The coat fit beautifully; Victor looked like royalty.

"Come on, Victor, live a little," teased Ryman. "You can buy Sandra a few strands of black Tahitian pearls with your next million."

Ten more minutes passed; the measurements were complete and Edward was tallying the bill. "With the discount, that will be $15,594, which includes all taxes and shipping, plus lifetime alterations, should we lose some of that baby fat."

Holy shit, Victor thought, *Sandra will have my ass!* Reluctantly, he gave Edward his American Express Card.

Edward entered the data into his laptop. "I'll make sure we keep your card on record; anytime you want to order additional suits, just ring the shop or email me. Here's my card. I'll staple it to the invoice. I've also taken the liberty of writing my home phone number down if you happen to be in London and would like another fitting. I'd also like to give you a little gift," continued

Edward. He pulled a beautiful black felt dress hat out of one of his wardrobe cases. "This is a hand-signed Giorgio Armani. It is an exquisite complement for your topcoat. Wear it in good health."

Victor looked in the full-length mirror. His makeover was complete.

23.

Las Vegas Penthouse Poker

Julie Jakowitz waited impatiently at the registration counter in his signature checkered jacket and open-collar shirt. Slot machines, blackjack, and craps tables played in high-volume stereo in the giant pink-and-red room.

Ryman and Victor walked in. Jakowitz approached with a smile. "Based on the way you guys are dressed, you must be from Wall Street." They shook hands. "The poker tournament in Sam's suite is running a little long. I don't understand how they keep score other than who wins the most money. How about we have a drink and then you freshen up in your rooms?" One drink quickly turned into two.

"How long have you known Sam?" asked Victor.

"We go back 60 years to the streets of Brooklyn," said Jakowitz. "During the war, we flew sorties together. He was a gunner and I was his co-pilot. Afterward, we both returned to Flatbush. I got my degree from Brooklyn College and became a CPA. Sam went into retailing. Occasionally, he needed to outsource some of his more complicated financial work, so he hired me. We became pretty good friends. I got to know his wife, Erica, and then the kids, Linda, Albert, and Kim. I'm the godfather of his oldest son, Albert."

"We're all New York City street kids," observed Victor.

Julie looked skeptically at Victor in his tailored blue pinstriped suit. "Street kids don't dress like that."

Trying to establish similar roots, Victor said, "I was born in Harlem and raised in the South Bronx by first-generation Italian immigrants."

Julie didn't really care; he went on with his own story. "Anyway, somewhere along the way, Sam convinced me to move to California and open a CPA practice with him as my lone client.

"And then he persuaded me to use some of my old military contacts to start an export company," Julie continued, "focused on bringing Korean products into the U.S., and finding low-cost sources of manufacture in South Korea for American companies. In the first few years, I made about thirty trips to Korea. Before I knew it, I had American companies asking if I could get rid of their excess merchandise in Korea. Likewise, I had Korean companies who wanted to distribute their excess in the States. Sam and I put our heads together, and soon we were doing a ton of deals. He was buying and selling stuff I'd identify, and he'd ask me to unload merchandise he found. We started to make a hell of a lot of money together."

"When did you begin to work for Sam full time?" asked Victor.

"No, no," scolded Julie. "I don't work for nobody. Sam and I are partners."

At 4:00 a.m., Julie checked his watch. "I think the game is probably breaking up about now."

~

Jakowitz escorted Ryman and Victor to Nachman's penthouse suite. The living room was the size of a football field, colored in flamingo pink and bone white. The poker players were shrouded in smoke around a crowded table. A gorgeous black woman wearing a skintight dress, stiletto heels, and long, shiny black wig greeted the new arrivals. "Hi, I'm Rita. I help Sam with his things."

"Fellas, this is the last hand," Nachman's voice boomed through the smoke toward Ryman and Victor. "Make yourselves comfortable at the bar or, if you prefer, watch these sharks wipe out poor old Sam."

The five other players laughed politely. Within minutes, the pot had risen to $40,000. Only Nachman and a wrinkled man with a salt and pepper goatee and a silver earring were still in the game.

"You're bluffing again," declared the beard, pushing in a pile of chips. "I'll see your $10,000 and call."

For a moment, Nachman feigned terror, then calmly placed four sevens on the table.

"Goddamn it! How the fuck do you do it every time?" The beard threw up his cards.

"Relax. It's only money," laughed Nachman. "And you've got plenty of it, Isel. Anyway, I've got to break for a business meeting. Let's reconvene in a couple of hours." Nachman was maybe five-foot-eight with a rounded, slightly obese belly and a short upper torso topped with a tiny, bald, peanut-shaped head. His gravelly, raspy tone was refined, almost gentle. He was a proponent of the thirty-second smell test: if your shit didn't stink in that time, you got his attention. Otherwise, you were history.

Rita sat on the couch behind Sam. "Rita honey," said Sam, "why don't you take a little nap in our bedroom while I talk to these nice men?"

"Sure, Big Daddy," she smiled seductively. "Momma always does whatever Daddy wants."

"Come on, gentlemen. Eat," urged Nachman, pointing at a giant plate of gravlax, cream cheese, mini-bagels, and all the fixings. "We can't do business on an empty stomach."

With a shared passion for poker and competition, Nachman and Ryman bonded instantly. When Ryman crowed about whipping Bjorn Borg's ass in Monte Carlo, Nachman countered with out-bluffing Leroy Neiman in poker at Cannes. Each took turns trying to outdo the other. Then they started on their houses. Ryman's hand included the Kings Point Mansion, a twelve-room townhouse in London's toney Knightsbridge; and the Sutton Place Penthouse in New York. Nachman's hand was stacked with his palatial Bel

Air mansion that overlooked the more modest homes of comedian Eddie Murphy and singer Englebert Humperdinck.

Nachman's kicker, though, was a flawlessly restored Spanish adobe in Santa Monica, once owned by Douglas Fairbanks. It looked out over the ocean, as well as an 8,000 square foot cottage with a tennis court and swimming pool on the grounds of the exclusive La Costa Resort in Carlsbad, California.

The finale was all business, with Ryman taking the lead. "The first ten million was cheap available seed capital. This next round of acquisitions should easily justify another fifty-million-dollar raise. The acquired companies wind up with some mix of cash and stock, plus earn-outs. If we achieve just normal growth and a modest P/E multiple of fifteen, everybody's stock will be worth thirty to forty times its original value. That's Jimmy Dean country."

"You mean the country and western singer who makes sausage?" asked Nachman, totally perplexed by the analogy.

"That's him. When Dean sold his company to Consolidated Foods ten years ago, he got a million in cash and ten million in stock for a company doing about thirty million in sales. Consolidated became the Sara Lee Corporation. They started acquiring companies left and right, splitting the stock eight times in the process. 'Big Bad John's' stock is worth over 400 million today."

"If we decide to pursue this matter, what are the next steps?" asked Nachman.

"We need to review your financials," said Ryman. "If everything is clean and you can show a substantial three-year earnings history, we'll make you an offer."

"That's easy." Nachman turned to Julie. "Make sure Marty Dawson gets Ryman a set of the latest numbers. Franklyn, when you're satisfied, let's meet at my beach house and talk deal specifics. If you have questions, ask Marty. He knows everything. He's family."

"Who's Marty Dawson?" asked Ryman.

"He's my consigliere, my number one man. Sam doesn't make a business move with him. The good news is that his firm, Delano Mondrain Hudson, is not far from you in midtown."

Victor imagined another spartan set of offices like that of Allyn Tishman; he just hoped they had more than water and peanut butter for refreshments.

Ryman wanted to keep talking, but Nachman had other ideas. "Rita, honey, call the boys. Tell them to come on back so we can finish our poker tournament."

~

Jakowitz shared breakfast the next morning in Nachman's suite. "What do you think, Julie?"

"Ryman's a piece of work, but I think we can work with him. Plus, I have a feeling that corporate guy, Victor, who sat there with his mouth shut, will run the thing. His rep is pretty first-class."

"You and Marty handle it," ordered Nachman. "Share our financials, assuming they sign a non-disclosure. But let me be clear: I want cash for the company. No Jimmy Dean stock deal. Dean got damn lucky, playing poker with his company like that. I'm an old-fashioned guy; all that matters to me in this world is how much cash you have."

"Which bring us to the ownership of the company product inventories," said Jakowitz.

"Is there a question there?" glared Nachman. "The $40 million in pre-acquisition inventories belong to me. And tell Marty our three-year earnings history should justify a purchase price of $30 million, net of fees to you, Marty, and whomever else."

Nachman spread cream cheese on his sesame bagel. "That's the money side," he continued with his mouth full. "Tell Marty I also want to be off the personal guarantees for our bank credit line. If ITI needs a little time to get their shit together, like twelve months post-financing, fine. But no more than that."

"Got it," said Jakowitz, like he was taking a deli order.

There was one last item. "We've also got to protect the Nachman name. So there needs to be a clause that if ITI goes belly-up, the Nachman name reverts to the Nachman family."

24.

Douglas Fairbanks' Beach House

The day Ryman and Victor returned from Vegas, Astrid signed for a registered mail envelope from the Nachman Company. As was her custom, she carefully opened it, made a copy of the contents for herself, and then carefully reglued the envelope before strutting into Ryman's office.

"This looks important. I think you might want to open it," she advised.

Ryman devoured the tasty documents. Not only did the reports meet all public-accounting standards, but the three-year earning history was substantially higher than he'd anticipated. Ryman shared the Nachman financials with Victor, who didn't quite grasp the full impact of their promotional value.

Ryman closed his door and began tossing tidbits over the phone to those he deemed essential. "Otis, I can't give you a lot of details but, as a major stockholder, I thought you'd like to know we are close to the acquisition of an important West Coast liquidator." It was like dropping bloody bait in the water.

As soon as Weinstein hung up, he made two phone calls to some of his Hassidic sources, who identified Sam Nachman as the likely acquisition candidate. Then Weinstein called Louisa Dothan to place an order for another million shares.

~

Ryman's next call was Marino. "Ryman, no long-winded BS; just get to the point," snarled Marino. "It's the middle of the fuckin' trading day."

Ryman leaned forward, accidentally hitting the speakerphone button. Astrid noticed, and started taking copious notes. "What if I told you we were close to a major acquisition, a company with a historically solid earnings stream?" Ryman dangled his loaded hook.

"You want the news to spread? Then put some fuckin' meat in the sandwich." On the way to the water cooler, Victor couldn't help but overhear Marino screaming on the speakerphone.

"How about thirty-five million in revenues and three million in after-tax profits?" declared Ryman.

"Where are you going to get numbers like that?"

"The Sam Nachman Company."

"The LA liquidator? How the fuck are you going to finance that?"

"Like I've done before: with consolidated 'subject-to' deals. The payoff is huge—so long as you hold up your part of the bargain."

"We are."

"Bullshit," snapped Ryman. "The stock price has got to climb. I've got to be able to close these deals with a lot of paper to make it easier to play with good-will allocations."

~

It was decision time for Victor. Did he confront Ryman about his questionable promotional tactics, or just put on ethical blinders? After Ryman was off the phone, Victor decided to approach him.

"Franklyn, I couldn't help but hear Marino screaming over the speakerphone. What was that all about?"

Ryman responded diplomatically. "I was briefing our underwriter about the Nassi situation. Part of my job as CEO is to ensure the public gets the right information."

Victor stared.

"Cut that holier than thou bullshit," scolded Ryman, trying to intimidate Victor. "What's your point?"

Victor pushed back. "Franklyn, as I told you in the beginning, I'm a street kid from the South Bronx. Intimidation doesn't work. First you give me a hypocritical speech about the quiet period, and then you turn around and spill your guts to our thug financier."

Ryman attempted to deflect the issue. "Marino is a legitimate investment banker."

"Ryman. Cut the horseshit. If Marino travels in the same circles as my Mafia cousin Antnee, he's at least part thug."

Ryman was cornered. He had no place to go. "Victor. We're partners, right? So let's call a spade a spade. Norwest is not exactly Morgan Stanley. Do you think I enjoy dealing with scumbags like Marino and Louisa Dothan? They couldn't shine our shoes. But we have got to be practical. We need them to get through the first door. But they're so dumb and slimy that we've got to hold their hand every step of the way to make sure they do what we need them to do."

Ryman paused. "So, are you with me?"

Victor knew he had just crossed another Rubicon.

~

Marty Dawson was clear about the offer Sam would accept. "The good news," said Dawson, "is that Sam is in no rush, which should give you time to organize a larger second round of financing. He also suggested you discuss the term sheet at his beach house in Santa Monica. The place is a kick. It used to belong to Douglas Fairbanks during the height of his career."

"You're going where?" asked Sandra sarcastically. "What the hell kind of businessman has an initial meeting during a Vegas poker game, and then invites you to discuss terms at Douglas Fairbanks's beach house?"

"Baby, it's all part of the money game," rationalized Victor.

"It feels more like we're playing a round of filthy-dirty Monopoly with no real rules." Sandra shuddered. "Is this really us now?"

Victor delivered his now-familiar speech about financial independence. Against her better instincts, Sandra acquiesced. "Careful what you wish for—one of these days, I expect to be a regular on these work-play trips. Agreed?"

~

A maid in a starched white outfit opened the carved, oversized dark green door to the beach house. She led Ryman and Victor past elegant bronze sculptures and trickling fountains made of carved granite, down a gallery-style hall with diffused light that flooded a wall with magnificent original works of art.

Nachman greeted the men with a big handshake. "Gentlemen, let's eat and then we'll do some business." Moments later, they were standing on a patio with ocean views, in front of a sumptuous lunch buffet that included three different caviars, five types of smoked fish, and beef, tuna, and salmon carpaccio.

Ryman stared up the beach toward the home on the crest where he himself had disappeared into the darkness two years ago. He thought to himself, *Have I returned to the light?*

Meanwhile, Nachman decided to let his hair down.

"Did I ever explain how the Nachman company got started? I was a mid-level merchandising manager for the old Whitefront appliance chain until I was 50. Desperate for some cash to put the kids through college, I got the idea to create a clearance sale with some old inventory. It worked great. I did another with the same results.

"Soon, WT Grant went into liquidation. I was confident my clearance sale strategy would work there, too. But the courts required a $100 million letter of credit as a security deposit before you could even place a bid. I managed to get a few wealthy friends to take a chance in exchange for 50 percent of the profits, if any."

"So, what happened?" asked Victor.

"We bid 30 cents on the dollar for the $800 million inventory, which was twice what competitors were willing to bid. Fortunately, the liquidation was more successful than anybody imagined, including me! Using progressive pricing and massive advertising, we sold the inventory for almost fifty cents on the dollar, after all expenses.

"Two years later, the $600 million Marshman-Ross inventory went into liquidation. I simply applied what I had learned from WT Grant. My competitors again thought I was crazy to bid 32 cents on the dollar. They laughed and called me the ultimate poker player."

"What happened that time?" asked Victor.

"Kid, we ultimately sold the inventory for 51 cents on the dollar, and I've never needed a financing partner since."

"Fascinating," said Ryman, and he meant it.

"Franklyn, I gather you've looked at the numbers, talked to my boys," said Nachman. "Hopefully, they told you whatever you wanted to know."

"They were all great," Ryman replied. "I understand exactly where your business stands."

"I like you," said Nachman, patting Ryman on the shoulder. "And I'd like to do a deal with you, so I'm going to tell you what I think is fair. But I'm not going to negotiate. Understand?"

Jakowitz and Friedway had prepared Ryman well. There were no surprises: $30 million in cash, ownership of the $40 million in existing inventories, a personally guaranteed credit line for twelve months, and the return of the Nachman name in case of bankruptcy.

"Your terms are fine," said Ryman, who knew dickering would be fruitless. "But I need a favor. I need you on the credit line for a couple of years. We need an operating history for the banks to provide ITI with the significant credit lines to do bigger deals. You know the business far better than me. If a deal comes along and we don't have the cash or the line available, we're dead."

There was a moment of silence as Nachman leaned back in his chair to study his hand. "Let me talk to Marty about that one," said Nachman finally.

"How about we add two million shares of stock to the purchase price, in exchange for the credit line extension?" asked Ryman, knowing The Street would not look kindly on an acquisition deal that didn't include ITI stock.

"While we're here," continued Ryman, "we should discuss salaries and earn-out formulas."

"That's Marty's area," replied Nachman, not interested in such details. "Whatever is fine with Marty is fine with me."

25.
Ryman Tries to Change the Deal

"Keep your mouth shut," ordered Ryman as he and Victor walked down Park Avenue to Dawson's office.

"Before we leave Dawson's office today, they're going to agree to split revenues generated by the sale of that $40 million in inventories sitting on their balance sheet."

"Didn't we already shake on deal terms?" asked Victor.

"Ahhh," grinned Ryman. "Nothing's ever done in a business deal until the ink is dry."

Delano Mondrain Hudson was nothing like Tishman's spartan world headquarters! The 150-year old firm's elegant lobby looked like an exclusive London men's club: stuffy wingback chairs and walnut-paneled walls, which were lined with antique Audubon lithographs and English hunting scene prints in gilded mahogany frames.

Dawson's matronly but pleasant assistant introduced herself and escorted them down a long hall, past a series of offices overlooking Park Avenue. Every member of the plush club checked them out as they walked by.

"Don't take the staring personally," Ryman whispered in Victor's ear. "Partners at big law firms are like pickpockets, always ready to steal a prospective client or force their way into a deal that's on the table. Anything that permits them to stake a claim to some of the lead partner's income."

~

Dawson sat behind an oval-shaped desk in a corner office the size of the Yankee Stadium infield. White shirt with the collar open, curly salt and pepper hair, charming and athletic, he looked like a decathlon competitor.

"Gentleman, good to meet you. I'm Marty," he said, hanging up and taking over. "Sam has spoken kindly about you, which isn't something he often does."

Marty wasn't alone. On the green leather couch nearby sat a bombshell blonde wrapped tightly in a black dress.

"This is Christine Polack," Marty made the intro. "One of the best paralegals in the firm."

"Martin, we are delighted to have a deal with Sam," began Ryman, who couldn't take his eyes off Christine even as he began to negotiate. "He's a great strategic fit. We need unconventional ways to redistribute inventories. That's why we are willing to give him such a generous earnings multiple."

Dawson smiled. He could see a slow curveball floating up to the plate. "Franklyn, let's get off on the right foot, eh? The name is Marty. Martin sounds like an arrogant medieval prince."

Victor chuckled. But Ryman didn't like public putdowns.

"We want Sam and the family to be happy with the deal. But there also needs to be some spirit of fairness," said Ryman, his eyes on Christine's twin mounds and working down her strike zone. "The fact that Sam will only leave the credit line in place for a year is difficult to swallow. What the company needs is a three-year string. We all know how important the availability of capital is to snatch those lucrative opportunistic deals."

Marty leaned back in his oversized leather chair. "As you know, Sam feels strongly about putting a ceiling on his credit line guarantee."

"That's why I'd like to propose a compromise," said Ryman. "Why not leave half the inventory in the company, like a cash reserve? If we need more credit than we have available for a given deal, we'll collateralize some of the inventory. At the end of four years, ownership of the remaining inventory reverts to Nachman."

Victor saw Dawson grimace, but he remained quiet.

"And suppose the inventory has materially depreciated?" interjected Dawson.

"Well, that's one of the risks of the deal," said Ryman. "We'll make our best efforts to ensure that doesn't happen."

"I've been in this business for over twenty years, and I can say with total confidence that there is nobody like Sam Nachman," declared Dawson, angrily leaning forward to put his hands on his desk. "He will bring significant revenue to ITI, as well as attract other valuable partners, both of which will help make your next financing a reality."

"I'm not asking for a new deal." Ryman tried his change of pace delivery. "I'm just asking you to consider."

Dawson swung away and connected. "Listen, let's cut this creeping incrementalism crap. You need Nachman. You need his good name, and you need his earnings. Nachman doesn't need you. Either take the deal as is, or let's just part friends."

"But..." started Ryman.

Dawson's stare shut him up. The inning was over.

"I'll have to confer with my advisors," concluded Ryman.

"You do that, Franklyn," said Marty. "But don't bother me again unless your *advisors* accept the deal precisely as you and Sam already agreed."

~

The following day, Ryman again met with Dawson. "Congrats, the ITI Board of Directors have approved the Nachman terms as outlined in the contract," said Ryman, lying like a rug. "ITI hopes to take full advantage of the company's considerable operating expertise."

"I wasn't trying to be difficult," replied Dawson smugly. "But, as you can appreciate, I was given a specific set of expectations by the family."

"I do have one question. Why is Sam so adamant about a clause that allows him to retain the Nachman brand in perpetuity after a five-year operating period?"

"You know lawyers. We are trained to think about the worst case. In the unlikely event that ITI goes down, I want Sam and the family to be able to return to the liquidation business with a brand name the world recognizes."

"What an academic issue. There is no way ITI is going anywhere but up."

"When can I expect a signed contract?" asked Dawson, choosing not to reply.

"I'll sign it today and have it messengered over," said Ryman.

"Let me save you a few quid," Dawson responded. "Christine can stop over and pick up the document. We're only a few blocks from you."

"Fine," said Ryman, visions of blonde curls dancing in his head. "I'll be here until lunchtime, and then I'm off to the Vertical Club for a workout."

Christine seemed to smile at something. Ryman noticed the erection in his pants.

"Marty, no worries if you're running a little late. I can always wait for Christine at the Club."

"Franklyn, forget about it. Christine is way out of your league. Understand?" warned Marty.

26.

Big Retainers Don't Grow on Trees

Ryman and Tishman agreed that the time was quickly approaching when the required legal services would be greater than Allyn's boutique firm could provide. Ryman gave Dawson a call.

"Marty, this is Franklyn. I want to compliment you on how you handled the Nachman transaction. My board has instructed me to ask if you and your firm would have any interest in representing ITI in acquisitions and future financings."

"Franklyn, I'm flattered, but I'll need to discuss the matter with my partners, some of whom may not comfortable with a public startup."

"What do you think would make them comfortable?" asked Ryman.

Dawson considered. "For sure, they would want to meet with you and Victor as the founders."

"Done. Anything else?"

"No financial exposure."

"Translate that into dollars?" said Ryman.

"We'd need a $150,000 a month retainer, plus all direct expenses, and Delano Mondrain would retain the right to void the relationship on seven days' notice." Ryman grimaced; 30-90 days was the standard, making a week a little hard to swallow.

~

The main conference room at Delano Mondrain Hudson was standing room only.

The Firm's managing partners, Sefton Delano and Theodore Mondrain, were as straightlaced as Marty was pragmatic and entrepreneurial. They were like a bookend set of square jaws, deep chiseled brown eyes, blue pinstriped Paul Stuart suits, $150 haircuts, manicures, and white shirts with boring club ties resting on English spread collars.

"Fellas, I'd like to introduce Franklyn Ryman and Victor Martini," said Marty, sound like a master of ceremonies. "They are the founders and primary ITI principals. We're here to discuss the possibility of taking on ITI as a Delano Mondrain Hudson client.

"I've explained to both that the Firm is not normally in the business of dealing with start-ups. However, in fairness, Franklyn and Victor have a pretty unusual concept and have already signed a contract to acquire our client, the Nachman Company. I think it's best for them to explain their vision directly to you."

Ryman and Victor wowed the all-male room for thirty minutes, seamlessly sharing the spotlight—bobbing and weaving, with rapid-fire combinations of corporate vision, preliminary projections, and acquisition candidates. When they were finished, Ryman lit up his signature Macanudo and took a few large puffs, unaware that his ashes were scattering on the table and floor.

Dawson knew what to expect from Ryman, but he was surprised at Victor's polish. "I must say," said Dawson, "you were smooth as silk with a pretty skeptical group."

Victor decided to pat himself on the back. "I've been wooing powerful, sophisticated clients ever since I was old enough to drink out of a cup."

Ryman wanted to vomit jealousy.

~

As they rode down the elevator, Ryman was determined to regain the lead position.

"The way, I explained the ITI story," crowed Ryman, "these guys will fall over themselves to be our corporate attorneys."

"I'm not so sure," said Victor.

"Okay, whiz kid, you've got the floor."

"To begin with, they didn't trust us. Those lawyers reeked custom blue-blood; we're off-the-rack. It wasn't about the money. It was about having the proper lineage. The only reason they even listened was because Marty's got clout."

"Who gives a shit!" responded Ryman assertively. "In the end, clout always wins."

"My guess is if Marty makes one mistake with that group of white-collar sharks, he'll be out. They don't like him any more than they do us. He's there because Sam brings in big fees between his deals, company matters, and homes."

Victor's growing command of the situation alarmed Ryman. He realized it would be harder to bully Victor than he initially assumed —and that extra effort wasn't part of his original plan.

~

The Delano Mondrain Hudson partners held their own meeting after the meeting with Ryman and Victor. "The whole thing stinks," said Delano. "ITI sounds like a sugar-coated pyramid scheme. I'll only go along if we're unanimous."

"I'm with Sefton," said Mondrain. "But $150,000 retainers don't grow on trees. Who the hell knows? We're lawyers, not business people. ITI *might* be able to do what they say."

Sefton turned to Marty, knowing it could be an ethical breach for Marty to manage interconnected clients. "Who is going to run this account to avoid conflicts of interest? The American Bar Association has rules."

Dawson was not about to disclose that he planned to be the lead on both, even if he had to give another partner a share of his share. "Sefton, let me think about the issue; I'm sure I can find an acceptable in-house solution."

Mondrain, preparing to leave, stared at Marty. "Make sure you collect the goddamn monthly fee upfront. If they stop paying, dump them! No second chances."

27.

Eddie's Magic Barter Credits

"Franklyn, now that our deal's done," said Nachman over Ryman's speakerphone. "I've got this clever friend, Ed Toothson, who you should meet."

"Who's Ed Toothson?" asked Ryman.

"After we won several liquidation bids in the courts, my competitors began bidding up the purchase price of available inventories by partnering with deep-pocketed investors," said Nachman in his soft, raspy voice. "I had to find another angle, because cash-only bids increasingly contained more risk and less upside."

Astrid entered. "Want some coffee?" she asked quietly. Ryman nodded without stopping his conversation with Nachman. She lingered on leaving and returning, taking copious mental notes in the process.

"One day, Toothson shows up at my office on Wilshire Boulevard unannounced. He says he's the president of Mansfield Communications. My son Albert says, 'Never heard of you,' and tells the guy to get lost. I hear the racket in the lobby. Toothson tells me he flew in from New York to propose a partnership. I'm curious; I ask, 'Why would I partner with you?' He replies, 'Receivable barter credits.' I tell him I have no idea what the hell he is talking about. He says 'Nobody does; that's why you need to give me ten minutes.'"

Ryman laughed.

"Toothson tells me he can bring deal flow and help close the contracts at no cost to me. I ask how. He starts explaining how his magical barter credits work. I figured it was worth a test. Before I know it, we're signing one client contract, then another."

"So," said Ryman sarcastically, "I'm listening."

"Franklyn, I think it's better if Eddie explains. After all, he invented them."

"Sam, with all due respect, Toothson sounds like a Nachman subsidiary. Our offering is about selling The Street earnings based on the historical success of individually acquired companies."

"Franklyn, you miss my point. Thanks to Eddie's invention, both Mansfield *and* the Nachman companies have made a ton in the last four years. We've closed a shit-pile of mega cash-barter deals with Canon, Mattel, and Panasonic, among others. My cash and reputation give companies the comfort that they're dealing with a reputable company. They know exactly how and where we were re-marketing their inventory—no black-box bullshit. And Eddie's credits allow them to avoid a write-off."

Ryman *sort of* got it. "So... Mansfield is a free-standing business with a recurring earnings stream?"

In his own office, the portly Nachman leaned back in his seat. "Relax, Franklyn. Relax. *Both* businesses are here to stay. Eddie fulfills the goddamn credits—at least once in a while—to keep the auditors happy," laughed Nachman. "He's even figured out how to make a profit on the barter-credits. And my office handles all the client books and records and profit distributions, so everybody's happy."

"Sam, am I missing something? You guys buy the merchandise for cash and barter credits, then profits when the clients use the credits. That doesn't make sense."

Nachman laughed. "Told you this guy was clever. But, as I said, you need to hear it straight from Eddie."

"Do you have Ed's contact information?" said Ryman. "I'll call and make a meeting."

"I've made Eddie a rich man. Just tell me when—he'll be available," said Nachman, who then called Toothson himself.

~

"Is this a news update?" smiled Toothson. "Or did you do a deal with ITI?"

"Eddie, this is your chance to cash out big. We got an excellent cash price for the business, plus some inventory credits and company stock. We're satisfied."

Toothson hesitated. "You know we have a good thing going, operating in the shadows."

Nachman knew he needed to keep working with Toothson post-acquisition, so he turned up the pressure. "No problem if you don't want to meet Ryman. Just keep in mind, as an ITI company, I will be required to do excess inventory deals with other ITI companies. That's the whole synergy thing. If you remain independent, you'll have to put up the cash," said Nachman, who knew Toothson loathed that kind of risk.

Nachman also knew Toothson had over $300 million in barter credits on the Mansfield books. He had fulfilled less than ten percent in his best year, barely enough to avoid legal complications and remain credible.

"If and when client management changes," continued Nachman, "the new people may scrutinize those barter credit certificates with your name on them. Suddenly, all those barter credits you issue like popcorn could become a huge personal liability. The way I see it, ITI offers you an easy way to become a rich, respected, legitimate businessman *and* to distance yourself from a pile of potential lawsuits. Don't be a schmuck!"

28.

Ryman Gives Away the Store

Toothson's offices, like Toothson himself, were one of a kind.

Ryman and Victor were led up a set of steep steps and down a long hall to a dimly lit conference room by a round-faced receptionist with a butch haircut and nervous twitch. The dark gray walls were covered with framed pictures and matching letters from various American presidents.

As the two were to learn, collecting White House memorabilia was a Toothson family passion. They found the stuff historically interesting, and it was an excellent long-term investment that was also very impressive to the underground deal makers. The latter would stop by from time to time with the latest pay-for-play insider inventory tips.

At five feet, seven inches tall and weighing over three hundred pounds, Eddie Toothson was hardly presidential. He had a warm smile, big bushy eyebrows, and significant stomach rolls barely hidden beneath his suit jacket. A big briar pipe was clenched in his teeth.

Ryman was about to light up himself when Toothson opened a wooden cigar box.

"Please," he offered. "Try one of these. They're better than a Macanudo and sold only in Cuba. I've got this newspaper in Puerto Rico, *El Progresso*, run by some Cuban expatriates." His eyes twinkled. "Somehow, my boys get them and, like magic, a box just appears in the interoffice mail. If we have a drought, Mona slips down there in her plane," smiled Toothson.

"Who's Mona?" asked Victor.

"My wife, the receptionist."

"How did you get into the barter business?" asked Ryman.

"My background is direct marketing," began Toothson. "I worked for the old Walton Watch Company, and then the Dawkins Record Club. We were big on marketing directly to consumers. At the end of every annual clearance drive, we had leftover inventory searching for a non-competitive means of disposal."

Toothson failed to mention that he himself bought some of that inventory for cash at bargain-basement prices and attempted to re-market the good overseas at a significant profit. Unfortunately, his overseas *partner* took title to the inventory and disappeared, leaving Toothson about $1.5 million in the hole.

He eventually declared personal bankruptcy, but he was able to find a court clerk willing to remove the bankruptcy from the public records for a small additional bribe. The default affected how Toothson conducted future business. He refused to put any of his own cash into a deal, hence his exclusive reliance on receivable barter credits to purchase inventories. Nachman still knew nothing of the bankruptcy; he just assumed Toothson was a chicken-shit cheapskate.

~

"Sam and I work well together," crowed Toothson. "We have complementary skills, and that makes us tough competitors. Sam decides how much cash to offer the manufacturer, what price to sell the goods for, and which distribution channels to utilize. I analyze a company's media needs and purchasing patterns, and then develop a supplemental media plan using our barter credits. Our staff then executes that plan, as requested by the manufacturer."

"Could you explain how a media barter credit plan works?" said Victor. "As you know, I've run some major advertising agency accounts in my day, but I'm not familiar with that idea."

Toothson's facial expression changed. "No, I didn't know that."

With a fresh smile, he continued. "Let's say a client carries the old inventory on his balance sheet for $100 million, but he knows it's only worth $5 million," continued Toothson. "Most managements want to avoid large write-offs, because they drain their earnings and their stock price, and can put their job in danger. That's where we come in. We offer $5 million in cash and $95 million in barter credits, which is our pledge that we will buy media in the future with the credits."

"How can you sell the old products at a deep discount and make enough to pay for the barter credits?"

"Oh, it doesn't work like that. To access the credits, they have to spend fifty cents on the rate card cost for the media option we offer."

"Still sounds like it could be a loss leader."

"Not really," said Toothson, smiling broadly. "We only offer media we can buy for 30-35 percent of the rate card."

"Are you saying that Sam makes a profit on the remarketing of the old inventory, and you make a profit when the client uses their barter credits?"

"That's about it," Toothson replied smugly.

"When do you and Nachman write off the unused barter credits?"

"Never."

"How is that?" asked Ryman.

"Our contracts state we will use our *best efforts* to fulfill your barter credits, so we have no accounting obligation to carry a loss reserve."

Ryman heard what he wanted to hear—big profits with little expense. "What are your annual earnings?"

"Hard to project.," said Toothson, who knew just how to tease a greedy little pig like Ryman. "I don't pay any taxes, and I've never been publicly audited, but I am willing to guarantee I can deliver a net of $3.5 million per year for the last three years, maybe a little more. My goal was to build a business I could sell, so we've kept *another* set of detailed books and records."

"Are you certain they could pass the scrutiny of a public audit?" asked Ryman.

"Absolutely. On my mother's grave," swore Toothson.

"How much do you want?" asked Ryman calmly.

"I recognize that as a private company, Mansfield is an attractive candidate to a select group of buyers, so I've discounted my purchase price to ten million dollars upfront, or about three times earnings. I'm prepared to earn anything above that on a performance basis."

"Sounds fair," said Ryman. "Sam said you were a straight shooter. We've met so many guys who are just after our pot of gold. That's why it's always better to do business with people you know, or who are referred to you by good people."

Toothson took a puff on his cigar as he slipped a little goodie under the radar. "There's a bit of inventory from past deals, as was the case with Sam, that would also add credit to my side of the ledger," said Toothson.

"How much inventory are we talking about?"

"The spreadsheet entry lists $30 million because I purposely overstate my balance sheet to enhance my credibility for sales purposes, but on a liquidation basis, the inventories are worth pennies on the dollar." Toothson, a natural salesman, moved to the assumed close with a little smokescreen. "As you can appreciate, since we're talking such a low acquisition price for Mansfield, I'd like to maintain and liquidate those inventories post an ITI closing."

"That seems reasonable to me," replied Ryman.

~

Toothson wasn't finished. "Franklyn, you've bought lots of companies; maybe you can help me think through another issue."

Ryman puffed on his cigar. "I'll do my best."

"For some years, under the advice of counsel, of course, we've accumulated earnings to avoid paying taxes. Consequently, we now have a rather large cash buildup that can potentially be distributed as either capital gains or ordinary income—an income tax differential of almost twenty-six percent. How do I make sure I take the money out before the sale without making a sophomoric mistake?"

"Not a problem; my lawyers deal with deferred assets all the time," volunteered Ryman. "How much cash are we talking?"

"About twenty-four million," replied Toothson.

Victor was incredulous. Toothson planned to strip the company of working capital and product inventories *before* the sale to ITT.

"But keep in mind Eddie," continued Ryman, "your books do need to meet public accounting standards. Audit fees to clean up the books are an expense to the seller."

"How much?"

"In the neighborhood of $100,000 for a three-year audit."

"Wow, that's a lot of money," protested Toothson for dramatic effect. "You're not dealing with General Electric."

"This is a deal point," Ryman insisted.

Toothson acquiesced, knowing he had given up squat because Mansfield was unmarketable without a Big Five CPA public audit.

"The only remaining matter is the *subject to* boilerplate in the contract," said Ryman casually.

Toothson's eyebrows rose. "What does that mean?"

"Like Sam, we give you a non-refundable deposit on contract signing and pay you the purchase balance when we raise the next round of capital."

Toothson smiled. "Sounds like one of my barter credit IOUs. What's the drop-dead date on your right to close?"

"I figure twelve months at the outside, but, like with Sam, we are asking for twenty-four months because this will be an unusual acquisition for the SEC to digest."

Toothson stood up. "Sam agreed to these terms?"

"Absolutely," said Ryman, lying through his teeth.

"If he's in, I'm in," replied Toothson.

"Sam is leaving his credit line in place for 12 months," said Ryman. "I assume you'll do the same."

"I'd be happy to do that, but I don't have a credit line. We always use Sam's."

~

Once outside the Mansfield offices, Victor turned sarcastically to Franklyn. "I think we just agreed to a *zero-net-worth transaction on the layaway plan.*"

"What the hell is a zero-net-worth transaction?" snapped Ryman. "Sounds like advertising jargon to me.

"'Zero-net-worth' isn't advertising lingo," argued Victor with surprising insight. "It's the true value of an acquisition after it has been stripped of its underlying real book value. We're paying ten million for Mansfield's historical earnings stream. Toothson keeps the company's accumulated cash and existing product inventories while we keep all the barter credit obligations that generated the cash and inventory in the first place."

"You're over-thinking matters," Ryman persisted. "It takes time to understand the subtleties of Wall Street; it's like no other place. I've completed hundreds of acquisitions; each has its own rhythm and individual peculiarities, partially based on the wants and whims of the seller. The trick is to give the acquired management the appearance they got what they wanted plus some, while never giving away any more than you initially planned."

"Is that what we just did?" glared Victor.

"Think about how I held the line when Toothson tried to nickel-dime us over legal and accounting fees," replied Ryman proudly. "That's just the way these characters are. You've got to be firm when it counts."

~

After a few subsequent meetings, Toothson concluded Ryman was part genius, part blowhard. He knew that when it came time to *renegotiate* a few final deal points in the final hour—a Toothson trademark—he needed a steady, sympathetic ear on the other side of the table. He had decided to take his chances on the greenhorn —Victor.

"Mona and I were wondering what you and your wife might be doing this Friday night," asked Toothson over the phone. "Since we're going to be partners, I thought we might get to know each other better. I hear your wife's a nurse. Mine was too, before she got involved in the business."

"Sounds great, but I need to check with Sandra; she's the family social director."

"I noticed you guys lived in Greenwich. We're over in Armonk, so we're not that far. You could come over, have a few drinks, and then my driver can take us to the Friars Club in Midtown. There's gonna be a roast of Chris Rock this Friday night. It should be a hoot." The members-only Friars Club had been Manhattan's landmark club where friends and peers roasted America's finest comedians and entertainers for the past 80 years. It took 30 seconds for Victor to decide this was a cool idea.

~

The Martinis arrived at the Toothsons' house at seven on the dot. Mona, already sloshed, had a spread of canapés and two large pitchers filled with dirty martinis and cosmopolitans on the media room table.

"Come on in," said Mona, slurring her words slightly. "You must de Saaandra. Ed has told me so much about you." In her hand, Mona loosely clutched a serving tray. "These teeny-weeny ones are Beluga Duga eggs," she giggled. As she laughed at her own joke, the tray started to waver in her hand.

Sandra came to the rescue. "Mona, these trays are so heavy; let me give you a hand."

Mona let go readily and gulped down another martini. "Sandra, dear, isn't it weird that they call these things dirty? It's like somebody scooped them out of the toilet."

"Honey, we've probably had enough," said Toothson, glaring at her. "Remember, you've got a flying lesson tomorrow."

Sandra was alarmed. "A flying lesson. Really!"

"Christmas gift from our kids to their mom. They plan to take pictures of their mother boarding her first training flight. Remember, dear?" He took the glass out of Mona's hand and set it on the table. "Time to go."

A wobbly Mona smiled at Ed, pointing her finger. "Ed is so right! He's always sooo right. What a guy!"

~

As the car sped down the Hutchinson River Parkway toward the Friars Club, Mona smiled and pulled a white napkin off a fresh pitcher of dirty martinis. "Abracadabra!" Soon the martinis were gone, and so was Mona. She passed out in Sandra's lap.

Toothson was embarrassed, but composed. "After twenty-one years," he shrugged, "she still has energy to burn."

To Sandra and Victor's surprise, Toothson left Mona in the limousine as they went into the Friars Club.

"John," said Toothson to his driver, "take her to the diner. Black coffee. Pick us up in about three hours."

~

Later, Sandra sat quietly in bed. Victor made believe he was reading, but she wasn't fooled. She put his Kindle in her lap.

"So?"

"So, what?" asked Victor.

"Is that what money does to people?" replied Sandra.

"I don't know; I've never had what the Toothsons have."

"They must be missing something. Mona is one unhappy lady."

"They're them, and we're us. That will never happen to us." Victor said confidently.

"Are you sure?"

"As sure as I was the day when I first saw you in that college lounge." Victor went to turn out the light.

"Humor me," said Sandra sweetly. "Could you explain to me again what ITI makes? I'm not sure I understand."

"We don't actually make anything. We buy companies that buy discounted inventories that nobody wants."

"And, what does one do with something that nobody else wants?"

"You get rid of the stuff in any way possible: in-store liquidation sales, on the internet, in sales sections at retail stores internationally. The reality is that there is a buyer for almost anything at the right price."

"But how do they sell it, and still make a profit, in a way that makes you want to buy the company?" asked Sandra.

"That's a long, complicated story involving a thing called receivable barter credits. Let's save that for another day."

"Are you having fun?" asked Sandra.

"I think so."

That was not the answer Sandra wanted to hear.

29.
Back to the Bigtime, with Conditions

With Nachman and Toothson under contract, Ryman knew the time had come.

Norwest Securities did not have the infrastructure or experience to raise the $75 million needed to close Nachman and Toothson, to expand company operations, *and* to identify other potential acquisitions.

Ryman's well-connected advisor, Johnathan Dothan, had been down this road many times before. He suggested a surprising *out-of-the-box* investment banking solution: the 75-year-old blueblood firm of Whitlaw & Company.

"Do you think they would consider us?" asked Ryman.

"You never know if you don't ask. I've done some pretty gamey deals with their managing director, Phillip Scarborough. Plus, we have our secret weapon: Victor's polished line of corporate bullshit."

~

Whitlaw had none of the usual Wall Street investment banker trappings. Located far from Wall Street in a landmark art deco building at Fifty-Eighth Street and Fifth Avenue, the lobby was awash in black and white Carrera marble and had a hand-painted ceiling that paid homage to the Sistine Chapel.

As the three men approached the reception desk, Dothan provided background. "Old man Herb Whitlaw Sr. started the firm with three grand in 1930; ran it with a steel fist. The family tradition continues as a virtual dictatorship under Herb Jr., although my guy Phil, a former university dean, has been the public face for twenty years attracting several large university pension clients like Harvard, Yale, and Stanford."

As the three men got out of the elevator on the seventh floor, a thin, well-dressed man in his late forties nodded at Ryman as they crossed paths. Neither said a word.

Julia, Scarborough's effusive assistant, introduced herself and escorted the group to a conference room. "Gentlemen, may I offer you some coffee?" said Scarborough, a short, warm, figure with a thick head of salt and pepper hair.

"Phil, perhaps I should give you some of my background first," suggested Ryman, fully pumped and ready to go. "And then tell you more about the business."

"I know precisely who you are," Scarborough interrupted. "But nobody on The Street knows your associate. Victor, how about a croissant and coffee while you tell me about yourself?"

Focused and relaxed, Victor filled in all the blanks. "Impressive background for such a young fellow," said Scarborough. "Could you summarize the ITI business from an operational perspective?"

Victor spun his Madison Avenue web, elegantly understating the potential and depicting acquisitions as an infinite pool.

"What are the risks?" asked Scarborough.

"To paraphrase our attorneys," replied Victor, "we're buying a bunch of entrepreneurial cowboys who have always run their own ranch."

"Can they be managed as part of a larger corporate enterprise?" asked Scarborough.

"We believe so," responded Victor.

"What kind of prospective financing does ITI need?" was the next question. Ryman wanted to answer, but Johnathan signaled for Victor to continue.

"We estimate the need for about $75 million to cover the first round of acquisitions and to establish an operating capital reserve,"

Victor replied. "Round two will probably require another $100 million."

Ryman's ego was desperate to be included in the conversation. "Phil," he jumped in, "you would be amazed at the early interest we've…"

Scarborough interrupted, looking hard at Ryman. "You know, Herb Jr. has reservations about another deal with you. He never forgot you teaching his daughter Chloe how to snort coke in his master bedroom."

Victor thought to himself, *Dear God, I'm glad Sandra didn't hear that.*

Johnathan came to the rescue. "Phil, what's past is past; Franklyn is clean. I can vouch for that."

"He'd better be," warned Scarborough. "I hate bullshit. It insults my intelligence. Franklyn, do we understand each other?"

Phil turned back to Johnathan. "Based on the preliminary documents you forwarded, I like the business and I think we can make a lot of money together. And that's what it's all about at the end of the day."

Victor had just learned a valuable Wall Street lesson: trust was unimportant if there was a lot of money to be made.

"Victor," said Phil. "your track record looks like you can run the company without letting Franklyn screw it up. But I still want to do my due diligence, to ensure none of Franklyn's lunatic friends are buried in the paperwork, before I expend my company resources."

~

As a first step, Scarborough and his attorney, Clive Davis, met with Marty Dawson in Delano Mondrain Hudson's main conference room, where he got right to the point. "Whitlaw & Company is seriously contemplating becoming ITI's investment banker. You've been dealing with ITI and a number of their prospective acquisitions. What does your gut tell about the management team and their financial projections?"

"Phil, we'd be happy to provide some off-the-record observations," said Dawson. "But Clive's presence," pointing to Clive Davis, "leaves all of us open to potential litigation from Whitlaw & Company."

"Pure nonsense!" objected Davis. "I attend all the due diligence sessions on Phil's deals!"

"What do you take me for, an idiot?" retorted Dawson. "Everybody knows you're part-lawyer, part-spy. How many times have you used inside information to bring suit when things didn't go according to your greedy expectations?"

"That's all hearsay. I dare you to cite one *documented* frivolous suit." Clive snapped back.

"Cool it!" ordered Scarborough. "This isn't a necktie party."

"Fellas, there's a simple solution," said Dawson, sounding every bit the statesman. "We understand the need for Whitlaw & Company to perform its due diligence. But to protect everyone's confidentiality, I suggest we sign mutual non-disclosure." Marty placed a preprepared privacy disclosure document in front of Clive and handed him a pen.

Davis paused. "Sign the damn waiver," barked Scarborough.

The initial focus of the Whitlaw due diligence was the senior management team. Davis's report concluded that Victor was a market-proven traditional corporate operator with no prior experience as an entrepreneur, while Ryman could not operate his way out of a paper bag and was a poster child for ragged ethics, personal hyperbole, and an excessive lifestyle. But he was also a master at persuading acquisition-oriented owners to do as suggested.

Scarborough's conclusion: "It looks like we're betting the ranch on their joint skills."

"Dangerous," warned Davis. "What if Ryman gets to him?"

"I hear you," agreed Scarborough. "If Victor catches 'Ryman-itis,' we blow the whistle up and down The Street. Agreed?"

~

The Whitlaw team then met with Dawson to discuss the recurring nature of Nachman and Toothson's deal-by-deal revenue profile.

"I don't think you need to worry about recurring revenues," volunteered Dawson. "Sam and Ed have been doing deals together for five years. They know how to find, structure, and execute them."

"Generally, I agree with Marty," said the more conservative Davis. "But this receivable barter credit treatment could be explosive. We may have trouble with the SEC in terms of income recognition, since Toothson has fulfilled only a tiny portion of the two hundred million or so outstanding credits."

Dawson responded, "Nachman-Toothson contracts clearly define a performance standard. They are only obligated to use their 'best efforts' to fulfill barter credits. Ed conscientiously makes available barter credit offerings in good faith. What the clients choose to do or not do is their business."

"And what about the proformas?" questioned Scarborough.

"The revenue projections are consistent with past histories," replied Dawson, "but we've made no allowance for the benefits of working under a public company umbrella, eliminating operational redundancies, and lowering finder's fees. My firm also has a group of attorneys with significant experience in dealing with the SEC."

~

Two days later, Ryman received the phone call that would return him to Wall Street's high-roller elite. He and Victor met with Scarborough to discuss.

"Franklyn, my partners and I have unanimously agreed to take the ITI engagement," said Scarborough, "with certain terms and conditions."

"I'm listening," said Ryman.

"Number one," began Scarborough, reading from a two-page document. "Before the final execution of acquisition contracts, Whitlaw & Company will purchase a ten percent position in the company at a discount to market for operating capital needs until the deal closes. This is typical company practice, with the money coming directly from the partners, including me. It's our commitment to the deal."

"What kind of discount are we talking about?" asked Ryman. "A purchase price of a dollar a share."

"The stock is three times that now," objected Ryman. "That's seventy percent haircut!"

"That's the deal," said Scarborough firmly. "At your current burn rate, you're going to need that million to stay alive until our financing closes.

"Number two," continued Scarborough. "The initial financing will be seventy-five million. Fifty would be equity or common stock and the other twenty-five a convertible debenture, a corporate bond with a coupon [rate of interest] of twelve percent to make it an attractive junk bond."

"That's a significant coupon premium given the prime rate," Victor countered. "What if we step to twelve percent in Year Two, but start with six percent in Year One to give the company some breathing room until we see the full impact of ITI's integrated activities?"

"Fair enough," said Scarborough, writing in the new numbers.

Ryman attempted to smile. He should have thought of that. "Plus, we may need a hundred million, not seventy-five," said Ryman.

Scarborough raised his eyebrows to the ceiling.

"Phil, I think Franklyn and I can tighten our belt and get by on the seventy-five," interjected Victor.

Scarborough chuckled. Ryman didn't. *How dare Victor intervene in my domain?*

"Number three," continued Scarborough. "To distance ourselves from the penny stock market trash, we need to execute a reverse split that yields an opening price of at least ten dollars.

"Number four. Concerning due diligence and ongoing diligence, our attorneys are to have complete access to everything —upon reasonable notice, of course—including all the records, minutes, etc., created by the attorneys and employees."

"Why don't you just bug our offices?" joked Ryman. "And tap the phones?"

Scarborough ignored the sarcasm, although he wanted to take Ryman up on his offer.

"Number five. Whitlaw & Company receive a fee of eight percent of the funds raised, plus three-year warrants at a fifty percent discount to market."

"Jesus! You're killing us," fumed Ryman. "A fee that is twice the market norm plus warrants with a two-year string at the opening price can have a serious effect on dilution and the bottom line."

"It will be a challenge," acknowledged Scarborough modestly. "But this is a deal few quality New York firms would even consider, much less underwrite. And one last thing. I meet all the acquisition candidates."

"Done,'" said Ryman.

Just before Phil left with everyone's signatures on the dotted lines, he was obligated to mention *one more, one last thing*. "This comes from Robert Sr. personally," said Scarborough coldly. Robert Sr. was Whitlaw's Chairman Emeritus. "You do dope, get caught with dope, or are anywhere near a dope bust, and the whole deal is null and void. Plus, Whitlaw & Company will see to it that the whole goddamn Street comes down on your neck!"

"Phil, I'm shocked. Everybody knows I've been squeaky clean for years. Victor knows the whole story. We have no secrets," said Ryman. Victor nodded as Ryman's massive ego kicked into high gear. "No question, Phil, I was a taker, but that's over. I'm giving back."

"My, my, isn't that admirable," said Scarborough with a smirk.

"I've even created a foundation to allow underprivileged kids to get a good college education," continued Ryman. "It's called the Wilfred B. Foundation, named after my two Newfoundlands, Buzz and Wilfred."

"Don't you have *any* conscience?" said Scarborough.

"What the hell are you talking about?" asked a genuinely surprised Ryman.

"The dogs. Herb's house." Ryman stared blankly.

"You don't remember, do you? During one of your drug binges, you fed his prized Newfoundland, Bertram, with dog food spiked with cocaine.

"Phil. That was a harmless prank."

"Tell that to Bertram."

30.

Sequential, Parallel Transactions

Louisa Dothan winced as her hubby Johnathan provided her with a blow-by-blow of the Whitlaw conditions in front of Ryman.

"Not good, but manageable," said Louisa.

"Now you're an investment banking expert?" responded Ryman cynically.

"No, I'm just a killer broker who knows your past. Let's make it easier for them to get behind the offering."

"Don't start lecturing. I'm clean."

"Franklyn, that's a given. I'm talking about appealing to Scarborough's greed. Let's get him a set of kick-ass restated historical earnings audits for Toothson and Nachman."

"I can have one of Friedway's contacts work on that."

"Friedway," She glared at Ryman. "Toothson and Nachman *are* our round one earnings story. We need to hire a well-respected public CPA firm which cleans up the numbers and provides an acceptable opinion on those crazy barter credits," said Louisa.

"Now, you're an SEC expert?" countered Ryman.

"Louisa's right," said Johnathan. "Whitlaw is going to insist."

"I'd suggest we hire Crofts Rockman," said Louisa. "They are a highly respected public accounting firm, and from my past dealings, certain engagement managers are very client-friendly—if you get my drift."

Ryman was sold.

~

The next day, Louisa, Ryman, and Victor were in an elevator heading toward the Rockman offices on the 40th floor of the World Financial Center with floor to ceiling windows and unobstructed views of the Hudson River.

As a closeted acrophobic, Victor anchored himself at the conference table in the middle of the room, directly across from managing partner Anthony LaMantia and his two lieutenants, engagement managers Michelle Anastasia Laton and Edward Wilton Wallace. Michelle was a snooty little tight-ass from Harvard with straight hair and a conservative, no-frills black dress. Edward looked like one of those preppy, arrogant news anchors who talked down to you over his tiny Bill Blass designer glasses.

By contrast, LaMantia exuded a folksy, second-generation Italian American charm that masked his slick, soft-sell pitch. "Our experience suggests that developing audited financials for private companies entering the public arena requires a more sensitive mindset than merely the rigid application of standard corporate auditing practices. Michelle and Edward have worked with me on some similar engagements, although I must admit the world of barter credits is new to all of us."

"Anthony, as Louisa may have mentioned," said Ryman, "our current acquisition contracts have performance triggers, so we are in a time crunch to complete the historical restatements. Do you have the available support staff?"

LaMantia socked it to them. "Franklyn, Rockman not only has the depth of resources but, equally importantly, we have the *right* resources."

"That's good to know," said Ryman, blowing more smoke. "This new financing is only the beginning. Our business plan calls for additional acquisitions and corporate financings. But, technically, we are still in a startup who has to watch their nickels and dimes."

LaMantia saw a pot of gold on the horizon. He shuffled to the window, projecting a pained reluctance. The reverse sell had begun.

"Ryman, to be perfectly honest, I'm concerned our fees might put too much of a strain on your operating budget."

"What are we talking about?"

"Ninety thousand a month, plus expenses."

"I assume that's net after Louisa's referral fee?" joked Ryman.

LaMantia gracefully covered his ass as he shook hands with Ryman. "I assume it's okay with you if we have the *same* professional warranties and representations as Delano Mondrain Hudson?"

~

After signing the engagement letter and receiving the first month's retainer in advance, LaMantia called Dawson.

"Marty, as you know, the first order of business is to recreate three-year financial histories for each of the companies. I figured we'd start with Nachman, since he's the largest acquisition and probably will require the most time. Who's the contact person for books and records?"

Dawson tooted the Nachman horn. After all, he was family, and he'd negotiated ten percent of the gross sale price, including existing inventory sell-offs. "For anything to do with the numbers, contact Controller Hyro Sanchez. He's been with Sam forever. I think you'll be pleasantly surprised. The Nachman books and records are clean as a whistle. Other than possibly a few expense adjustments, the audit should be a breeze."

"Great," said LaMantia, thinking he'd heard that one before. "While I've got you, who's the Mansfield contact?"

Dawson's tone changed as he established distance. "I have no idea; you'll have to ask Ed. I'm Nachman's guy."

"Does Sam carry any reserve against income on Nachman-Toothson transactions for the barter credits issued by Ed?"

Dawson remained elusive. "I have no idea how Toothson accounts for his side of the Toothson-Nachman transactions. It's just never been a concern."

LaMantia thought Dawson's comment odd, since more than sixty percent of Nachman's revenues were derived from Nachman-Toothson joint ventures. "How can they split profits equally, and yet you don't know anything about his accounting? Isn't barter credit fulfillment a deal expense?"

"You're getting into Toothson's wheelhouse," dodged Dawson. "All we knew is Sam does numerous transactions with other third parties besides Toothson. Sam maintains a strict code of ethics. We never ask to look at our partner's books. Bad faith. My advice is to talk to Toothson directly."

~

"Ed, I'm a virgin when it comes to the world of barter credits," admitted LaMantia during his first phone call with Toothson.

Toothson began his convoluted explanation. "We're a relatively simple business. Our focus is on manufacturers who want to get rid of their excess inventories and need to avoid a write-off. Getting ten cents on the dollar in straight cash doesn't work for a lot of clients. We buy their inventory at full wholesale value and pay them in barter credits."

"Could you explain a barter credit in layman's terms?"

"It's our best-efforts-pledge to offer our clients the opportunity to obtain cash discounts on goods and services they use in the normal course of their business."

LaMantia was incredulous. "You mean, companies let you take title to their inventory for nothing?"

Toothson retorted, "No, we pay them in barter credits." LaMantia asked if they always used the credits. "We offer goods and services, but they are under no obligation to accept our offerings," said Toothson, slowly and precisely. "The credits have a shelf life — typically, three years."

LaMantia then created an example to see if he got it. "Let's say Mansfield buys ten million dollars in computers. You generally offer savings of how much?"

"Conservatively, twenty-five percent."

"That means a company would have to buy forty million dollars of something for Mansfield to fulfill the contract. How many credits have you issued?"

"We currently have about three hundred million dollars on the books."

"And how many have you fulfilled?"

"I'm not sure, but we can develop a current number," said the Teflon-coated Toothson.

"I'm a little surprised you don't have that information right at your fingertips, since that's a core business expense," said LaMantia, increasingly suspicious. "I'd need that data to complete your audit."

Toothson tossed a change-up. "Look, we're all on the same team here. Right? I'm much more a salesman than an operations guy. My accountant, Benjamin Stein, takes care of the numbers. Why don't I have Mona organize a date for you guys?"

"Why stand on ceremony? Let's call him now," pressured LaMantia. As he dialed, Toothson hoped Stein was unavailable or, better yet, out of the office entirely. It wasn't Toothson's day.

~

"Hi, Ed. What's up?" said Stein.

"Benjamin, I'm on the speakerphone with one of Croft Rockman's senior managing partners, Anthony LaMantia. He's got some questions relative to barter credit fulfillment for the ITI audit. I figured we'd go right to the source of all Mansfield wisdom," smiled Toothson. "Is this a bad time?"

Stein caught the clue. "Great, no problem. How can I help, Anthony?"

LaMantia was as subtle as a sledgehammer. "Frankly, Benjamin, I'm having trouble believing a company would transfer title to their inventory for Mansfield barter credits."

Stein proceeded cautiously. "Anthony, I don't believe whether a company does or doesn't do a deal with Ed is an audit issue. We have a ten-year track record in doing these transactions. How can I help you with the audit?"

LaMantia had been outmaneuvered. To make matters worse, he knew Stein was correct. It was time for a counterpunch. "Benjamin, you're right. That's not an audit issue. But how is it that Ed takes no reserve against earnings for the future fulfillment of these credits? Isn't he grossly overstating earnings, or have I missed something?"

Stein then took LaMantia for a ride around the block.

"Typically, Ed doesn't look at a transaction that way. He makes a profit on every barter credit he fulfills."

LaMantia was genuinely perplexed. He was in unfamiliar territory despite all his experience. "Ed makes a profit on the goods and services he provides in exchange for the inventory he previously sold for cash? That doesn't make sense!"

Stein knew he needed to talk to Toothson. Alone. "Anthony, we can show you the history. Just give me a few days to pull the data together. If you guys don't mind, I have people waiting for another meeting."

LaMantia was convinced barter credit fulfillment was all 'smoke and mirrors.' He needed to relate his bookkeeping discovery to Ryman and Victor. "Ed, that reminds me, I've got another meeting myself. Let me get back to you with a due-diligence checklist."

LaMantia was on his mobile to Ryman immediately.

~

"Gentlemen, based on what I heard at Toothson's, there is no way Crofts Rockman can create a historical audit. His business is based on pure fabrication!" declared LaMantia. "He tells me he makes money on fulfillment, but he has no idea how many credits he's fulfilled and his accountant was evasive."

Flustered, Ryman struggled to construct a coherent response. Victor came to the rescue.

"Anthony, I'm confused. Didn't Ed explain his business was a series of *sequential, parallel transactions?*"

"Sequential, parallel transactions?" repeated LaMantia.

Ryman relaxed. He knew Victor had some new Madison Avenue bullshit up his sleeve. "In Part A, Ed takes title to the merchandise, selling it for cash. His profit is the gross revenue received, less total selling expenses. Do we agree?" asked Victor. "In Part B, clients buy stuff from Toothson for cash that they use in the normal course of their business. He becomes their purchasing agent. Like any good purchasing agent, he buys and resells the goods at a discount to current market prices. OK? Like any good businessman, Ed also makes sure he makes a profit on the sale. I mean, would you start a business to sell products at a loss?"

"Obviously not. That doesn't make any sense."

"Precisely," said Victor. "Does that help you?".

The logic was irrefutable. LaMantia softened. "Well, approaching the audit in that fashion could work. We'll just apply a smaller reserve for barter credit fulfillment against Part B of the transaction." That was not the answer Victor wanted, so he kept spinning the web.

"Anthony, how do you justify a loss reserve in Part B when every sale over the past ten years has made a profit — about five to eight percent net?" Victor had LaMantia on the ropes. Another one-two combination and he would have a TKO. "Let me draw an analogy. Procter & Gamble is in business to sell Tide detergent at a profit. Would you add an adjustment to their sales because you thought they might sell their product at a loss at some point in the future? How long do you think P&G would retain you?"

Ryman was impressed by Victor's commanding exhibition. He could not have done better himself.

"Victor," said a now confused LaMantia, "how do I get my management to certify such a nonstandard accounting practice?"

That was LaMantia's problem. "Ryman and I are not asking you to do anything you don't want to do. Toothson's business is his business. We can't change that. If you don't want our audit business, we understand. We came to you first because of Louisa."

LaMantia was history. "Let me talk to my technical group so we can determine the best way to package Mansfield's historical performance to pass muster in Washington."

After LaMantia left, Ryman shook Victor's hand with a huge shit-eating grin on his face. "That was one outrageous, incredible sales masterpiece!"

31.

Parker Bloomberg Primes the Pump

"Marty was right. Nachman's books are clean. No audit issues of any kind," said LaMantia. "I've got some more good news. Due to some adjustments, Nachman's historical earnings will be a little higher than your original projections."

Ryman's eyes lit up like three-hundred-watt bulbs. "How much?"

"About three million per year, or nine million over the most recent three-year period.

"What about Toothson?" asked Ryman.

"A little more complicated," replied LaMantia. "We've provided a favorable earning opinion on about eight million per year, but I wouldn't be surprised if the SEC calls us down for a conference. Let's cross that bridge if and when it comes."

Ryman was delirious. At twenty times earnings, his net worth rose about $160 million. He made like Paul Revere, galloping around the office and broadcasting the audit results.

None of the admins understood what the hell he was talking about—except Astrid, who made like a CNN analyst.

"How does that affect our initial capitalization? Does the purchase price increase? Is our earnings multiple more attractive?" Ryman provided detailed responses, seemingly oblivious that her questions were very sophisticated for an administrative assistant.

Minutes later, Ryman's telephone console was blinking like a Christmas tree.

Astrid took the first call. "Franklyn, a Parker Bloomberg is on line one."

Ryman had a love-hate relationship with the tall, burly, curly-headed man who always looked like he just got out of bed. The pushy Bloomberg was an acknowledged sleazebag market-maker who had made millions on Ryman deals just by gathering scraps of insider information any which way, then *reinvesting* the profits in a cocaine home delivery business to Manhattan's rich and famous.

Ryman waved Astrid off. "Tell him I'm in a meeting."

"Sorry, Parker; Ryman's tied up with the press. Do you want to talk to Victor?" asked Astrid.

"Waste of time," replied Bloomberg. "He's as green as a Granny Smith apple." Bloomberg did not want to take no for an answer. He knew Astrid was a coke addict. "Honey, I understand you like to trade information for nickels and dimes."

"Sometimes," she said brazenly. "It depends on the trade terms."

"How about you become a Parker regular? Feel what you hear and see, and I'll make sure you never want. How does that sound?"

"I'm not sure," said Astrid. "I've already been busted twice."

"The Bloomberg delivery company is guaranteed discreet. One call and you can have eighty-five percent pure delivered to the door, twenty-four hours a day, seven days a week."

"Do I have to do anything else?" said Astrid.

"Let's talk more about that when we share our first toot together."

"Franklyn, I'm putting Parker through. He said he just needs a few minutes."

~

Bloomberg had done his homework—he knew the details of the LaMantia call and the Nachman results. "Christ, good news does fly fast," chuckled Ryman.

By noon the following day, there was buying frenzy in ITI stock. Over twelve million shares changed hands. The stock jumped thirty percent, to $4.25.

~

Ten minutes after the closing bell, a concerned Scarborough called Ryman. "Franklyn, did you see today's closing numbers?"

"Phil, I'm running a business; we don't subscribe to those minute-by-minute LED readouts like you Wall Street guys."

"*Twelve million* shares changed hands today," said Scarborough, smelling foul. "What the hell is going on?"

"Phil, you know how things are these days. The market is like Vegas. One rumor and everybody starts placing bets." Ryman changed the subject. "Did LaMantia call you on the Nachman audit? Great news, isn't it?" As Scarborough listened, the foul odor became intense.

"The Nachman deal is starting to look better and better, eh Phil? Once the post-acquisition operating synergies kick in, this business is going to explode. The Street's already started to factor that into our multiple."

Scarborough knew there was only one way The Street could calculate revised multiples on projections that had yet to be officially released. But he chose to turn the other cheek. After all, a rising stock price only increased market demand for the pending Whitlaw & Company financing, making him and his firm millions richer in the process.

32.

Prince Charming Becomes THE Ryman

"So how was Prince Charming's day?" Sandra smiled at Victor as they sat at the corner table in their favorite Greenwich restaurant, Jean Louis.

"Why ruin a perfectly romantic dinner?" Victor groaned.

"Maybe just a few headlines? Your clients used to say I was a pretty savvy adman's wife."

"Trust me," Victor responded, "Wall Street is like a mysterious planet in another galaxy where residents live in black boxes and communicate in a peculiar mumbo-jumbo dialect."

Sandra persisted, and Victor eventually gave in.

"First thing this morning, Crofts Rockman gave our audit a clean bill of health. Within hours, The Street got wind of the details; our share price jumped 35 percent. Soon, Phil Scarborough was on the phone screaming while Ryman denied any knowledge of the leak."

"How does this stuff happen?"

"I assumed one of the usual suspects—Ryman, Katz, or Dothan—was priming the pump."

"Why didn't you say something?"

"I was going to until I spoke privately with Janet. You know her. She says, 'Boss, you got it wrong. I overheard a guy named Parker Bloomberg on the phone with Astrid. He bribed her for inside information by offering her some coke.'"

"Did you confront Franklyn?" asked Sandra.

"He said I was imagining things. Stock volatility is just part of the market."

~

Sandra didn't like what she heard but was curious. "How much is the ITI stock price now?"

"About four and a quarter and rising."

"And how many shares do we own?"

"Twenty million."

"Oh my God, you're kidding," said Sandra breathlessly, realizing their net worth was now more than $90 million. "I don't know if I'm horrified or elated. One side of me says, let's get back to the way we were before we lose all perspective; the other side is thrilled at the prospect of being super-rich."

"Honey, I feel the same way. But my instinct tells me we cannot turn back now. We're so close; I can taste it."

~

TWO DAYS LATER

"Babe, you would have been proud of me today," said Victor as he opened the door.

"Where's my kiss?" teased Sandra. "Business used to be second."

As they sat in the library with cocktails and a roaring fireplace, Victor decided to play the sensitive husband. "So, my beautiful wife, how was your day?"

"You may not want to know. It was so sad."

He just let her talk.

"This lovely man in his 60s had a massive stroke caused by a seriously blocked artery. I told his wife to stay calm; her husband was in caring, experienced hands. By the time we got him into the operating room, the patient's vitals had plummeted. My anesthesiologist tried to quickly sedate him, so we could perform a triple bypass, but the man coded right on the table.

"The team was so upset. They asked me, as the team leader, to comfort the family." A tear formed in Sandra's eye; Victor waited while she composed herself. "And, how was your day?" she said finally.

"I don't think this is the time or place."

"No," insisted Sandra. "I could use a break from my realities."

"My day started with this hotshot accountant telling Ryman and me we can't do this, and we can't do that. He's literally about to blow one of our big acquisition deals out of the water. So, your hubby dug into his bag of Madison Avenue tricks. When I was done, he was convinced that owing clients millions of dollars in barter credits can increase profits!"

"That makes no sense," replied Sandra.

"Not if you think about the activities as *sequential, parallel transactions!*" crowed Victor.

"What are sequential whatevers?"

"I have no idea; I just made them up and the professionals bought into the idea."

"What did Franklyn say?"

"He laughed his ass off."

Sandra noticed a disturbing Machiavellian smile on Victor's face. After 17 years, she wondered if the man in the chair was still the man she had married.

"Victor, I'm getting a little scared," said Sandra. "It is starting to feel like you've become more like Ryman than you think."

"What's so wrong with being more like Ryman? He's made a fortune on Wall Street by knowing the right buttons to push."

33.

Professional Fees, Conflicts of Interest

Marty Dawson's workload was at the max: negotiating the Nachman sale, handling the Whitlaw due diligence demands, and trying to create an SEC-friendly financing document.

He decided to solicit the firm's SEC specialist, Thomas Kugle, for assistance. Kugle, a graduate of Harvard Law School, was as proper, preppy, and risk-averse as they came. He was from a Greenwich neighborhood, went to Greenwich schools, married a Greenwich woman, and owned an antique colonial Greenwich home.

Despite Kugle's hefty earnings, Dawson knew he was awash in debt trying to keep up with his pretentious Greenwich neighbors—and his wife's appetite for the best of everything, from the kids' wardrobes to the private schools they attended.

Dawson approached Kugle with a simple deal. "Tom, if you can take some of this SEC work off my plate, I'm willing to share the ITI monthly retainer after the firm's overhead and profit deduction."

Initially, Kugle expressed reluctance. "Marty, what you're saying is Delano Mondrain would represent both the buyer, ITI, *and* the seller, Nachman, with the SEC. That conflict of interest feels like a potential lawsuit waiting to happen."

"I beg to differ with you," challenged Dawson. "The firm is well aware of my dual responsibility. We had that discussion before taking ITI as a client. The agreement was that if I felt something was not kosher, I'd drop ITI immediately."

"How much are we talking about?" asked Kugel.

"The partner's net from ITI fees is about $75,000 a month *before* my expenses. I was thinking a 25 percent share of my net."

"I guess it can't hurt to see if we can make it work," said Kugle.

"Just remember," reinforced Dawson, "you are the SEC specialist. I still make the final calls on all ITI legal matters."

~

The introductory Kugle-Ryman meeting did not go well. Kugle probed the validity of receivable barter credits.

"Why all these questions at $850 an hour? We've been over this with Marty," said Ryman impatiently.

"My job is to get you SEC ready, then act as spokesman for your case in Washington, D.C.," responded Kugle.

"*Our* case," glared Ryman.

On the way back to the office, an unimpressed Ryman said, "Kugle is just what we need—a boy scout that has to be trained. Once we get through the SEC, I'm going to move *my* account to a legal firm with the resources to handle large, international corporations."

~

Four weeks later, LaMantia disingenuously dropped the ITI audit certification letter on Kugle's desk. "Marty told me this is your baby now. I hope you guys are satisfied." His furrowed brow suggested a man who had been cajoled, persuaded, prodded, and coerced. "Under the circumstances, we've done a hell of a professional job with this offering."

"What are you trying to say?" asked Kugle.

"Best-case scenario is Ryman and Martini make a big score, and Crofts Rockman is professionally ostracized for taking shortcuts and turning a blind eye. I keep wondering, why did I expose us like this?"

Kugle knew the unpleasant truth. Despite LaMantia's professional veneer, he was a pig like everybody else. High profile start-ups with $90,000 per month retainers didn't grow on trees.

And if ITI grew into a billion-dollar enterprise, LaMantia became a slam-dunk for senior managing director, which guaranteed another $250,000 in his pocket. Not bad for a thirty-eight-year-old kid from Hackensack.

An electrical fire in the train tunnel delayed Kugle's ride home to Old Greenwich. And the battery on his cell phone went dead, so he didn't get home till 1:00 a.m., but he knew Victor would want to know. "Victor, sorry for the hour, but I wanted you to be the first to

get the good news: Rockman delivered their certification at the close of business today. We should be submitting our paperwork to the SEC by the close of business tomorrow. Congratulations."

"Thank goodness; we'll finally be operational!" said Victor. "I had no idea how much legal mumbo-jumbo was involved in preparing a goddamn prospectus."

"The first one always seems the longest, and this one certainly had a few bumps in the road. But Victor, remember: we've still got to get final SEC approval, so don't start spending the money just yet."

"How long should that process take?"

"Typically, about ninety days, depending upon the complexity of the issues they raise."

"Holy shit, that long?! The Norwest IPO only took thirty."

Sandra awoke.

"The last time, you guys were just a concept company," said Kugle. "This prospectus portrays a company with earnings, complex footnotes, and a host of subtilities. The good news is my sources indicate the SEC has a lighter than normal backlog, so we might slip through a little faster than usual."

~

"Who the hell was that? It's almost one-thirty in the morning," mumbled Sandra.

"It was Tom Kugle. He said Mona Toothson just called looking for my cell phone number. She wanted to apologize for passing out on the way to the Friars Club, and to invite me to go for an apology plane ride."

"Have fun," smiled Sandra. "Just tell her not to drink and fly. I want you to see me spend lots of money on Rodeo Drive when we're filthy rich."

34.

Accounting Fiasco at the SEC

The good news: the initial SEC response arrived at Delano Mondrain Hudson in only forty-five days.

The bad news: they raised several substantive issues.

Anxious to conclude the matter, Ryman and Victor canceled their afternoon schedules to meet at Kugle's office.

About an hour later, in a Delano Mondrain Hudson conference room, Kugle summarized the situation. "There are two primary SEC issues."

"Only two?" commented Ryman with a touch of arrogance. "Based on my experience, that means we're almost home."

"Normally, I would agree," said Kugle. "This time, I'm not so sure. The SEC has concluded Nachman and Toothson are one company because of their extensive joint venture activity. Reading between the lines, they view the offering as a neatly veiled stock scam designed to allow related parties to cash out at the public's expense, instead of the execution of a legitimate third-party industry consolidation strategy."

Ryman went ballistic. "Those bumbling bureaucrats took forty-five days to fuck up the facts! Let's get them on the phone. I'll explain the situation."

Tom remained outwardly calm despite bristling at Ryman's arrogance. "While I agree they're mistaken, you and I both know there is a protocol to follow. We need to document that the three companies were formed at different times, in different states, and do significant business with other third parties."

189

"How dare they! I've never been a party to a shareholder scam," ranted Ryman. "My integrity is beyond reproach!"

Tom sneered. "Franklyn, let's stick to the facts about the related parties issue. Going elsewhere might dredge up a few unpleasant surprises."

Victor interrupted. "Let's just move on. The documents to support our case are readily available."

"The second issue," reported Kugle, "shouldn't surprise anybody, since it's been raised by Crofts Rockman—the income-recognition treatment of non-cash transactions, section 154, paragraph 3 of the Code of Standard Accounting Principles. The SEC believes Nachman and Toothson's historical proforma incomes are overstated due to the absence of an expense reserve for barter credit fulfillment."

"How do you suggest we handle this one?" said Ryman.

"This subject is so involved that it could take months through the mail," observed Kugle. "I suggest we request a committee conference. Direct interaction should eliminate any potential technical miscommunications. Maybe we can even bring the related parties issue to a close at the same time. Let me chase down Anthony's availabilities so we can get something scheduled in Washington as quickly as possible."

"Tom," said LaMantia a few hours later from a cell phone somewhere in South Jersey. "I'll agree to attend the meeting on one condition—Ryman remains invisible at the SEC. The last thing we need is the involvement of a Fuller Brush salesman."

Scarborough readily agreed with LaMantia's assessment. "We'll just tell him flat out his advisors are unanimous that he's not going to Washington. Remember, subtlety is not his strong suit."

Ryman took the news surprisingly well, but put his own spin on it when passing the info on to Victor. "I just heard from Tom. The SEC meeting has been confirmed for Tuesday at 10:00 a.m. Since you're the company's resident expert on the income recognition of non-cash transactions, I told Anthony and Tom you should represent us." He smiled. "Besides, technically, you are the ITI treasurer and chief financial officer!"

~

On the plane to Washington, LaMantia thought about the potential damage to his professional reputation if the SEC took unkindly to the audit methodology. "Victor, I've been thinking. You should take the lead with the SEC on all income recognition issues. Our accounting treatment is sound, but it may appear more convincing if a senior corporate officer explains the fine points."

"Am I missing something?" responded Victor. "Isn't that representation part of your ninety-grand-a-month retainer?"

"No worries. We'll be right there if you need technical support," smoothly assured LaMantia.

Kugle said nothing, because he'd been instructed by his bosses to cover *his* ass rather than allow Delano Mondrain's squeaky-clean image to be damaged. "Victor, Anthony makes a good point. I also think it would be best if you took the lead on related party issues; you live with these acquisitions every day."

~

In downtown Washington, the SEC headquarters was twelve floors of army-issue, battleship gray walls, covering floor-to-ceiling cinderblock construction. The three men walked toward the reception desk and announced themselves. An emotionless matronly woman with brown hair pulled back into a tight bun instructed them, "Take a seat until the Accounting Committee is ready for you."

Once summoned, Kugle, LaMantia, and Victor entered a sterile white room where three stone-faced figures sat at the far end of a long table. No warm-ups were offered, no introductions, merely a curt order: "Gentleman, the meeting is yours."

Victor rose. "Thank you for your time; we are here to respond to the primary issues raised in your correspondence, file number 23665, dated August 12th. Specifically, ITI's contemplated acquisition of selected companies as related party transactions and the company's income recognition practices regarding non-cash transactions."

The man in the center introduced himself as Altman Bridges, head of the SEC Audit Division. He also briskly introduced the man seated to his right as East Region area manager Michael Costello, and the man on his left as West Region manager Bert Vaupen.

"Are you Mr. Ryman?" asked Costello.

LaMantia introduced himself and Victor. "Mr. Martini is the company's chief financial officer and treasurer. We all felt he is eminently more qualified than Mr. Ryman to deal with the issues raised."

"That's unfortunate," said Costello, glaring at LaMantia as he addressed his colleagues. "According to the public record, Mr. Ryman has been challenged by this office concerning aggressive income recognition practices in previous ventures. Would that be a fair characterization, Mr. Bridges?"

Victor ignored the sarcasm and stayed the course. "Perhaps we should begin by discussing the related parties issue."

Bridges corrected him. "Mr. Martini, let's be clear. *We* are not here to *discuss* anything. *You* are here to demonstrate that ITI's potentially fraudulent securities violations are frivolous."

Victor spent the next thirty minutes summarizing the business of each acquisition—their genesis, their independence, and their unrelated managements. He also produced books, records, and individual client lists, and a series of case histories where corporate titans such as AT&T, Time Warner, and General Electric joint-ventured with firms they eventually acquired.

Bridges called for a recess. The three bureaucrats adjourned to a private room.

"Tom, how are we doing??" Victor asked.

"Don't know. I've never seen anything like this at the SEC before," said Anthony.

The group returned. Bridges declared, "The SEC recognizes

the company's rebuttal and documentation thereof, and withdraws its opposition to the related party issue."

~

Victor thanked the SEC for their rapid response and then moved to the second issue, ITI's aggressive income treatment. He began explaining the construction and implementation of barter credit transactions as separate activities. He ended with letters of endorsement from clients and their legal departments about their acceptance, booking, and use of company-issued credits. Victor's pitch was flawless; he felt like he was back at A&J again, mesmerizing clients.

The increasingly frustrated SEC tribunal fired questions for almost two hours. Finally, a flustered Bridges spoke. "We have no more questions."

Kugle broke his silence. "Does that mean the income recognition issue is resolved?"

"No, said Bridges, "it merely means we have no opinion on the way the company recognizes revenue at this time."

~

Kugle decided to make a pit stop before leaving the building. He was in a bathroom stall when Costello and Vaupen entered the men's room. Neither realized Kugle was present. "We've got to convince Bridges to put these ITI guys on ice until we figure out how to mandate adjustments in their numbers," said Costello.

Vaupen agreed. "That Martini is slick."

"That reminds me," said Costello, "was the FBI able to dig up any dirt on Martini?"

"Not a goddamn thing," said Vaupen.

~

Kugle waited to tell Victor and Ryman about the bathroom conversation until the official SEC response arrived two days later.

"I think we're got big problems with the SEC."

"Why?' asked Victor. "Their follow-up letter seems innoxious."

"Trust me. This letter will lead to another letter, and another, etc. The SEC is the undisputed champ of delay tactics: *Never say no, just never say yes.*"

"Outrageous," bellowed Ryman. "Let's take them to court!"

"Franklyn, my sources suggest Bridges' problem is intensely personal."

"What the hell are you talking about?" glared Ryman, confused.

"About six years ago," said Kugle, "Bridges' daughter, Yvonne, was an up and coming Hollywood starlet who got hooked on cocaine after attending your 50th birthday orgy at your Malibu Beach House."

"That was her decision," replied Ryman.

"Yvonne passed out in your bedroom. When the police arrived, you were gone, and she started beating the shit out of one of the officers with the point of her stiletto heels. The cop lost an eye, and Yvonne got three years for assaulting an officer."

"That's not true," said Ryman.

"Which part?" asked a horrified Victor.

"Any of that being my fault. Yvonne meant nothing. I was disappointed in my lifestyle; I left that night to start over."

"What happened to Yvonne?" asked Victor.

"She was branded a convicted felon with a habit; she never recovered, and eventually committed suicide."

Victor was stunned. "Who else knows about this?"

"Nobody," replied Kugle. "My job is to protect you. Phil's got his money agenda, and Franklyn's so-called advisors would sell anybody down the road for 30 pieces of gold. I'm not even sure if Marty's on our side anymore."

"Does that mean Delano's going to bail?"

"Naw, there's too much money on the table. My senior partners realize $150,000-a-month retainers don't grow on trees. Plus, we don't have any liability here. Remember the representations and warranties you guys signed?"

"That's comforting," said Ryman, leaving in a huff.

Kugle looked at Victor. "Word to the wise. The odds are not in your favor. To survive, you will have to make a deal with the devil to learn to think precisely like Ryman. Is that really what you want?"

Victor had reached the point of no return. His reply was his answer. "How much does Marty know about the bathroom conversation?"

"Nothing."

"Let's keep it that way."

35.

Ivanka, Sam's Traveling Pro

Ryman and Victor concluded that the key to beating the SEC was to argue the case until the SEC was out of bullets. That meant getting a longer contract extension and line of credit guarantee from Nachman.

"If Nachman steps up," said Ryman, "Toothson will fall in line. The trick is to schmooze Sam into an extension agreement before Marty tries to extract another pound of ITI flesh."

Kugle was surprised at Ryman's lucidity. He knew it was the right strategy for ITI, although not necessarily the right one for Victor, nor for his firm, and certainly not for his relationship with Marty.

The battlelines had been drawn. Delano Mondrain Hudson was now a willing party to the ultimate conflict of interest: two senior partners who represented clients with conflicting agendas.

~

"How about I arrange an in-person meeting with Sam to congratulate him on his appointment as Chairman of the ITI Advisory Board?" asked Victor. "While I'm sucking up, I'll casually drop in the need for a contract extension; maybe I can even get a signed piece of paper."

"Sounds like a plan," said Ryman. "But what the hell is the ITI Advisory Board?"

"Haven't got a clue. But it's all the rage in the agency world. Clients think it adds an experience cache. I'll whip up a preliminary charter on the plane."

~

"Sam, it's Victor. We just had a board meeting while waiting for the SEC to get off their asses. The Board thinks it might be useful to start developing specific programs to increase deal flow when we're officially family. Since you've got the most significant operating experience, I thought it might be invaluable to pick your brain for a day or so."

Nachman bit immediately. "Why don't we make it a business retreat?" suggested Sam. "Fly into LA, stay overnight at the Beverly Hills house, and after breakfast, Mary can drive us down to the La Costa house. You'll love it. We can brainstorm, bask in the sunshine, and play a little tennis."

"Mary? I thought your wife's name was Erica."

"Mary Jones is our housekeeper, who has worked for me for twenty years." Sam started laughing like he had told himself a private joke. "Play much tennis?"

"Sam, I'm a city boy. There weren't too many tennis courts in my hood in the South Bronx."

"Not a problem. I'll bring along my tennis pro. *She* can give you a few lessons right at the house."

~

That evening Victor explained his sudden travel plans to Sandra.

"Hon, I've got to schlep out to the coast for a few days to babysit Sam Nachman. The SEC is taking longer than expected to approve the offering, so Ryman thought I should do a little schmoozing with Nachman at his Southern California home."

"Well, Franklyn certainly picked the right person," said Sandra. "Your clients used to tell me you were the king of schmooze. So, what have the boys organized?"

"Honey, it's not that kind of trip. The guy is sixty years old, for Christ's sake! My mission is to get a contract extension. I'm going to feed his ego by making him the chairman of an imaginary ITI steering committee."

"Is there a problem?" said Sandra, concerned.

"Relax, babe. Tom said the SEC currently has such a backlog; everything is taking longer to review and process. The extensions are just insurance."

"Mind if I come? I've got some extra vacation days. Southern California is beautiful this time of year."

Victor had painted himself into a corner, but Ryman had been a great role model in learning how to solve such menial problems. "Honey, what a great idea! Just be aware, we're meeting at a little retreat he owns in the desert, about forty miles from San Diego, so that we won't be disturbed."

"No problem; I'll play with Sam's wife in LA."

"You may have to entertain yourself; Erica is babysitting their youngest grandchildren at her son's house in Thousand Oaks."

"What a guy! I can choose between watching you guys fall asleep snoring in the desert, or play babysitter with somebody's screaming grandkids."

Victor shrugged his shoulders.

"I'll think I'll take a rain check," replied Sandra.

~

A blonde with a body to die for entered Nachman's limousine at the LA Airport.

"Victor, say hello to Ivanka Sokolov, my traveling tennis pro. She'll be making the trip to La Costa with us." Nachman smiled lecherously. "We've arranged for Ivanka to give you all the lessons you need. Right, hon?" She rolled her tongue around her moist lips, undressing Victor with her eyes.

Soon, Ivanka, dressed in a revealing tennis outfit, began to warm up on Nachman's court. "Hon, time for your first lesson," she said, as she titled her derriere into Victor's crotch. "This is the best position to serve with power and accuracy." When she sensed Victor was sufficiently warmed up, Ivanka took a detour. "Victor, let's see how well you volley." Moments later, Ivanka had him huffing and puffing all over the court to punctuate who was in charge.

Nachman laughed his ass off. "Victor, tomorrow we'll give you a break. You can play me."

Ivanka gave another scintillating performance at dinner. Her mouth erotically caressed and chewed and swallowed as Nachman and Victor sat mesmerized. Two nightcaps later, everyone retired to their respective bedrooms—Nachman to the master at one end of the house, Ivanka to a guest room at the other end, and Victor to a 2000-square-foot guest suite, dead center on the second floor with a magnificent golf course view. Restless, he fantasized about Ivanka as the television flickered, the door slightly ajar. Ivanka's shadow tiptoed past Victor's door to Nachman's bedroom. The clock read 2:00 a.m.

The next morning, Nachman and Victor shared breakfast as Ivanka slept. Victor got right to the point. "Sam, we've run into a snag with the SEC because of the related party transactions between you and Ed. In plain English, they claim you guys are not two separate companies, that you're using the financing to bilk the public."

"We're not going to let them get away with that, are we?" said Nachman, personally affronted.

"*Absolutely* not! But it's going to take some time to work through the issues. You know bureaucrats. Bottom line, we need a contract extension."

"Who else knows?" asked Nachman.

"Nobody. We came to you first. Franklyn, Whitlaw, and I all know the Nachman Company is *the* critical round one acquisition."

"How long do you need?"

"On the safe side? Another twelve months, including the line of credit guarantee."

"Let me talk to Marty; I'm sure we can work something out. Consider it done."

Business concluded, Mary took a few group pictures of Sam, Victor, and Ivanka with Nachman's old Kodak camera.

"What the hell is that?" Victor laughed when he saw the ancient device.

"You young people and your digital images. I still like to hold a printed picture. Mary, take Victor's address and send him a set when they come back from Santa's workshop in the North Pole!"

~

"How was the trip?" asked Sandra.

"Jesus, do I have to explain every last detail every time I come home? I don't ask you to explain every patient crisis," exploded Victor uncharacteristically.

Sandra was shocked speechless for a moment. "Victor, I was making conversation. I haven't seen you in four days. Why are you being so rude?" Sandra paused. "Did something happen out there?"

Victor ran his hands over his face. "The meeting with Nachman turned out to be a little more complicated than I thought. That's all." Victor saw his response would not suffice. "I had to negotiate a few deal points behind Marty's back because Franklyn and I knew Marty would never agree without holding us hostage again."

"Who's Marty?"

"Nachman's shitbag, high-powered attorney, whose favorite negotiating tactic is a dagger through the heart."

Sandra then threw a dagger of her own. "By the way, a lady by the name of Ivanka called. She said you left your tennis racket on Sam's tennis court." Sandra waited for a response.

"During one of our breaks, Sam suggested we finish our business at his La Costa place, which was only about 30 miles away. I didn't realize he was such a tennis buff. Next thing I know, I'm watching him huff and puff on his tennis court. When he got tired, he handed me his racket, and said, 'My gift; your turn.' Then he had me volley around the court with this muscular woman that looked like she could play tight end for the New York Jets." Victor rolled his eyes for added effect.

But Sandra wasn't fooled; she laughed sarcastically. "You make such a crappy liar. Ivanka also wanted to know if you liked the pictures that came in the mail. Now, which one is she? The bald fat guy, or the blonde with her breasts popping out of her blouse?"

"What do you want me to say?"

"How about starting with the truth?"

36.

Throwing Victor Under the Bus

It was time to update Phil Scarborough on the current situation. Ryman decided to throw Victor under the bus. "You handle the meeting, since you were the one that went to Washington and La Costa. Phil seems to respond better to your bullshit version of the truth."

"Phil, I guess the Washington trip didn't go quite as reported," Victor started. "Kugle called to say he had just received a three-page request from the SEC for more information. Clearly, they are trying to redline us."

Phil glared at Ryman. "I guess your past reputation precedes you. That's probably why they are asking more questions about our $100 million offering than they asked AT&T about a $10 billion financing."

"Phil, I think my past is…" Ryman began.

"Maybe I should explain to…" Victor broke in, but an impatient Scarborough interrupted him.

"Franklyn, enough; let's just focus on replying to the SEC—even if it takes months."

"Phil," said Victor reassuringly, "the SEC delay is undoubtedly a setback, but Franklyn and I anticipated we might need extensions for the acquisition once larger-than-expected audits were finalized. I'm just back from La Costa, where Sam agreed to a twelve-month extension on the acquisition and credit line."

"What does he want?" asked Scarborough.

"I not sure he wants anything," said Victor naïvely.

"Trust me; he'll want something!" said Scarborough, "they always do. I know. Victor, what about Toothson?"

"I haven't spoken to him yet, but I'm pretty sure I can get Ed to follow suit."

"Victor, you better move quickly; I'm willing to make visits, place calls, whatever it takes," volunteered Scarborough.

"Not to worry, Phil," said Ryman, doing his impersonation of a knight in shining armor. "I'm planning on taking it from here, but considering his lack of experience, Victor's done an admirable job thus far."

~

Scarborough's barfed at Ryman's balls. His real issue with the SEC roadblock was the potential damage to the Whitlaw reputation, and to their investors' families. Based on Scarborough's representations, Whitlaw investors expected a substantial return on investment for stepping up first—a financing deal had to get done.

"Given the SEC's resistance to another ITI public financing at this time," said Phil, "I suggest a change in strategy from a public financing to a private placement." With a private placement, early investors would be able to buy non-liquid company stock at a deep discount to the fair market price.

"Phil, a private placement is a hell of a lot more expensive than public money," retorted Ryman. "Besides, it will look like…"

Scarborough exploded. "Ryman, get off your high horse. Haven't you noticed? Rome is burning! You're worried about saving a few dollars. But if we don't get the financing done quick, ITI is history, and Whitlaw & Company becomes the laughingstock of Wall Street. I'm simply not prepared to let that happen!"

Scarborough got up and stood in Ryman's face. "Franklyn, I should caution you that even a private placement won't be without pain. We'll have to call in a lot of favors from long-time Whitlaw investors, and the pension funds who have made billions on

Whitlaw deals that the traditional investment banking houses have dismissed."

Victor was all-in on the change in strategy. The last thing he wanted was to see his *paper wealth* disappear.

~

"What's the minimum you need to close the deals and maintain an adequate operating cash reserve?" asked Scarborough.

"Fifty million will get us through the first eighteen months. By then, we should have some solid operating results, and we'll be able to return to the public markets for expansion capital," replied Ryman.

"We also need to make a couple of other changes," said Scarborough, directing his conversation exclusively at Victor.

"To be perfectly blunt, ITI's cash-management sucks. So, effective immediately, I want to be appointed to the board of directors to maintain a tighter rein on operational matters. As far as the additional costs of the private placement, I'll run a tab and deduct those costs from the gross proceeds at the closing."

Phil then turned and glared at Ryman. "And I want you to stay out of any further extension negotiations. Victor and I will handle that; I want to avoid giving away the rest of the store!"

37.

Never Surprise Family

After learning about the ITI cash flow crisis, Scarborough called an emergency partners' meeting for the following morning. He knew rule number one at Whitlaw & Company was to never surprise family.

The boardroom contained the scent of old money and the fumes of expensive cigars. Whitlaw had twelve senior partners, organized in teams containing two or three young bankers reporting to each senior partner. Teams had areas of specialization: retailing, banking, telecommunications, networking, fiber optics, semiconductors, etc.

When a team found a deal they liked, they presented to the entire family of partners. Before the firm would underwrite any deal, a majority vote of the senior partners was required. At that point, each team had to personally invest a minimum of $100,000, although there was no upper limit. Team members could split their investment as they saw fit; sometimes it was proportionate to dollars invested, sometimes not. The senior partner ultimately made that determination.

Instituted some forty years ago, this rigorous process was credited with the firm's enviable record of success. Clients knew Whitlaw & Company had never failed to complete financing once the partners endorsed a deal, and the firm's ability to pick winners was legendary.

Unfortunately, Scarborough had the embarrassing obligation to inform his Whitlaw family that ITI might be the first financing failure in the firm's illustrious history.

Scarborough went right to the bottom line. "Gentleman, late yesterday I received a disturbing briefing from ITI management. The public offering is in peril. They *have* had some bad breaks, but, candidly, I should have watched the store more closely." Scarborough laid out the issues precisely and efficiently, sparing nothing. After twenty-two years, he knew how the game was played at Whitlaw & Company; the problem was his to fix.

"To give the company time to resolve its differences with the SEC, I'm recommending we shift from a public offering to a private placement. I also agreed to personally provide the company a two million dollar unsecured, noninterest-bearing bridge loan to alleviate cash-flow pressures until the placement is completed."

A battle-hardened, chunky, sun-tanned partner, Stanley Starker, challenged Scarborough's logic. "Phil, while it's admirable you're willing to throw more of your own money at the deal, we need to ask ourselves if we're throwing good money after bad. While I wouldn't be happy about losing a hundred grand, it's not exactly the end of the world."

"Stan, I'm not ready to close up shop yet. I still believe these guys have an enormous business concept," responded Scarborough. "But, I'm not a hundred percent sure anymore; that's why I'm willing to take most of the risk."

"Phil, I think I speak for everyone here," said the tall, slender chairman, Herb Whitlaw Jr. "The firm will support your decision. You're closer to the deal than any of us. And, if you say go, we'll work our butts off to call in favors. However, on a purely visceral level," he added, "Ryman has a stench about him, even ten years later."

~

Scarborough knew it was time for a come-to-Jesus meeting with Victor. "Can you come over for lunch tomorrow? I want to speak to you privately."

Victor was confident Whitlaw & Company wanted out. But he

decided to remain silent in case there was a way to salvage his 20 million shares.

"Be delighted, Phil. What time?" asked Victor, feeling the guillotine.

~

"Good afternoon, Mr. Martini," said the cheery face at the elevator door. "Mr. Scarborough is waiting for you in Dining Room C."

"Hope you don't mind. I took the liberty of having Chef Duane prepare some lunch," said Scarborough, placing his hand in Victor's. "Is Veal Saltimbocca okay?" Victor looked around. The sun-filled dining room overlooking Fifth Avenue glowed with fresh flowers, paisley print linens, Lennox China, and Waterford Crystal. *Hardly the stuff of a felon's last meal,* thought Victor.

Gratuitous opening ceremonies were ditched. Scarborough sprinted for the finish line as the ice water was poured. "Victor, I've gained a great deal of respect for your business acumen in the short time we've worked together. Giving credit where credit is due, Franklyn is a great promoter. But the truth, to him, is what he thinks you want to hear at that moment!

"I'm in the throes of a genuine dilemma," he continued. "I'm not sure I want to go forward with the financing. I am reluctant to put my reputation and that of the firm on the line, given the cast of characters. At the same time, I am a pragmatist. I smell money, big money. I didn't get rich by walking away from deals! Since you've been on the inside since day one, I thought perhaps you might share your true feelings, particularly without Franklyn breathing down your neck."

Victor, like Scarborough, would have preferred to be straight, but that was impossible. If he spilled the beans, Whitlaw & Company would vamoose, shattering Victor's dream of becoming filth rich. It was time for an Oscar-caliber performance. "Phil, Franklyn and I have become very close in the past year. There is no doubt in my mind Franklyn wants ITI to be a first-class organization. We both recognize that our round one acquisitions are strange characters with strange ethics, but in a perverted way, they admire Ryman."

"Victor, I could care less who likes Ryman. You're the guy who has got to make the companies work together; Ryman's not an operator." Phil looked him in the eyes. "Can you pull this thing off?"

Victor played the sincerity card. "Truthfully, it will be a challenge, but I'm up for it," he said. "ITI's pretty unconventional, but hell, so was Microsoft in the beginning. Who would have thought a college dropout would create an operating system to run eighty percent of the world's computers? I think ITI has that kind of potential upside for Whitlaw & Company. There are literally trillions of dollars of excess inventories around the world. That's our potential."

38.

Sex Over St. Patrick's

"Victor, I think I want out," said Sandra. "The promise of some future pot of gold is not worth it anymore. We're becoming people I don't like."

"You can't be serious." Victor was incredulous. "I just agreed to work closely with Phil Scarborough and the Whitlaw family."

"What the hell happened to Ryman?"

"He's still there, but…"

"What is that supposed to mean?"

"Phil said Whitlaw would like me to take over company operations and leave Franklyn in the back room."

"You know his ego will never let that happen."

"I'll figure out something. Trust me."

"This is starting to feel like an episode in *The Sopranos*," said a visibly unnerved Sandra. "Each day gets a little dirtier. One lie leads to another. When does it all end?"

~

The next evening, Victor was in the living room in front of a crackling fire, reading his *New York Times*. He was drawn to a bizarre story in the business section about Jason Eldridge, the CEO of the NYSE United Brands Corporation and a former Episcopalian minister, who had donated millions to the Guggenheim, the Museum of Modern Art, and the Metropolitan Museum of Art.

Eldridge's fortune had been estimated at almost $6 billion, but apparently it did not generate the inner satisfaction he sought. The previous afternoon, he had jumped out the window of his office on the 44th floor of the Pan Am Building on the corner of Park Avenue and Forty-Seventh Street, leaving no note of explanation and, to the best of everyone's knowledge, no obvious family or business motive.

To Victor, the story was disturbing. Why would a charter member of New York's Obscene Wealth Club find suicide as the answer?

Sandra wandered in and saw Victor staring blankly at the newspaper. She assumed his mood was a remnant of the reservations she had about ITI. "Baby, if Mama can't share her true feelings after all these years…"

Victor interrupted. "Sandra, it's not you or us or anything like that. Just… look at this story in *The Times*."

She glanced at the Eldridge story. It did not arouse any sympathy. "How could I feel sorry for a guy like that? It's sick; a guy with all that money couldn't think of anything better to do with his life than jump out a window?"

"Maybe the guy had demons he couldn't overcome. The mind can do strange things," said Victor.

"What has that got to do with us?" asked Sandra.

"At this moment," smiled Victor, "the only thing I know for sure is that you're my soulmate. So how about you and I take a night off from Ryman and all the other lunatics, and get back to being us?"

~

It was like old home week at the Four Seasons restaurant on Fifty-Third Street. The bartender waved. Victor introduced Sandra. The reservations manager welcomed him by his first name: "Your table is ready and waiting." The maître d' shook his hand as they walked into the Pool Room and were seated at the restaurant's prime power table, directly in front of the fountain across from the room's entrance.

"I'm impressed," said Sandra, beaming. "I've seen some pretty heavy-duty couples at this table in *Town & Country* magazine."

Captain Paolo Maione arrived, shaking Victor's hand warmly. "The usual?" Victor nodded. "And for the lady?"

"Paolo, this is no lady; this is my wife, Sandra."

Paolo kissed Sandra's hand. "Ahhh bellissimo, bellissimo."

"Victor, I appreciate your friend's enthusiasm," whispered Sandra self-consciously, "but Paolo's fuss is making everybody stare at us."

Victor figured this was his chance to make amends for the Ivanka fiasco. "They're simply wondering who the most beautiful woman at the best table at New York's most expensive restaurant is."

Sandra melted. Her eyes glowed. "You are still the sweetest man in the whole world. I'm so lucky."

Somewhere between the gravlax and the salad course, nature called.

"Honey, will you excuse me a minute?" It was Sandra's turn to freshen up. As she walked away, Victor realized, perhaps for the first time in a while, that Sandra was still as sexy as the day they had gotten married.

~

As dinner concluded, Victor asked, "Have you ever seen the top of St. Patrick's Cathedral lit up at night?"

"And how would I do that?"

Victor took her hand and said hello to Bill, the head of the Seagram's security. Bill smiled, unlocked the door to a sleek brass elevator, pressed the button to the 54th floor, and tipped his cap.

"Welcome to our offices, my queen," smiled Victor, standing in front of two large carved wooden doors at the west end of the building. He then began searching his pockets. "Damn, I left my office keys with the garage attendant."

It was now midnight, and Sandra had a 7:00 a.m. meeting with the chief surgical officer and his staff. "No problem. Some other time," she said sweetly, "I've got an early staff meeting anyway."

"Absolutely, positively not!" replied Victor. "Stand back."

Sandra wondered what her impetuous husband was thinking. Suddenly, Victor made like a Kamikaze pilot, running down the hall straight for the double doors, screaming, "AHHHH!" His shoulder crashed into the doors, popped the lock, and swung the doors open wide. "My lady, your humble abode anxiously awaits you." Sandra went from horrified to hysterical to intensely pleased.

After showing her around the opulent ITI office digs and the spectacular skyline views, they headed for Victor's corner office. "This view is breathtaking. I guess this public company mumbo-jumbo has its advantages."

As she stood admiring the lights on the roof of St. Patrick's, Victor began to caress her breasts and purr in her ears. Slowly he led her toward his deep, wide, designer couch.

"Not here, not now," she protested weakly.

"How many times have you had the opportunity to do it on the boss's couch?" Victor's gentle insistence won out. They necked and made love like it was the first time, all over again.

39.

Irene Katherine Remembered

"Victor, I've been organizing the roadshow," said Scarborough. "We'll start with an investor group in Los Angeles and cover three more cities in six days.

"Before we go, why don't you and your wife come over for dinner on Saturday evening? I've heard nothing but nice things about her."

~

"Honey, it's quite a compliment to be invited to a dinner at Phil's home. He's one of the most influential investment bankers on Wall Street."

"What exactly does an investment banker do?" asked Sandra.

"Phil has two roles. His firm, Whitlaw & Company, gives us exposure to major investors, so we have the funds to close the acquisitions. Secondly, his firm acts as our advisor on our Wall Street strategy."

"What should I wear? What should we bring? Who else will be there?" asked Sandra.

"God, wear whatever you want to wear! I never heard Gordon Naye complain about anything you wore to an A&J event," Victor reminded her. "In fact, why don't you splurge and buy yourself a new outfit? Remember, you're now a multi-millionaire; you might want to play the part."

~

Riverside Drive in the West 90s was eight blocks of elegant, four-story carved stone residences with lead glass windows, pointy spires, carved gargoyles, and spectacular views of the Hudson River. As Scarborough was fond of saying, he was "minutes from midtown, miles from the madness."

Scarborough greeted Sandra and Victor warmly. One virgin margarita later, Sandra had the same warm, fuzzy vibes she used to get around A&G Chairman Gordon Naye. She sensed Scarborough was also very fond of her Victor.

"How about a little tour before dinner?" The rooms were as gracious and comfortable as Scarborough himself. "These Kandinskys are my pride and joy," pointing to two stunning canvases displayed above the mantelpieces in the living and dining rooms. The house's seventeen rooms were a study in contrasts. Restored antique eighteenth- and nineteenth-century furniture were surrounded by enough modern art to double the Guggenheim's size, including originals by Dali, Picasso, Johns, and Warhol.

~

They stopped in front of the soulful portrait of an elegant woman. "This is beautiful," said Sandra. She noticed the initials IKS in the corner. "Who was the artist?"

"The initials stand for Irene Katherine Scarborough," said Phil in a disarmingly wistful tone. "That's a portrait of my late wife. I had the artist place her initials in the corner. She was the love of my life. We did everything together; she was the perfect soulmate. Sometimes, when Victor talks about you, it brings Irene back to me in full Technicolor."

Sandra was flattered, yet uncomfortable. She wanted to know what had happened but didn't dare to ask. Scarborough filled in the blanks. "Ten years up in smoke when that car crashed into us. I sometimes wonder, why her and not me? Anyway, that was a long time ago."

~

"Sandra, I'm not sure how much Victor has told you about the ITI saga," Phil commented.

"Bits and pieces, here and there. Victor has always preferred to separate family from business. But frankly, I *am* curious. I thought the hours he spent at A&J were intense. What do you fellas do all those days and nights?"

"Sandra, I'll spare you the sordid details. But your husband's been a real trooper; if it wasn't for him, I'm not sure Whitlaw & Company would still be in this deal." Scarborough played the highlight reel—the good, the bad, and the ugly. Sandra was horrified. An almost apologetic Wall Street powerhouse was calmly articulating her worse fears.

Finally, though, he offered her some reassurance. "Sandra, despite our little bumps in the road, we are making progress. During the next two weeks, Victor and Franklyn will be traveling around the country with me on what we're calling a roadshow."

She smiled. "Sounds like a Vaudeville routine."

"In a way, it is. Franklyn and your husband will be explaining the ITI vision and its prospects to my firm's best institutional customers to persuade them to invest in the company. These are companies run by high-net-worth individuals that see deals before they go to the stock market."

~

Sandra decided to be blunt. "So, how do you feel about their prospects?"

"I believe the demand is there. We'll be visiting lots of heavy hitters in the next two weeks. They've shown tremendous preliminary interest in the deal, so unless Ryman pulls a Ryman, you two will eventually be wealthy and free to do whatever you want with whomever you want."

"Will Ivanka be there?" smiled Sandra.

Victor was horrified.

"Who's Ivanka?" asked Scarborough, confused.

"That's our *little* joke," replied Victor hurriedly.

"Like in one *little* blonde bombshell joke," echoed Sandra.

Scarborough smiled with a knowing twinkle. "No worries,

Sandra; I'll be with the boys every step of the way."

~

Scarborough had given Sandra the answers she wanted to hear. "Enough business for one night. Let's celebrate our forthcoming victory." Scarborough escorted Sandra and Victor to a carved stone wine cellar, which occupied much of the first floor. The room, a perfect fifty-six degrees, was cluttered with dusty labels from legendary vintners: Chateau Margaux, Mouton Rothschild, Chateau Beycheville, Calgon Segur, and Haut Brion. The vintages? The best of the best: '45, '47, '61, and '69.

"Collecting wine is my passion," said Scarborough modestly as Victor gasped at the inventory. "Henri has prepared Beef Wellington as the entree and a carpaccio medley for the first course. Let's go with something light, perhaps a '61 St. Emillion for the carpaccio, and maybe a '47 Margaux for the Wellington. How does that sound?"

"Wow, a 1947!" said Victor. "Shouldn't you save that for a special occasion?"

"This *is* a special occasion," said Scarborough, looking warmly at Sandra.

The meal was sensational, the wine exquisite, and the conversation engaging and non-stop. Scarborough volunteered that he began in academia and eventually planned to return, perhaps as the dean of a business school. But he wasn't there just yet-there was too much money waiting to be made. Dinner ended somewhere after 3:00 a.m.

On the way out, Scarborough handed Victor a manila envelope that contained detailed profiles of every prospective roadshow investor. "Victor, here's a little weekend reading, compliments of Whitlaw and Company."

40.

Survival of the Fittest Begins

The following Monday, Victor arrived just in time to overhear Astrid on the phone, in the middle of one of her Bloomberg news updates.

"Parker," she said in a hushed tone, "other than the fact that we've stopped ordering fresh flowers, everything appears to be business as usual. Gotta go, Victor just walked in."

"How about we trade," said Bloomberg. "Your notes and observations for an ounce of the good stuff."

"Two ounces and a Cosmo. Usual place," replied Astrid.

"If I didn't know better," laughed Bloomberg, "I'd say you were part Hasidic Jew."

~

"Victor, Parker Bloomberg's on line one. Franklyn's at the Club, so I told him you'd take the call."

"What the hell is going on?" shouted Bloomberg. "You guys haven't even hinted at any new acquisitions. And Ryman's been as quiet as a goddamn monk about the financing. The rumor is *boggsville at the SEC*, and your operating capital is running low."

Victor did his Ryman impersonation. "Parker... Parker. Why the hell all this angst? There's a simple explanation. Whitlaw & Company told Ryman to keep his big mouth shut since we're about to go on a six-city investor roadshow."

Bloomberg bit. "Scarborough's optimistic?"

"Let me put it this way," whispered Victor, as though he was delivering the most critical information in the world. "Turns out

Crofts Rockman certified the Nachman's and Toothson's historical net incomes and operating margins were about 40 percent higher than Franklyn originally expected. We assumed the SEC would be pleased—you know, better shareholder value and all. But our lawyers said the SEC might try to drag their feet on our offering because nobody buys acquisitions that cheap!"

"That's the dumbest thing I've ever heard," said Bloomberg.

"I know, I know, but what can I tell you?" said Victor, laying more pipe. "That's why Phil suggested we go private placement. He figured it might cost the company a few dollars more in fees, but Whitlaw investors will take the paper in a heartbeat."

"Fantastic," said Bloomberg, chomping at the bit to spread the news.

"I could be wrong," said Victor with humility. "You're the market expert. But I would think early shareholders will be delighted."

~

No sooner did Bloomberg hang up than Johnathan Dothan called Victor, assuming Ryman had shared their ITI market research scam.

"Thanks to you guys, my brother Steve's reputation as a market analyst could be in big trouble!"

"Calm down," said Victor, trying to figure out what was going on.

Dothan continued, "I just learned *Forbes* magazine is planning to publish a major feature story next month demonstrating how phony research reports support clever stock scams. The story names *everybody* at ITI." Victor was speechless. "That means Steve's reputation goes sayonara, I'll lose my security licenses, and Louisa's brokerage business go down the tubes, because she put a lot of heavy hitters into the stock who are not exactly nursery school teachers."

"Great, so where does that leave me?" Victor finally asked.

"My guess? Nowhere," replied Dothan. "You were never in the

report. Franklyn said you guys had agreed that once ITI was fully operational, he was going to realign the management team to make it more Wall Street-savvy."

Victor realized Ryman was more Machiavellian than even he had estimated.

"Suppose," said Victor, "your sources provided some tasty information—*off the record, of course*—to discredit the Forbes story before it's published. Would that solve the problem?"

"Absolutely."

Victor paused. Could he trust Dothan? Did he have a choice?

"I had lunch privately with Scarborough over at Whitlaw & Company on Friday. We spoke for a couple of hours. Given the SEC issues, Whitlaw & Company recommended switching to private placement. *I gave him the green light.* He's organizing a roadshow with his best investors as we speak. He and Herb assured me they'd call in favors to get the deal done in a couple of weeks, that we just needed to make sure we secured a Nachman credit line extension."

Dothan smelled a bloody coup. Something about Victor's wording, *I gave him the green light,* reverberated in Dothan's head. Soon, he was on his cell phone, desperately seeking Ryman. A flabbergasted, angry, and bitter Ryman screamed into the phone. "That little two-faced shit! I *made* him somebody!"

Victor had just committed two fatal errors. He had played politics with the wrong people, and he had broken trust among thieves. *It was now survival of the fittest.*

~

Ryman's campaign to destroy Victor began with an appeal to his rapidly inflating ego. "Let's follow Phil's guidelines," Ryman suggested, "and get Nachman's line extended."

"Agreed," said Victor.

Ryman smiled. He wanted no part of another negotiation with Dawson. "It might be better if you wrapped up the extension with Marty and Sam while I hold the fort down here. You know what they say about too many cooks in the broth."

Ryman assumed Victor would be way over his head, and he, Ryman, would then come to the rescue to reinforce to Phil that he was still firmly in control.

Meanwhile, Victor knew he needed help. He gave Thomas Kugle a call.

"Tom, how about lunch? I heard that the new Armenian restaurant El Habib on Forty-Eighth is pretty good," said Victor, who had never eaten Armenian food but knew Kugle adored the stuff.

"Nice pick," said Kugle. "They have the best tabbouleh salad in the City, according to *The New York Times*."

Sitting at a tiny table with a cheap brass chandelier dangling above their heads and unfamiliar smells permeating the air, Victor framed the issue.

"Tom, I don't know if you're aware, but I'm supposed to meet with Marty to discuss another Nachman contract extension. But something doesn't feel right. With 20 years of history, Marty's first loyalty has got to be Sam, his family, and maybe even Toothson."

"It is unusual," agreed Kugle, knowing what was coming.

"Tom, Franklyn *and* I would like you to be our senior counsel on all ITI matters."

"Victor, please; Franklyn didn't say that."

"Okay. *I* want you to represent us."

"Victor, I'd like to help, but I'm a partner at Delano Mondrain. I think it best if you asked our managing partner to make any decisions about the ITI assignment."

~

Two days later, Victor discovered that the clever Dawson was way ahead of him.

"Victor," said Dawson on the phone, "I've been thinking; trying to represent two clients in the same deal is not fair to either one. I think Tom should represent ITI."

Dawson titled back in his chair.

"Don't read anything into this change in counsel. Sam is still one hundred percent committed to the success of ITI. I've already got him to agree to the latest contract extension terms, except for the line of credit; that remains at a year. And, there is no quid quo pro. He's not even looking to reduce the size of his $20 million personal guarantee."

"Marty, under normal circumstances, that would be an excellent compromise," said Victor, lying through his teeth. "Franklyn has already had a few preliminary meetings with his banking contacts. They like the deal but consider ITI a start-up, despite the individual acquisitions' significant operating histories. They want to see a year or two of post-acquisition operating results before extending ITI an unsecured line of credit. Leaving the Nachman credit guarantee facility at twelve months leaves no margin for error."

Dawson remained unconcerned. "Boys, a deal is a deal."

~

Ryman saw Dawson's squeeze play as his opportunity to restore some luster to his own ego.

"Phil, with all due respect, you're getting in a lather over nothing," said Ryman as he and Victor visited the Whitlaw offices the following day.

"Weeks ago, I anticipated the need for additional lines of credit as soon as we completed our next financing," said Ryman. "Turns out my old United Medical lending officer is now the senior loan officer at Security Pacific, the largest commercial lender on the West Coast. I've already got his verbal approval for an ITI unsecured twenty-million-dollar line of credit."

"Based on what?" challenged Scarborough.

"Based on Nachman's and Toothson's historical financials."

"Ryman, need I remind you? There's nothing to collateralize.

Did you happen to mention to your buddy that Nachman and Toothson are *zero-net-worth transactions?*"

Alarms went off in Ryman's head. Hadn't Victor invented that bullshit Madison Avenue lingo? Scarborough using that term could only mean one thing—Scarborough and Victor were becoming thick as thieves behind his back!

"Dawson's got us over a barrel," said Scarborough.

"I'm not sure about that," interjected Victor, seeking to score more points. "The way I read it, Dawson never even mentioned the credit line extension."

"So," said Scarborough.

"So," said Victor, "I have a plan. Phil, you and Franklyn play along with Dawson. Quietly, I'll fly to the coast to meet Sam one-on-one. I'll tell him we need his input on some potential excess inventory contracts. Sam loves to have his ego stroked. That will be the moment I bring up the *misunderstanding* about his credit line."

"What bullshit," said Ryman. "Dawson will cut your balls when he hears you met with Sam about legal matters without him," said Ryman.

"Screw Dawson. Once I've got the agreement signed, what's he going to do?" replied Victor.

Ryman fumed. "Let's put your crazy idea to a vote with our advisors."

Scarborough glared. "That's *me*! Victor, make the call."

~

Getting Nachman's signature on a contract extension was pure Hollywood.

A tall, burly man, holding a sign that said "V. Martini" met Victor at the frenetic Los Angeles Airport baggage claim.

"I'm Rodney," said a gruff voice with a New York accent behind the smoked glass divider of the pink-and-white limo. "So, how do you like the bus? My girl's an interior decorator. The leopard skin seats are custom."

Victor, who had never seen so much bad taste in one small space, replied warmly, "Rodney, no doubt about it: your lady has got a touch."

"Da boss wanted me to inform you about the plans. Game

foist, dinner later. Okay, wit ya, Mr. Martini?"

"Sure, fine. Whatever."

The limo stopped in front of the players' gate. An usher opened the door. "Welcome to Staples Center, Mr. Martini, home of the world-champion Los Angeles Lakers. Mr. Nachman asked me to escort you to his seats." Victor followed the usher down the aisle, past the $3500-a-pop VIP courtside seats. They stopped at the end of the Lakers' bench. There sat a smiling Nachman in his signature Fila jumpsuit, in Laker purple and gold. To Nachman's left was Rita, the black chick Victor had met during Sam's poker game in Vegas.

"Victor, sit down, sit down. I want you to meet some people." To Nachman's right was a ruggedly handsome man in his early thirties with jet-black hair and warm, generous, deep blue eyes, and a long-legged, red-haired model draped over his shoulder. "Victor, this is my son Albert and his girlfriend. Honey, I'm sorry, what was your name again?" Victor thought to himself, *Isn't this quaint? Two happily married men with loyal wives and six kids, out on an intimate double date with 20,000 of their closest friends!*

"Albert, this is the extension I was telling you about."

"Sam, before you look at it, you need to be aware that I did make one change from what we agreed with Marty. I increased the credit line guarantee to twenty-four months. We really need it. I've been talking to the banks."

"What did Marty say?"

"I didn't tell him."

Nachman laughed. "Kid, you have a pair of big brass ones." He then handed the three-page extension agreement to Albert, while the entire arena cheered and screamed as the game headed into overtime. Albert studied the document as if he were in a private conference room. "Dad, it's fine. It's exactly as you and Marty agreed. Except for the personal guarantee."

"Do I have the right to cut Ryman's balls off if he leaks my company information?"

"Yes."

"And do we get our company name back if they screw things up?"

"Yes."

"Rita, honey," said Sam. "Would you mind bending over?"

"Daddy loves Mommy's booty, doesn't he?" smiled the noticeably pregnant Rita. Nachman took a pen out of his pocket, rested the document on her back, and signed both copies. He patted Rita on the ass then gave one copy to Albert and the other to Victor.

"No more business; let's enjoy the rest of the game! And send me a picture of Marty when he finds out," laughed Nachman.

41.

Dr. Vedderman's Spinal Cocaine

Scarborough gave Victor and Ryman a roadshow update.

"With the collapse of so many start-up tech companies promising the moon, there is a renewed interest in emerging growth companies with a clear path to profitability, like ITI.

"So, as you can imagine, investor response to our roadshow has been gratifying. We start in LA and have full houses in Columbus, Minneapolis, Chicago, Atlanta, and New York."

"New York and Los Angeles, I understand. But why those other places?" asked Victor.

"Typical myopic New Yorker," chuckled Ryman, trying to score a few points with Scarborough. "Believe it or not, there's a lot of money between the two coasts. You do know more than ninety percent of personal wealth lives outside of Manhattan and Beverly Hills, right?"

"Victor, just keep in mind that our institutional investors are a unique breed," continued Scarborough. "That's why last Saturday night, I gave you that detailed profile of every roadshow investor you'll meet."

Ryman didn't like what he heard, but that was for another time.

~

The day before leaving for LA, Victor did the unthinkable!

Over Sandra's protests, he decided to alter the direction of the waterfall at their pool by rearranging two large rocks. Straining mightily, he managed to move the first rock. As he bent over to push the second, a bolt of pain shot down his back, causing him to collapse. Unable to move, he called Sandra on his cell phone. "Honey, we've got a bit of a problem. I just pulled something in my back. I'm lying by the waterfall. I can't move."

Nurse Martini appeared. "You look like a damn beached whale. What in the world made you do something so stupid the day before your trip?"

"Honey, I appreciate the lecture, but I'm in a lot of pain. Get a doctor, an ambulance. Something."

A few minutes later, Victor's next-door-neighbor and orthopedic surgeon, Dr. Joe, was chuckling over his prognosis. "Sandra, our weekend warrior strained his back. Three or four days in bed and a bunch of aspirin should get him back into action."

Nurse Martini then called the local volunteer fire department and asked for a favor—two strong men and a stretcher—to carry Victor the three hundred or so yards up the hill to his bedroom.

"Hey macho man, you'd better alert Franklyn," said Sandra, sticking the phone in Victor's face.

~

"Franklyn, this is Victor. We have a bit of a problem here. I can't make the roadshow."

"What the hell are you talking about?"

"I strained my back pretty bad," Victor admitted sheepishly. "I'm laid up in bed."

"Christ, get the hell up! All those investors! Phil will be furious. He knows I can't play solo," responded Ryman candidly. "I've had some past misunderstandings on the coast."

"Franklyn, I don't think you fully understand."

"Not to worry, Victor, I've got an idea. Just wait right there."

"No problem," said Victor sarcastically. "I'm not going skydiving till 6:00 p.m."

Soon, two guys who looked like they carried trucks on their backs for a living pounded on the front door. "Mrs. Martini? Mr. Ryman sent us to get Mr. Martini. He's made an emergency appointment with Dr. Vedderman, a back specialist in New York

City. Where might we find Mr. Martini?"

Sandra pointed down the hall. Before she could say much more, the two aides gently secured him onto a hardwood stretcher and carefully loaded him into the ambulance, which then rushed to Dr. Vedderman's street-level office on Park Avenue, between Fifty-Fifth and Fifty-Sixth Street. At the nurse's insistence, Victor was lifted off the stretcher and placed in a cold steel chair in the middle of the doctor's office. Victor moaned like a dying whale.

"I know it's uncomfortable, Mr. Martini. Just be patient. The doctor has dropped his other cases and will be here momentarily." Then the door swung open and a little white-haired man, no more than five feet tall and wearing the obligatory white coat, walked into the room. His face was weathered and wrinkled. He also sported a sizeable brown wart on the side of his nose and two steely dark brown eyes, which were topped with thick, bushy brows.

"I'm Doctor Vedderman; where does it hurt?" he said with a thick German accent.

"Center of my back and down my leg," Victor gasped out. "I can't move."

The doctor told Victor to relax, reassuring him that everything would be all right. There were no further questions. There was no examination. He turned his back to Victor and began working at a table. "I'll be right with you. Start counting backward from sixty, out loud," said the doctor with his thick accent.

"Sixty... fifty... forty-five, forty-four..." at about thirty-seven, the doctor turned around and looked directly at Victor. In each of his pudgy hands, he held a foot-long barbeque skewer masquerading as a flexible medicinal rod. A wet cotton ball sat at one end, and spiral handles at the other. On the table behind him was a dark brown-tinted bottle full of fluid.

"Now, Mr. Martini, relax; this will not hurt. Lean your head back on the headrest."

Victor was terrified! The doctor slowly and gently slid the first skewer down Victor's nose. Moments later, only the little curly handle was visible. The doctor slid the second skewer down the other nostril.

"See, that didn't hurt, did it? How do we feel?" Victor noticed the pain had dramatically subsided. "Let's talk for a few minutes. Then I want you to get up and sit in my waiting room for another fifteen minutes. We remove the treatment rods when I call you. Yah?"

After Vedderman had removed the skewers from Victor, he expressed his appreciation. "Doc, you saved my life! I have an important trip tomorrow across the country. Do you think I can make it?"

"No problem. When you return, I would suggest treatments once a week for about three weeks. After you are conditioned, we can schedule treatments for as often as you like."

~

Victor walked spryly through the door. "Jesus, what happened to you?" asked Sandra.

Victor explained the skewers, the treatment, and the brown bottle. Sandra knew immediately. "Oh, I've heard about that. Liquid cocaine non-invasively applied directly to the spinal column."

"Liquid cocaine!"

Sandra calmed her hypochondriacal husband, "Oh, honey, it's no big deal; it's common knowledge within the medical profession that, under certain circumstances, we use the stuff to manage patient discomfort." Like Ryman, she didn't want Victor to disappoint Scarborough. Besides, she was having a surprise putting green installed next week. Victor *had* to go!

"The trick with spinal cocaine is to minimize retreatment because it can become highly addictive," said Sandra reassuringly.

42.

The Roadshow Turns Sideshow

The ITI roadshow started with lunch on the Polo Lounge's patio, in the Beverly Hills Hotel on Sunset Boulevard. It was vintage Tinsel Town.

Thirty-two casual entertainment-types, in their $800 Marciano Italian silk shirts and $400 Gucci shoes, came out for the show. They were sucking down papaya and carrot juice and munching on fresh black Italian figs and mangoes while they waited.

In his custom-made, English tailored blue pin-striped suit with modified single-breasted lapels, Ryman practically screamed *outsider*. "Are you auditioning for a sequel to *Wall Street*?" cackled a razor-thin figure with a gray mustache and oily tan. "Didn't you get the memo? Oliver Stone has already resigned Michael Douglas."

The crowd roared.

"Gentlemen," said Scarborough to the all-male gathering, "I want to thank you for taking time out of your busy schedules."

"Like Herb gave us a choice!" chided an anonymous voice in the crowd.

"He was just concerned about the quality of life in your golden years," bantered Scarborough. "A couple of million each in this deal, and you've got lunch money after the next box office bomb."

~

Ryman and Victor were about ten minutes into their dog-and-pony show when the media crowd, accustomed to one-page storyline pitch sheets for $200 million movies, grew impatient.

"Enough already. I get the excess inventory story," teased one.

"What kind of a deal can you make for 6000 reels of studio turkeys?" asked another. "I'll take payment in crushed ice for my martini bar."

Ryman whispered in Victor's ear, "This is one tough crowd. Just roll with the punches. When they finish kibitzing, we'll go for the close."

As if on cue, the crowd became businesslike. "All kidding aside, what's your name?" said a forty-something, tanned, slicked-back-hair-type who was staring directly at Victor.

"Victor."

"Victor, what is your projected annual return on investment?"

"As you know, an early-stage business typically takes twenty-four to thirty-six months to break even."

"Not in Hollywood!" came a response followed by more kibitzing.

"I understand that," said an unflustered Victor with a winning smile. "That's why an ITI investment should look pretty damn attractive. Our acquisition of successful operating companies means substantial revenues and profits in Year One. It's also a safe bet that the goodwill allocations will be more than offset by the increased revenues derived from operating synergies and the elimination of functional duplication." Victor sounded impressive.

The crowd took one last shot: "Do your projections incorporate your obscene salaries?"

Victor chuckled. "Yes, they do. But that begs another question.

Where do you guys hide your obscene salaries when you create those share-of-profits contracts every star bitches about?"

"I'm curious about that answer myself," said TV star Jason Alexander of *Seinfeld*, now standing in the corner. Everybody was crowing and pounding on the tables.

The nightclub act was about to end. Scarborough stepped in for the close. "Does anybody have any other questions about the business?" There was silence.

"You all know the drill. The ITI deal is an institutional sale. My assistant, Stan Shackman, will collect individual commitments. We'll then bundle them as studio investments. Any questions?"

"When do you expect the placement to fund?" asked director Myron Slotnik.

"About twenty-one days. So please keep that in mind when you wire transfer," said Scarborough, now all business.

~

"Phil, can you give us a Year One earnings estimate?" asked another bald participant in a silk Hawaiian print shirt.

"Frank, you know the rules."

"Sorry. Let me rephrase that. Based on past operating performance, I guestimate that Year One earnings will be between seventeen and twenty cents a share. Does that seem like a reasonable projection?"

"I would say so," smiled Scarborough.

"I have one last question for Franklyn." The voice was Orem Luckler, the powerful studio exec who had once thrown Ryman out of a party after catching him trying to teach two of the studio's prize starlets how to snort coke. Ryman was terrified. Was he about to be embarrassed? Luckler continued, "I love the tailoring in your suit. Who made it?"

Ryman posted a relieved grin. "Orem, I still use Edmund Sexton from Oxford Street in London."

"I heard he's gotten pricey," shot Orem. "Well, if you were making suits for the Royal Family, wouldn't you charge a few quid? Fact is, he's still the best."

Victor sensed one last ego-stroking sum-up couldn't hurt. "As you gentlemen all know, going first-class means knowing where to go and when. That's what makes ITI such a unique investment opportunity." Phil rolled his eyes.

"Thanks to Whitlaw, your participation in this private placement means you get the best at a substantial discount to intrinsic market value."

The money meetings were over. It was now playtime.

43.

No Thanks, Sherrie and Barbee

The afternoon sun burned brightly above the Beverly Hills Hotel's pool. The place was abuzz with agents, starlets, and business-types wanting to be seen.

"So, Phil, how did we do?" asked Ryman, sipping a Bloody Mary in one of the VIP tented cabanas.

"Well, I haven't talked to everybody, but Orem and a few of the other big hitters have committed. So, it looks good… very good… at least, here in LA."

"Bring on Minneapolis!" said Victor.

"Fellas, I just got a call from Herb. I've got to go back to New York on the redeye tonight. Just remember: the key player in Minneapolis is Emmet Jacobs. He knows the liquidation basis, so you should be fine—particularly since you've got an extra night to rest up."

Victor decided to take a nap in the cabana as Ryman searched for some action. He fell into a deep sleep while Ryman went out and began chatting up two blond starlets.

"You girls up for dinner tonight?" said Ryman, thinking ménage a`trois.

"Could be," said the statuesque Sherrie. "How do I turn 'could be' into 'definitely'?"

"Find a companion for my friend Barbee. The two of us are a bit much for one guy."

"Can't blame a guy for trying," smiled Ryman, smoking his cigar. "Girls, come on over to my cabana. I'd like you to meet somebody." Ryman, Sherrie, and Barbee stood over a snoring Victor. "Barbee, give Victor a little hello kiss," said Ryman.

Victor woke up to Barbee's tongue in his mouth. He was stunned and aroused. The group started chuckling. "Victor, say hello to our dinner dates, Sherrie and Barbee." Victor attempted a half-hearted excuse, which Ryman ignored. After seventeen years of marital fidelity, he was concerned about the temptation that stood before him. At the same time, he was just a man, and a unique Hollywood opportunity had arrived 3000 miles from home.

"Girls, how about a drink so we can get to know each other better? I hate dining with strangers," said Ryman.

"I quite agree," said Barbee, giving Victor the once over.

"They make a great raspberry-infused cosmo here," offered Victor. He picked up the phone inside the cabana. "Lars, we'd like to place a drink order. Two of your famous cosmos, light on the Triple Sec, and two bloodies, heavy on the Belvedere."

A few minutes later, a luxuriously tanned, sculpted, middle-aged guy without an ounce of body fat who was dressed in white shorts appeared with the drinks. "So nice to see you again, Mr. Martini. The house account, I assume?" Victor nodded. The girls were impressed, while Ryman foamed at the mouth! Naïve, green Victor had a house account at the Beverly Hills Hotel? Something was wrong with this picture.

"By the way, Mr. Martini, John is here today. As I recall, he was your favorite masseur. Shall I make arrangements?"

"Not today, Lars." Victor paused. "Girls, how about you?

John gives a great massage. Lars, tell John to give the girls a nice deep tissue massage." Victor turned to the girls. "John's hands will put you to sleep. His massage is so relaxing." Ryman watched Victor's act in utter disbelief. "And, Lars, just put John's fee and tip on my account."

"So, what does Ryman do for you, Mr. Martini?" asked Sherrie, trying to make conversation.

Victor smiled. "He doesn't work for me; we're more like

partners. And, please, I'm Victor."

"Like in eighty-twenty partners?" smiled Barbee, confident Victor was just being modest.

After a few hours at the pool, the girls went to their rooms to freshen up while Victor made a quick call home. He was delighted and relieved to get the answering machine. "Just thought I'd call to say all is going well. Off to dinner with some of these Hollywood investors. What a bunch of characters."

Victor, Ryman, and the girls met in the lounge at about seven; they had a few drinks and then headed for La Maisonette on Santa Monica Boulevard. Somewhere between the appetizer and the main course, Barbee decided to freshen up. As she left the table, a small Getty Museum catalog fell to the floor.

"What's this?" asked a genuinely surprised Victor.

"I'm a big fan of French impressionism. The Getty has a great exhibit on loan from the Hermitage in St. Petersburg."

"You're kidding," said Victor, thinking it was an unusual interest for a lady of the night.

Barbee assumed he was asking about the exhibit. "A lot of people don't realize the Russian tsars were great collectors. The entire top floor of the Hermitage is filled with works by Cezanne, Van Gogh, Monet, Degas, and especially Matisse, which have never been viewed in the United States." Victor sat speechlessly. Barbee picked up the vibe. "I guess you assumed you were buying a bimbo dinner in exchange for a cheap trick. Suppose I told you I got my degree in fine arts from UCLA? Would you believe me?"

"Should I?"

"The answer is yes. I'm eventually hoping to curate at one of the major museums here or abroad. My normal day job as a guide at the Getty doesn't exactly pay the rent in LA. In the meantime, a girl has to do what she has to do."

The evening ended with nightcaps at the Polo Lounge. Barbee, an emerging traditionalist, had two Sambucas with warm coffee beans floating on top.

It was 1:00 a.m. Ryman announced, "I have a surprise for everybody. Let's take a walk." As the foursome walked past the fireplace in the lobby lounge, Ryman took a sharp left down the path behind the Polo Lounge, where a few opulent bungalows had been discretely tucked away for Hollywood royalty since the 1930s. Ryman walked up to the largest one, a two-story job, put a key in the door, and waved his hands at the girls. "Me ladies, welcome to your castle for the evening."

The girls squealed like giddy teenagers. Ryman wasn't finished. A waiter carrying two bottles of Dom '87 appeared at the door.

"Put one in each of the bedrooms," directed Ryman. And then, with a final stroke of bravado, he handed the waiter a $50 tip.

At that point, a guilt-ridden Victor did the unthinkable. "Guys, I've had a great time tonight. I really did. But I'm happily married to the girl of my dreams. I've got to go."

As he turned and started walking back to the main hotel, Barbee called out. "Victor, please wait." He stopped. She walked up to him and smiled. "Your wife is one lucky lady. I really envy her."

Barbee tenderly kissed him on the cheek before returning to the bungalow with Ryman and Sherrie.

44.

Quick, Somebody Call 911!

"Sam, sounds like the roadshow was a big success," said Dawson to Nachman over the phone. "Just be here next Thursday to sign the closing documents and pick up your check."

"About goddamn time!"

"Ryman and Victor are panting to close the deal. I'm pretty sure we can put the screws to them one last time. Anything on your wish list?"

"Marty, they're not bad guys. Give them a break. You did good! We got a great purchase price, all our accumulated cash tax-free, and I'm off the personal credit guarantee in twenty-four months."

"Twenty-four months? Sam, it's a year."

"Jesus, I'm sorry, Marty. When Victor came out with the extension, I agreed to give them an extra twelve-months to make sure we get the financing done. Just update the closing docs."

"Son-of-a-bitch. The little fucker sneaked that one by me," said an enraged Dawson.

"Easy, Marty, it's not that big a deal."

To Dawson, it was a huge deal. He prided himself on being the fucker, never the fuckee. "Okay, so it's twenty-four months. But suppose we reduce the size of your guarantee from twenty to ten million."

"How are they going to do deals if they don't have the lines? I want them to succeed. Remember, my name and reputation are part of this thing," said Nachman.

Dawson persisted. He wanted his pound of flesh. "How about

a few more perks, so you don't take a dime out of your pocket?"

"Like what?"

"How about unlimited travel and entertainment and limos for you and the family?" suggested Dawson.

"That's pretty Mickey Mouse."

"Sam, I've got to get you *something* after that curveball," said Dawson. "Sam Nachman doesn't let people walk all over him." Nachman knew Dawson was talking about Dawson. Nachman himself had other more important concerns.

"Who's negotiating for Ed? He seems determined to transfer those barter credit liabilities, so make sure they are not a deal-breaker."

"Toothson's cheapskate lawyer, Dan Boyar, was originally supposed to negotiate that with Ryman, but Ed has asked me to step in. He doesn't think Dan's got the balls."

"Probably right."

"You okay with me handling it?" said Dawson, relishing the idea of having two shots at Victor.

"Babe, you're the best. If it were my call, I'd have you turn the final screws for every acquisition," laughed Nachman.

~

The final details meeting at Delano Mondrain Hudson, held the afternoon before the closing, quickly degenerated into a violent, bitter, screaming-and-yelling session that lasted well into the middle of the night.

The conference table was littered with papers, stained coffee cups, rancid paper plates, and wilted food scraps. On one side of the table sat Dawson with his collar open, tie dangling, and dark rings under his eyes. To his left sat an exhausted, bored Nachman and a fresh, alert Toothson. To his right sat the lusty blonde paralegal, Christine, her shapely legs protruding through the revealing slit in the front of her skirt, squirming restlessly.

Across the table sat the ITI contingent: Kugle, Scarborough, Ryman, and Victor. Scarborough was angry, Kugle appalled, and

Victor and Ryman in an elevated state of shock.

The clock on the wall read 3:30 a.m. "Fellas, fellas, what Sam and Ed are asking is not unreasonable under the circumstances," began Dawson, for perhaps the twentieth time. "Let's review Sam's situation. The purchase price of $15 million is eminently reasonable, given the Crofts Rockman historical audit earnings increase. And we're not quibbling about the additional twelve months you guys weaseled out of him on the personal guarantee. But respectfully, the request to provide Sam and his family with on-demand limo use is just good business. I would think you'd want him in a positive deal-making frame of mind after the closing, right?"

Scarborough was insulted. "Sam, for goodness' sake, you're the world's most successful liquidator, a part-owner of one of the world's most valuable NBA franchises, a world-class poker player, and an entrepreneurial legend. How can you be so Mickey Mouse at the last minute? I didn't think that was your style."

Scarborough had managed to simultaneously massage Nachman's enormous ego and tastefully embarrass him in front of everybody.

"Phil, you're right; that's not my style," replied Nachman.

"Well…" Scarborough paused.

Nachman looked at Dawson, whose eyes bulged as if to say, *Don't you dare!* "Marty, I can live with the deal we've struck. Let's sign the papers."

"Are you sure you want to do that?" glared Dawson.

Kugle passed the contract across the table. After Nachman's signature dried, Scarborough turned to Toothson.

"Now, Ed, I also have to appeal to your sense of fairness. You've stripped Mansfield bare. We've accepted that. But to ask us to pick up all the liabilities for the barter credits you previously issued to get the money we gave you…"

Ed was not about to budge, and Dawson knew that. "Phil, this is a deal-breaker. Ed feels strongly about this."

"Marty, you're a damn pig," said a short-tempered Scarborough.

"Phil, that's the deal. Take it or leave it."

Kugle knew nobody was going to get anywhere with Dawson or Toothson, so he tried an end-run by appealing directly to Sam. "Sam, you were gracious enough to accept what is fair. Can't you tell…"

"Tom," interrupted Dawson. "Don't go there."

"Don't go where?" glared Kugle back.

"Screw you," said Dawson rising from his chair.

"Screw you too," said Kugle, ready to climb across the table.

~

Nachman broke into a cold sweat and started to rub his chest.

He was visibly uncomfortable. "Marty, let's…"

"Sam, be quiet! This is none of your affair."

Nachman bolted out of his chair, fists clenched. "Nobody talks to me like that, least of all my goddamn attorney!"

Dawson tried to physically restrain Nachman as he gasped for air and collapsed on the floor. Christine ran over to check his pulse. "Jesus Christ, his pulse is beating a mile a minute and it's irregular as hell! I think he's having a heart attack! Quick, somebody call 911!"

The place was in chaos. Christine remained by Nachman's side, keeping him calm and relaxed. The emergency paramedics arrived in minutes. They placed an oxygen mask on the fallen Nachman and began a series of tests.

The medics provided their prognosis. "This morbidly obese senior just had a mild heart attack. I don't know what you folks are doing here at this hour, but the stress got him. I'd suggest we bring this gentleman home so he can get some rest."

"Why don't I go with EMTs back to Sam's hotel?" suggested Christine. "I'll stay by his side. We can talk about tomorrow later. Call me at the hotel when you finish."

"Fine," said Kugle. "Let's take a break."

Kugle, Scarborough, Ryman, and Victor retreated to a separate conference room. "What the hell kind of firm do you run here?" said Scarborough. "Marty seems to speak for everybody!"

"Phil, I agree Marty's behavior is unethical," said Victor, determined to get the deal done at any cost. "But, at the moment, we've got bigger fish to fry."

"Tom," said Scarborough, "how do we get out of this mess?"

"Phil, I'm afraid Ed has you over a barrel. Either you give, or he walks."

~

Scarborough went ballistic. "Bullshit! I demand you call Sefton Delano. Tell him if he doesn't get the terms of this deal resolved right now, Whitlaw & Company will file a professional ethics complaint with the American Bar Association tomorrow morning. We'll shut down your whole goddamn firm!"

Kugle calmly walked over to the phone, knowing his career and Dawson's could be in jeopardy. The phone rang five times. A voice answered, "Hello, hello..." Kugle paused. He was silent. The voice continued, "Hello, who the hell is this? It's four o'clock in the morning."

Kugle took a deep breath. "Sefton, this is Tom Kugle. I'm sorry to wake you, but we've got a situation here that needs your attention. Do you mind if I put you on the speakerphone? I've got the Whitlaw & Company Managing Director Phil Scarborough and the ITI Company principals here with me."

"What the hell is going on?" said Sefton.

"As you know, the ITI financing is scheduled to close tomorrow, I mean later today, at 10:00 a.m. Well, Nachman and Toothson have made several last-minute material requests. We resolved the Nachman matter, but Toothson won't back off or compromise. He is threatening to walk."

Delano was furious. "Screw that! Have Marty tell their attorney to take a hike. How dare they? From what I recall, ITI has already taken off its pants and spread its legs for these bastards."

"Sir, the other attorney is Marty."

"What the hell are you talking about?"

"He's representing both Toothson *and* Nachman."

"You gotta be shitting me! Put Marty on the phone and take me off the goddamn speakerphone."

Kugle walked into the other conference room. "Marty, Sefton is on the phone. He wants to talk to you."

"Sefton, you don't quite understand the subtilities of the situation…." Dawson began.

Sefton interrupted. Marty just listened. Kugle had executed a double reverse right under Marty's nose. Dawson put his hand over the phone and glared at Kugle. "You disloyal little shit, I'm going to have your ass fired after the closing!" Marty returned to the phone, taking orders. "Yes, sir. I understand, sir."

"You better figure out a fair compromise; otherwise, I'll make sure you never practice corporate law in this city again—ever! Do I make myself clear?" continued Delano.

Magically, thirty minutes later, a compromise was struck. ITI agreed to assume barter credit liabilities for those deals completed since the original acquisition term sheets were drafted eleven months before. And Toothson remained liable for the rest.

Despite all the ITI professional firepower, by the time Toothson's accountants adjusted the books and records, he was liable for less than a third of the barter credits; the other $200 million-plus in barter credit liabilities magically became ITI's responsibility.

45.

Mona Toothson's Other Life

Thanks to ITI, Toothson was not only *legitimately* wealthy, but he was also out from under hundreds of millions in potentially litigious barter liabilities.

And, if he was every challenged in the courts, he now owned an acceptable general accounting opinion from the internationally-recognized CPA firm of Crofts Rockman.

As Toothson packed his attaché to leave the closing negotiation, Dawson's secretary approached. "Mr. Toothson, your son James called during the meeting; he said it was extremely urgent."

Toothson wondered what could be that urgent at 4:00 a.m. He quickly found out. "Mom crashed her plane *again*. The tower said she just missed the runway at Westchester airport. Sis and I are at Armonk Hospital."

Toothson was alarmed but calm. "How bad is she?"

"She's lost a lot of blood and broken some bones, but the doctors say she's stable and should recover. They are monitoring her overnight in the ICU. She's been asking for you."

"I'll be there after the closing later this morning."

"The woman with her was not so lucky; she's on life support." James paused.

"What woman?"

"I don't know," said James. "Why would mom be with another woman at 4:00 a.m.?"

Toothson knew Mona's drinking and appetite for sexual experimentation had increased in recent years. But he never let on to the kids about all that. When Toothson confronted Mona on numerous occasions, she had emasculated him by pointing out that women gave her the kind of affection she craved from him. "I bet Mom was just showing off to a friend," replied Toothson. "Mom was very proud of her new flying license."

Toothson knew that he should remain supportive for the sake of his kids, but the movie was getting old—this was Mona's third crash in the past six months. Each time he ran to her side, and each time she promised she'd take more flying lessons, but she never actually did.

Things were different now. In less than six hours, he would become a legitimate business executive; he wasn't in the mood for a public litany of apologies and painful pledges of sobriety.

"James, why don't you and your sister get some sleep? I'm sure they've sedated Mom. Tell her I'll be there as soon as I can after the closing."

"Will do, Dad."

After he hung up, Toothson went back to his pied a `terre to get a few hours' sleep.

~

The phone rang. Sandra groggily rolled over in bed. The alarm clock read 4:00 a.m. "Where are you?"

"At our attorneys'."

"I don't believe you."

"Tom, help me out here," said Victor, handing the phone to Kugle.

"Tom, what the hell is going on?" demanded Sandra.

"Oh, we just finished a typical ITI day," said Tom calmly. "Marty found out Victor screwed him. So he tried to screw Victor back, in front of Sam. Then everybody started screaming at everybody, and Sam had a mild heart attack. Once the ambulance left, Ed threatened to pull out of the deal unless he got another million. Phil called everybody disgusting pigs, so my boss Sefton Delano decided to fire Marty after the closing."

"You couldn't make this stuff up," said Sandra. "Thank God you're there."

"I didn't tell you the worst part," Kugle deadpanned. "I had a mountain-high pastrami and corned beef sandwich during the festivities and got a serious case of heartburn—with no Pepcid insight."

~

By 10:00 a.m., the conference room was festive and pleasant once more. Victor counted thirty-six people present, including representatives for the seven investors; the acquisition principals, including Nachman, Toothson, their families; lawyers; accountants; public relations people; and two photographers. And three caterers were in the adjoining conference room, setting up a buffet lunch.

"Ladies and gentlemen," said Kugle, who had been instructed by Sefton Delano to chair the meeting. "After we get pictures, I'd like everybody to take a seat so that we can execute the closing documents. We've got enough paper in this room to sink the Titanic."

Soon, the investment group signed their documents and handed $75 million in bank checks to Kugle. Scarborough rose after all the documents were notarized. "Certainly, this has been one of the more challenging closings of my career, but then, who could expect anything less from the one and only Franklyn Ryman?" Everybody smiled and applauded as Ryman took a modest bow.

~

"Ryman and Victor, would you come up here?" invited Scarborough. "In commemoration of this particularly important event in our company's history, and as a thank you for appointing Whitlaw & Company as your investment banker, we would like each of you to have a little gift—an engraved gold desk clock from Tiffany's."

Ryman also decided to say a few words about increasing shareholder value. Victor and Scarborough rolled their eyes.

"Now that business has been concluded, we've got champagne and lunch in the conference room next door, compliments of Delano Mondrain. Just fill your plates and enjoy the afternoon," said Kugle.

Sefton Delano entered the room and whispered something in Kugle's ear. Kugle nodded and walked to the front of the room. "Could I have everybody's attention for one more minute? My boss, Delano Mondrain Hudson's Managing Director Sefton Delano, would like to say a few words."

"Like Phil and Tom," said Sefton, "we'd like to thank everybody for their contributions to making today's closing a reality. I've decided to close our offices for the day, so there's no need to rush on our account. Besides, I think there is a Dom '87 in those buckets, compliments of Phil Scarborough."

The group applauded.

"I also wanted to make one last announcement. In recognition of his years of service and his hard work on this particular transaction, the board of Delano Mondrain Hudson elected Tom Kugle as managing partner earlier this morning."

~

Toothson, pleased the deal was done, finished the obligatory toast before walking outside with his cellphone to call home. "Mom died about an hour ago," said James, crying.

"What the hell happened?"

"Dad, I don't know. We feel asleep in the visitor's lounge. Next thing I know, some doctor wakes me up and says, 'Your mom's heart just stopped beating. I'm sorry.'"

"What about the other woman?"

"Hard to believe, but they've taken her out of the ICU. They say she'll make a full recovery."

~

Toothson wanted Mona's service to be understated. He invited a few close family and friends, and his long-time cantor, Josef Newton, composed a farewell prayer, *Peace at Last*, that wished

Mona inner peace in her new home.

Unfortunately, as Toothson searched her belonging to find a few personal mementos to place beside her in her casket, he discovered a woman he never knew. A box of love letters to a woman named Lydia Rand covered the last ten years and cases of empty vodka bottles were neatly stacked behind a false door in her master bedroom closet.

About two weeks after the service, Toothson was served with papers from Rand, which claimed half of Mona's estate as her common-law wife. The legal documents suggested intimate knowledge of the forthcoming sale of Mansfield, including the purchase price, retained earnings, and such.

Toothson called Dawson, who advised him to negotiate a settlement rather than drag the kids through the courts. "I'm guessing I can settle the matter privately with Ms. Rand. I've done some checking. It turns out she's married to a high-profile national politician; she's got three kids and a storybook marriage."

"How much?" asked Toothson.

"Under the circumstances, I'd bet she'd go away for $2 million and a non-disclosure that we won't reveal her other life. Hell, we can bury it as a finder's fee adjustment on a previous deal. Nobody will be the wiser."

"Let me think about it," said Toothson.

Three days later, CNN ran a story about the accidental drowning of Lydia Rand Paul, the wife of the distinguished United States Senator Jamerson Paul of Massachusetts. In a tearful video clip, the senator said he was comforted by the fact that she died doing something she loved—scuba diving.

The official corner's report listed the death as cerebral hypoxia caused by a break in the line to her oxygen tank.

46.

The First ITI Operations Meeting

The first-ever ITI operating committee meeting could have been a skit on Saturday Night Live. The mood was relaxed and the meeting structure was completely nonexistent.

On one side of the conference table was Ryman, in his signature custom English single-label pinstriped suit; Victor, in his baggy Brooks Brothers' blues; and Scarborough, in a plaid cashmere sweater vest and tie, looking very much the college professor.

On the other side sat Nachman, in a Fila silver and gold Lakers jumper, and Toothson blowing smoke rings with his briarwood pipe, dressed in a worn sports jacket with leather arm patches. "Fellas, thanks for coming to our initial meeting," began Victor, attempting to sound in control.

"We've got two agenda items. First, we need to discuss expanding our corporate awareness by building your brand equities," said Victor. The room was so quiet you could hear a pin drop.

"Victor, would you translate that Madison Avenue double-talk into English?" smiled Toothson. "We're simple folk here."

Ryman decided to have a little fun at Victor's expense. "Finally, somebody else has noticed Victor's Madison Avenue double talk."

Victor got the message. "How about we lease and build out a corporate booth at the Consumer Electronics Show in Chicago? It's the biggest and most important goddamn trade show of the year."

"A booth. Why not just walk the floor? It's cheaper," said Toothson.

"Aren't you guys getting a little long-in-the tooth to scratch and claw for every deal?" challenged Victor, who made like Billy Graham waving his arms on a pulpit. "Guys, you're now a legitimate public company. Like in NASDAQ. Given the proper stroking, prospects will come to us. We provide reliability, credibility, and accountability."

"Sounds good to me. I'm in," said Nachman.

"Anybody disagree?" No one dared. "Good," said Victor. "Give me about a week to whip up a CES marketing plan. How does everybody's calendar look for the weekend of December twelfth? We'll need to go over the plan and make arrangements."

The date worked for everybody. The venue didn't. "Jesus," said Toothson. "It's nasty in New York in December. Sam, you're always bragging about sunny, glorious Southern California."

"Done. The next meeting is at my place in Bel Air. And forget the hotels; we've got even suites for everybody."

~

"Moving on," said Victor. "Next topic: deal flow. If you look at this chart, you'll notice the group executed twenty-nine deals at an average gross of three million dollars each during the twelve months before joining ITI. Our goal this year is to close thirty-five deals at an average gross of five million. That would give us consolidated revenues of more than $160 million for our first full year of operation." Victor paused a moment for everyone to take in the numbers. "If we earn ten percent pre-tax, we'll have hefty market capitalization that should boost the price of our stock and make our acquisition program even more attractive to entrepreneurs looking to sell their company."

Scarborough liked what he heard. Victor owned the room. Ryman, however, had mixed emotions. He certainly didn't want to be the operations guy for a bunch of blue-collar millionaires. But, with his massive ego, he didn't want to lose control either. ITI was his idea. ITI was his company! Victor was the guest.

"To pull this off," continued Victor, evermore confident, "we need to know where the deals are at all times. I've created this simple weekly Excel template to help with that. Just put somebody in charge of filling in the blanks and email it to me every week. Anytime you want to see what everybody else is doing, give our office a call, and we'll email you a consolidated report like this."

"I'm impressed," said Toothson. "Listen, I'll do anything to help you guys meet or exceed our goals."

"That will make the stock run, as you guys take bags of cash to the bank!" responded Victor.

"That's just what Eddie needs," kidded Nachman.

"Sam, that's not the point. Money is just a nice way to keep score." They all started laughing. Ryman seethed; Victor had absolute control of the meeting—and now Ryman needed to remind Victor who was the real boss here.

~

When the meeting ended, Ryman decided his student needed a little lesson in physical intimidation.

"Victor, grab your gym bag and let's go for a quick workout at the Vertical Club as we summarize today." Ryman expected the usual cascade of excuses, followed by generous amounts of arm-twisting.

"You're on," responded Victor. Another surprise: the receptionist and the club trainers knew Victor by his first name.

As they stood on the running track stretching their hamstrings, Ryman reacquainted Victor with the ground rules. "We'll do three warm-up laps, then pick up the pace on the second four, and, if you're still with me, we'll sprint the final three."

They jogged side by side for the first three laps without Ryman generating a bead of sweat. He smiled as the sweat formed on Victor's brow. "We've got to put a full-court press on these bastards to produce," said Franklyn, as he quickened the pace at lap four.

"I think we'll be okay," said Victor, who continued alongside Ryman stride for stride. Franklyn turned the pace up another notch at lap five. As they circled the track, the neon lights blinked overhead, and Rod Stewart's "Maggie Mae" blared over the loudspeakers. Franklyn and Victor overtook the other joggers, who moved to the slower inside lanes.

Out of the corner of his eye, Victor noticed Ryman starting to grimace from Victor's newfound endurance. As they hit the seventh lap, Ryman attempted an all-out sprint, his size-fourteen sneakers in high step and knees churning. Victor did likewise, except more gracefully, more effortlessly. By the eighth lap, Victor was twenty yards in front of a panting, perspiring Ryman. Victor looked back and waved as if to say, "come on." Victor finished the tenth lap almost a hundred yards ahead of Ryman. To punctuate his conquest, Victor waited at the finish line, casually leaning against the railing. A gasping Ryman crossed the finish line, incredulous at what he had just witnessed.

Lunch also had its share of surprises. Ryman ordered a healthy, low-fat pasta salad, and iced tea while the staff prepared Victor's formulation of carrot juice, beets, celery, apples, and papaya. He also wolfed down a handful of supplements with exotic names like Magnesium Glycinate, Coenzyme-10, and Bromelain. So much for Ryman's lesson in humility.

Ryman found a bright spot in his loss, though. He told Victor he had injured his Achilles and would be unable to attend the CES show in Vegas. Victor thought Ryman had something up his sleeve, but the fact was he and Astrid had made plans.

~

To everyone's surprise, Nachman, Toothson, and their support staff were treated like rock stars at the CES show. Finders offered new inventory deals; potential acquisition principals held private "advice" meetings; and the city's main newspaper, *The Las Vegas Sun*, decided to do a front-page business feature. The headline read "Going from Back Street to Main Street." The story included a prominent picture of Sam, Ed, and their *new owner* Victor Martini, standing outside the ITI corporate booth.

The day after the story ran, the stock rose 15 percent and Parker Bloomberg called to congratulate Ryman. "Franklyn, a hell of a story. We need more stuff like that."

Ryman sent Astrid to the out-of-town newsstand in Grand Central. When he saw Victor's picture, he went ballistic. It was time to cut his partner's balls off. He just needed the right plan at the right moment!

47.

The King Takes Ryman to the Cleaners

"Based on our deals-in-progress report, we're going to burn through Sam's line of credit pretty quickly," said Ryman over cocktails with the Dothans.

"Franklyn," responded a skeptical Louisa, "let's see the report."

"Who carries reports around when they are having cocktails with friends?"

"Franklyn, you're not trying to bullshit me, are you?"

"Trust me," said Ryman, lying through his teeth, "$20 million is not enough. That's why we need to launch *my* Barter Bank concept. It will revolutionize the barter industry, just as I did with the hospital management industry."

"I'm listening," said Louisa.

"Owning a bank focused on providing capital to the barter industry means we'll never run out of capital to fund ITI inventory deals or for additional acquisitions. We'll also be able to offer competitors capital at a reasonable rate of interest *and* receive a share of profits on every one of their deals."

"And how do we plan to fund this magic?" asked Louisa.

"By completing a public financing for a spin-off offering."

"Johnathan, you heard it here first," said Louisa. "Franklyn's going to ask the public to fund a subsidiary that will increase the value of his ITI shares before the ink on the private placement is dry. And I assume he plans to add more founder shares to his war chest."

"Louisa, be nice to Franklyn; he's made us a lot of money. The new scheme sounds pretty creative. The question is, will Whitlaw agree?"

"Johnathan, just tell your buddy at Whitlaw to start salivating about the underwriting fees from a new $100 million financing."

"Recommendations cost," reminded Louisa.

"How much?"

"Just four percent founder equity in the subsidiary, so our names don't appear in the prospectus—same as Allyn Tishman got in the hospital deal."

"But Allyn was an ongoing company advisor," protested Ryman.

"Bullshit," growled Louisa. "Johnathan and I and have spent more time on ITI than your so-called advisor who completed a few filings, then quietly placed his entire position into some tax shelter in the Cayman Islands. When was the last time you even talked to the two-faced bastard?"

Louisa had hit a hot button. "Fine. Four percent."

"I think I might also be able to help you with the Victor-Phil lovefest," said Johnathan.

"How?"

"Recruit some name management talent that will put your junior partner in his place."

"I'm listening," said Ryman.

~

Johnathan Dothan returned a few days later.

"My old friend Marc Melrose told me he's looking to explore new challenges," said Johnathan.

"Are you talking about the Chairman of Billingham Trust Company?" asked the wide-eyed Ryman.

"Yes," replied Johnathan. "And, he loves your Barter Bank concept. Louisa and I believe with Mark as Chairman and CEO, a barter bank offering would fly out the door. Could even be bigger than ITI itself."

Ryman was hooked. "Arrange a meeting."

~

Marc Jacob Melrose IV's 53rd-floor office on the tip of Manhattan Island seemed the stuff of feudal kings: twelve hundred square feet, paneled in richly-veined, imported English satinwood. Melrose's enormous, rectangular, black walnut inlaid desk had more drawers and brass knobs than a turn-of-the-century apothecary cabinet.

Melrose projected royalty. He had a full head of neatly groomed black hair atop the taut, lean figure of an impeccably dressed man who spoke in vague philosophical terms. "Franklyn, the concept of a worldwide barter bank has a certain caché. It's a constructive business concept consistent with my publicly declared interest to assist the less fortunate third-world economies." Dollar signs danced in Melrose's head as he imagined his net worth exploding into the outer reaches of the ozone layer.

An expert negotiator of a different sort, Melrose sensed Ryman's anxiousness to close a deal. So, he teased Ryman into a state of frenzied desperation by ponderously meandering through the availability of Somalian sapphires, Ivory Coast gold, and Indonesian rubber.

"Marc, I'm an intuitive animal by nature. We'd make an excellent management team, initially with the Barter Bank and eventually over the entire ITI holding company."

Melrose took out a couple of cigars and handed one to Ryman. As they lit up, a thick cloud of smoke engulfed them. "Ryman, I was under the impression you had an accomplished heir apparent that has been with you from inception."

"You must be referring to Victor Martini," said Ryman. "He's a nice young man with an advertising background, but he's not CEO material. He and I recognize your corporate finance experience dwarfs what he could ever accomplish. My thought is to strike a deal to get your feet wet as CEO of the Barter Bank; then, at the appropriate time, appoint you CEO over the whole enchilada."

"And what about you?"

"Hey, I'll be content to be honorary Grand Poohbah or something. I plan to buy an island—maybe Fiji or Bali—and bask in the sun. If you need me, I'll be available via satellite," smiled Ryman.

"And Victor?"

"Don't worry about Victor. I've made him a rich man. He's a big boy. You can bring in whoever you want." Ryman had just initiated his latest dump-Victor plan.

Now it was Melrose's turn to close. "Ryman, I don't know... Chairman of Billingham Trust to the chairman of a start-up Barter Bank? I'm not sure it would be appropriate to burden a young company with my kind of compensation requirements."

"Why don't you let me worry about that?" said Ryman with an air of braggadocio. "What range are we talking about?"

"Well, my total package is in the $950,000 range. But I can live on less, assuming the equity position justifies the reduction."

"What do you need? I'm not asking you to negotiate. I want to know what's the minimum you need to maintain your lifestyle. You've got to be satisfied or it doesn't make any sense."

"Assuming I have about thirty-five percent of the deal, Eleanor and I can probably get by on $60,000 a month or so. That's about $700,000 a year." Melrose nailed Ryman right into a corner.

"Not a problem. With a $100 million raise, nobody will blink an eye at those numbers. Not with your track record."

But Marc wasn't finished. "I also assume we are talking about a seat on the board?"

"Obvious!"

"There are a few other details," commented Melrose.

"How about we let the lawyers handle them? They've got to justify their retainer somehow," smiled Ryman.

"How long before you're ready to go to market?" asked Melrose.

"I would guess about sixty to ninety days."

"That would provide an adequate timeframe to conclude matters here," said Melrose, who had an urgency to close the deal. The Billingham auditors were excruciatingly close to uncovering more than forty high-risk, Melrose-approved, unsecured international loans, which had earned him millions in finder's fees that were now cleverly buried in a complex maze of offshore corporations.

Melrose also knew from Dothan that Ryman had personal cash-flow problems. "So, John tells me you are part owner of the Aspen Club. Great facility. My wife Eleanor and I have stayed there a few times."

"Thanks, but frankly, it's a huge black hole," said Ryman. "When cash flow didn't matter, losing a couple of hundred thousand a month was no big deal. Plus, I got to hobnob with celebs from all over the world. Right now, however, until the ITI registration period is over, I'm drawing heavily on my assets."

"I had no idea," said Marc. "Could the club use a working capital line? Perhaps I could introduce you to one of my friendly loan officers." Marc figured he had enough time left for one or two more unsecured loans. While this one had no finder's fee per se, he planned to leverage the introduction when the lawyers got around to the final detail.

48.

Ryman & Melrose, Partners in Crime

The Melrose employment contract meeting at Delano Mondrain Hudson resembled opening night at the Metropolitan Opera House.

Ryman, Tom Kugle, and paralegal Christine, assigned to Kugle after Dawson's sudden departure, represented ITI. The Melrose entourage included two lawyers—Sol Lieberman and Manny Poltakin—one accountant—Rebus Barton III—and Melrose's longtime administrative assistant, Gertrude Raantone.

Kugle thought the size of Melrose entourage was a bit odd, since Ryman had billed this as a "details" meeting. "Franklyn, where's Victor?" he whispered.

"I left him at home; he's not involved in the Barter Bank. This one's way over his head." Kugle smelled a rat. He just had no idea how big it was.

Lieberman, the lead attorney, took charge of the meeting, distributing copies of Melrose's employment agreement. "Tom, since the basic compensation and equity percentages have been previously agreed upon between Marc and Franklyn, I thought the most efficient use of everyone's time might be to focus on Section Twelve, captioned 'other considerations.'"

Kugle almost had a cardiac arrest as he glanced at the paragraph entitled 'base compensation.' Five years, starting at $750,000 and rising $150,000 per annum to $1.5 million. The equity positions were equally staggering: thirty-five percent of the spin-off, pre-dilution, plus 1.4 million ITI stock options at a strike price of five dollars.

"Fellas, before we begin, I was wondering if I could have a few words with my client?" said Kugle. The two left the conference room. "Franklyn, as your attorney, I must advise you that these numbers you've supposedly agreed upon are reckless and irresponsible. No startup pays $750,000 bases. If you think we have SEC problems now, wait till they see this. In my opinion, they are going to…"

"In your opinion… in your opinion," said Ryman, eyes bulging out of his beet-red head. "To hell with you and your opinion! What has that gotten me so far except three million dollars in legal fees? Remember what you told me about our last deal? 'We should have no trouble clearing the SEC; they're not that busy right now.' So much for your opinion."

"What does Victor think?"

"He's in complete agreement. Why?" Ryman and Kugle stood face-to-face like two heavyweight boxers at a weigh-in. "Melrose's name brings instant credibility to the deal. The Street will love it. That alone will pay for his salary," exclaimed an irate Ryman. "He's also insurance that the SEC can't pull that 'related party' bullshit."

"Franklyn," said Kugle talking to Ryman's nose, "you think life is a series of shortcuts. One continuous promotion. Well, it's not! Do you think everybody's …"

"Listen, you little shit; I invented this fucking company. Nobody's going to tell me what to do! In case you didn't realize, you work for me. I'm not paying you big fees so you can cover your ass with the SEC! Now let's get back into the conference room and wrap this deal up!"

"Franklyn," said Melrose moments later, awash in integrity, "I want to be straight up with you because that's the only way partners should operate. I've added a few items we didn't discuss previously."

"Such as?" asked Ryman.

"Eleanor insists on a five-million-dollar life insurance policy."

"Done. Next?"

"I've added a $16,000 disability income policy."

"Jesus Christ!"

In point after point, Ryman acquiesced. Kugle noticed the quirky option award language. An initial grant of 15 million ITI options at a 50 percent discount to market was, in effect, a signing bonus of $14 million. Tom leaned over to Ryman. "This option award is incredible: 1.5 million shares with a strike price at half the current market. I'm not even sure that's legal without approval from the Board."

Ryman face turned beet red. "Kugle, get with the program. ITI is my company, I control the Board, and you work for me.

Understand?"

~

Delano Mondrain's monthly legal bill was about twice the usual, thanks to the protracted Melrose negotiations. Kugle felt obligated to give his friend Victor a heads-up, since he was aware cash flow was starting to become an issue. "Victor, I don't want you to faint when you see a bill for $202,000."

"For what?"

"Last month's legal expenses."

"How is that even possible? We're waiting on the SEC, so there can't be many hours there, and we've slowed our acquisition activity while we assimilate the first group."

"The fees are for time spent on the Barter Bank."

"The Barter Bank? I thought Phil told Franklyn to turn that dial down until we increase revenues and earnings."

"I don't think Franklyn got the message. He's going full speed ahead with Marc Melrose on compensation, management duties, the prospectus, spin-off financing…"

Victor now knew why Ryman didn't have time to go to LA or Chicago. "Son-of-a-bitch," he muttered.

"Didn't you know anything?" said Kugle.

"No. And who is Marc Melrose?" asked Victor.

"He's the president CEO of the new bank, and its second-largest shareholder, since the other day when the two of them agreed on the terms."

"Thanks for the heads-up on that," said Victor sarcastically.

"Franklyn said you guys were in complete agreement on all the deal terms."

~

Two days later, Ryman beamed as he watched Melrose sign a mountain of personal agreements, including (but not limited to) his employment contract, equity agreements, and life & disability insurance applications. With an exaggerated gesture, Melrose placed a period after his last signature. "Well, I guess that makes it official: we are now partners in crime," smiled Melrose, peering over his tiny granny reading glasses.

"Marc, I'll have Johnny get the press release ready," said Ryman.

"Whoa, hang on," said Melrose. "Franklyn, that's a bit premature. I would feel much more comfortable knowing the financing was completed first—that's the conservative banker in me."

"I understand," said Ryman, who didn't understand at all.

"By the way, who is Johnny?"

"Oh, he's my internal jack-of-all-trades."

"With all due respect," said the smooth-talking Melrose, "your record of success demands a real public relations agency. The right media exposure to business leaders in *The Wall Street Journal* can only be good for the stock price."

"*The Journal?*" said Ryman. "I can't imagine they're going to cover our little company."

"Franklyn, I'm talking about coming in the side door," smiled Melrose. "You've got to be subtle and classy. For example, getting an article published with your byline as CEO of the world's first publicly traded international barter company couldn't hurt."

Ryman was like a mouse in search of cheese. "How can we make that happen?"

"Claxton Harlington," said Melrose.

"What's Claxton Harlington?" chuckled Ryman. "Sounds like a brand of Matzos."

"Claxton Harlington is the most influential PR firm on The Street," replied Melrose. "He'll know exactly how to position and write the story. And, most importantly, he'll know who to pitch at *The Journal* to get into print. Claxton has worked closely with me for seven years at Billingham. Why do you think people consider me an international banking expert? Don't get me wrong; I know my stuff, connected than I am. But he is New York's reigning master of first-class hype. Jack Welch, Ted Turner, and Larry Tisch are all clients.

"Matter of fact, I was telling him about you at dinner the other night. He was intrigued. I sense if you guys have a chemistry match, and if we provide an appropriate retainer, he might be persuaded to take the assignment."

Ryman chomped on the cheese, closing the trap. "Fees are not an issue. Like I've always said, 'People that don't go first-class have no class.' What kind of retainer plus goodies are we talking about?"

"I can't speak for Claxton, you understand...." Melrose and Ryman began sending smoke signals with their cigars. Melrose stuck his hand out. As far as he was concerned, the meeting was over. "I look forward to working with all of you."

"Tom, you can turn the meter off. Marc and I are going to have a cup of coffee before I go back to the office."

Ten minutes later, Ryman and Melrose were sitting in a quiet corner of Café Allegro at Grand Central Station, sipping cappuccino grandees and nibbling chocolate biscotti. Melrose explained that Harlington had made other business leaders filthy rich with his public relations spins and was looking to trade his experience for founder stock in a few selected situations.

"Not a problem," said Ryman. "Since some of my current advisors are not participating in this spinoff, there's room for a few percentage points."

"Good, good. But you're not talking about cutting Dothan out, are you? After all…"

"I promised that shitbag a taste, and I always keep my word. I figure I can goose-egg Victor and Johnny."

"That raises another question. I noticed Victor was not at our meeting. When I had lunch with Phil, he seemed very high on Victor. Talked about how critical Victor was to ITI's success. Doesn't he need to remain involved and incentivized?"

"Naw," said Ryman. "Victor's fine. Besides, Phil has misread Victor's importance. He's doing a good job and all. But critical? Hardly. The Barter Bank never even came up."

Melrose quietly concluded the situation between Ryman and Victor was an emerging political cesspool. He decided the wisest course was to ingratiate himself with both parties until somebody shot himself in the foot.

"Ryman, I didn't want to mention this in the conference room, but the committee approved your Aspen Club credit line. We're putting the final touches on a three-million-dollar unsecured credit agreement at prime minus fifty basis points, our best customer rate. That should give you some breathing room until the club is sold. The loan papers should be on my desk when I get back to the office."

"Like I was saying," said Ryman, "let's hold on the press the Barter Bank announcement until the offering is completed. In the meantime, I'll wet Phil Scarborough's beak."

49.
Enough is Enough

Ryman arrived all smiles at Scarborough's favorite cafeteria—
the five-star La Grenouille on Fifty-Second Street.

"Phil, thanks for seeing me. We rarely get the opportunity to
talk about operating issues between board meetings."

Scarborough knew Ryman had a personal agenda; the last thing
he was interested in was day-to-day operations. "Franklyn, I was
delighted with the results of the deals ITI made at the Consumer
Electronics Show," said Scarborough. "Looks like Victor was right;
that booth increased our brand visibility, especially with that news
story," said Scarborough, placing a copy of the *Chicago Tribune* on
the table. "He made our acquisition teams look like titans of
industry. I bet they ate it up."

"Phil, I'm not so sure we got full value received at the CES
show. Victor spent a lot of money."

"Franklyn," asked Scarborough, "have you ever read Jimmy
Breslin's novel *The Gang that Couldn't Shoot Straight?* The cast of
characters in the book has amazing similarities to our off-beat band
of multi-millionaires. Every member of the gang did things their
own way, but somehow it worked. I don't know how Victor
maintains his sanity dealing with those guys day after day," smiled
Scarborough, shaking his head.

"Phil," began Ryman, "I know you're fond of Victor. So am I,
but some performance issues have started to emerge."

"Like what?" Scarborough said, confident Ryman was about to
take a cheap shot.

"My financial manager says he's incapable of keeping expenses
under control, which, as you can appreciate, is fatal for a chief
operating guy. He also seems oblivious to our cash flow

management. Spending a million dollars to promote our brand awareness for business development activities seems pretty excessive."

"Really? I was under the impression that our company managements thought our marketing programs had caused a dramatic increase in the quantity and quality of our deal flow, and their return on investment exceeds expectations."

"Who told you that?"

"I was talking to Sam Nachman the other day."

"There's also a lot of other little things," said Ryman, increasingly paranoid that people were talking behind his back.

"Like what?" asked Scarborough.

"Nothing that I can put my finger on specifically."

"Franklyn, are you seriously trying to throw stones at the only person that's spending 100 percent of his time growing the business?"

Ryman backpedaled. "Let's make sure we don't have any misunderstandings. My objective is to identify areas for improvement, not to engage in character assassination. And, most importantly, to find creative new ways to raise operating capital as we grow."

Phil raised his eyes. "I heard you took a meeting with a major Wall Street banking executive about that far-fetched Barter Bank concept. Tell me it's not true?"

"With all due respect, Phil, the Barter Bank is not far-fetched, and…"

"What does Victor think of pursuing a Barter Bank spinoff?"

"He's in complete agreement," lied Ryman, making no mention of the compensation agreement he had signed with Melrose.

"Funny, he's never even mentioned the Barter Bank in any of *our* conversations. You do realize solving our SEC redline problem is the foremost priority? Unless we bring that issue to closure, I see zero opportunity to raise another dime for additional acquisitions, Barter Bank, or whatever."

Ryman intentionally digressed. "In all my years of experience, the SEC's conduct right now is an outrage. It's libelous, and it's defamatory. The nerve! We're just trying to build a business with shareholder value…"

"Franklyn, please, this is me, Phil, you're talking to. Enough with the bullshit. There is only one way to cut through the SEC redlining. Show them they're wrong. Make the company an operational success and deliver some solid operating profits," sneered Scarborough. "You know, like in building real shareholder value. To that end, I have a radical idea. Why don't you play to your own supposed strengths and let Victor handle the day-to-day?"

"What do you mean?"

"From what I can see, the best way to get the SEC on our side is to close more deals. And to close more deals, you need increased credit lines, because I'm guessing Nachman is not about to extend his guarantee a second time. What initiatives have you taken to obtain additional lines of credit? After all, you're supposed to be the king of fundraising. Where are all your old buddies?"

~

Ryman got Scarborough's message. He boarded the next plane to Los Angeles to meet banker and former bar buddy Jason Garrett for dinner at the bustling, trendy Palomino Restaurant on Wilshire in Beverly Hills.

A conservative lending officer by day at United Pacific Bank, Garrett was anything but conservative on the LA night scene. Dressed in a black silk sports jacket, a beige silk shirt, and slacks, Garrett looked like a Nicholas Cage with slick black hair, on the prowl as he scanned the bar for fresh flesh, only half-listening to Ryman do his ITI promotional song and dance.

"According to our projections, we only need about $20 million in additional lines. Since we've worked together successfully before, I thought I'd give you first shot at the business."

"Franklyn, I appreciate your loyalty," said a sarcastic Garrett. "But the bank's got a long memory. You were a great customer at

United, no question about it. And we made a lot of money. But when you conned us into financing your Chicago Clearing House business, we lost everything, plus some."

"Jason, you know that wasn't the same Ryman that ran United Medical."

"Ryman, I'm well aware of that, but the Bank doesn't discriminate between losses created by drug-crazed CEOs who make irrational decisions and squeaky-clean CEOs who simply make bad decisions. I can offer you a $20 million credit facility with a personal guarantee though, assuming the underlying assets are there."

"I'm just not in that position to do that right now," replied Ryman.

"Are you telling me you blew the whole fucking thing? You were filthy rich. You had it all." Ryman was pathetically silent. Garrett threw him a bone. "Franklyn, let's get real. No accredited commercial bank is going to provide you an unsecured lending facility. You've got to locate non-conventional sources of financing —guys like Moshe Selman, Chairman of American Reliance Insurance in New York. Tell you what, as a favor to an old friend, I'll call Moshe and make the introduction. He's always willing to look at deals with higher returns for taking higher risks."

"Thanks," said a humbled Ryman.

"Do me a favor this time," smiled Garrett. "When you make it back, put something away for your next rainy day."

~

"How much did you get?" asked Victor, assuming Ryman had a successful trip with his former banker. Ryman misunderstood. He thought Victor learned he had been shut out and was trying to humiliate him.

"Think you can do better?" sneered Ryman. "Those West Coast pigs wanted an exorbitant interest rate, your two children, and my next three wives."

Victor realized he had accidentally bruised Ryman's fragile ego.

He backpedaled. "We'll find a way."

Ryman regain his composure. "Agreed. In fact, on my way back to the airport, I put a few calls into my contact list."

"Any nibbles?"

"By the time I landed, I had a voicemail from Moshe Selman," trumpeted Ryman.

"I thought he was chairman of an insurance company."

"He is, but he's got so much spare cash he does private investment deals too, just for sport. We've talked in the past, but nothing ever made sense. ITI barter deals are right in his sweet spot."

One call and Ryman had made a date.

"Mind if I tag along for the experience?" asked Victor.

"Normally, I'd say no problem, but I think Moshe might smell desperation, which could cost us some unnecessary loan origination points. We've already got enough warnings about cash flow; I'd like to make his line as cheap as possible."

As usual, Astrid finalized Ryman's travel plans—and then traded the information for a dime bag of cocaine from Bloomberg.

~

From the moment Ryman arrived, the arrogant Selman represented himself as *the king of real deals.*

Born into poverty, Selman ruthlessly climbed the corporate ladder to become the youngest president ever of Reliance Insurance Company. In the process, he accumulated incredible wealth through a series of side deals with company vendors.

Selman loved bargain hunting. He had bought his modest thirty-four room pre-war Park Avenue apartment at a distress sale twenty years ago for $271,000 in cash. Now crammed with seventeenth- and eighteenth-century antiques, mostly repossessed French baroque, the home had been featured twice in Architectural Digest and was estimated to be worth around $24 million, not including furnishings. As they toured the opulence, Ryman and the flamboyant Selman became instant buddies. "Rodin created this bronze in 1859," Selman said, "a few years after 'The Thinker.' Exquisite, isn't it?"

"Jason was right. Your collection is exquisite," said Ryman, awkwardly trying to establish credibility. Moshe knew why Ryman was there. He smelled blood. The price would be outrageous. "Moshe, by any chance do you know an old friend of mine, Costa Marvas, in Monte Carlo?"

"Know the name. But we've never met. Why?"

"He's also a Rodin aficionado. He has recreated Rodin's entire studio, as it was, in his home. I'm guessing he has a dozen originals. Your bronze got me to thinking."

"Did he pay retail or wholesale?" asked Selman.

"Wholesale? Unlikely," said Ryman. "We're talking world-class art."

"That's bullshit, Franklyn! Everything can be bought for wholesale. Just gotta have the eye, some cash, and two big ones," said Selman flicking his cigar ashes on the sixteenth-century Persian Nain rug in the study. "How about a little Armagnac?" Selman dropped huge pours of a 1924 vintage into oversized brandy snifters like he was doling out Budweisers.

~

"So, Ryman, what have you got for me? Jason said something about needing lines of credit."

"We're in the excess inventory business; we find deals, buy them, and creatively re-market the stuff based on mutually agreed guidelines. We…"

"Cut to the chase. I know from excess. I like the business. I'm the guy who bought the DeLorean car inventory and all the extra parts when John DeLorean's dream blew up in smoke. What a jackass! Making US luxury cars in Ireland." He rolled his eyes. "But what the hell. We sold a ton of them to antique car collectors based on futures. Would you believe those dumb buffs paid more than the original retail? Antique DeLoreans? What nonsense. How much is an antique Studebaker or DeSoto worth today? I'll tell you

—squat, nada. Except for those dumb buffs." Selman, like Ryman, loved to hear himself talk.

"What do you think was your best inventory deal?" asked Ryman, not really caring about the answer.

"That is easy: hands down, the Andrea Doria. We pulled that sucker up out of the deep for bupkus, then made a fortune selling everything on the ship, including the junk! The free publicity from the salvage activity gave people the impression they were buying Titanic memorabilia. One guy paid $25,000 for a pocket watch!" Moshe looked at him suspiciously. "Why the question?"

"Moshe, I think we have some inventory deals, signed or on the drawing boards, that might rival your best. We've signed so many contracts that we've exhausted our credit lines. We're looking for a financing partner."

"Not a problem. Just get me the inventories and what you pencil the deals to be worth. I'll review the stuff with my Board and get back to you with a specific proposal."

"Any estimates on how long your internal process might take?

We've got some pretty tight timetables," said Ryman.

"Ryman, not to worry. I own eighty-four percent of the stock. Is a twenty-four-hour turnaround quick enough?" smiled Selman condescendingly.

Back at the Seagram Building, Ryman declared victory. "Victor, consider the credit line issue solved. Bring on the deals!"

"I'm impressed," said Victor.

"As I suspected, Selman is my kind of guy. I wish we were dealing with businessmen like him all the time. They're so much more predictable and rational than the Nachmans and Toothsons of this world."

~

The inventory specs were hand-delivered to Selman that afternoon. As promised, twenty-four hours later, a financing proposal was sitting on Ryman's desk. Unfortunately, the terms were beyond outrageous: the first return of principal, 18 percent fixed interest, and 35 percent of the net profits from each deal. "The bastard's a crook!" said Victor after looking at the terms.

"Victor," said Ryman calmly, "let me ask you a question. What options do we have? Either we accept his terms, or we miss our revenue estimates and watch the value of your stock drop fifty to a hundred million. I'd like to be there when you tell Sandra that!"

Ryman also put his spin on Selman's usurious terms with Phil Scarborough.

"Franklyn, based on these terms, I don't see how we can make any profit. The only benefit might be some positive cash flow, *assuming* the resale estimates hold."

"I realize they're a little steep," said Ryman, "but once we take possession of the inventory, we can renegotiate. Moshe won't walk away from all that money."

"Franklyn, you are completely out of control. Herb and I have decided enough is enough. It's time we hire an experienced CFO with mainstream bank contacts—and the power to control your self-destructive urges."

50.

Sleazeball CFO from Hell

Scarborough wanted the CFO search done yesterday!

"An obvious source of qualified candidates has to be your accounting firm, Croft Rockman," said Scarborough. "They certainly know the terrain, and their referral might even save you fifty grand or more in headhunter fees."

"Let me think about it," said Ryman.

"There's nothing to think about," directed Scarborough. "Get LaMantia to identify a candidate you *and* Victor like, then I'll interview them before you make an offer." Ryman again noticed Scarborough's insertion of Victor but said nothing.

Initially, LaMantia was concerned about dropping a Crofts Rockman referral into the strained relationship between Ryman and Victor, the acquired owners' personality quirks, and the SEC's complex income recognition issues—but a $90,000 a month retainer was a $90,000 thousand a month retainer.

After conferring with his partners, LaMantia identified Jeremy Singleton, a technically skilled CFO with baggage. He had been dismissed suddenly by one of Croft Rockman's biggest clients, the Rubbermaid Corporation, a multi-billion-dollar consumer goods conglomerate. The official reason: the new CEO wanted his own guy. Fairly standard corporate American business-speak, but LaMantia knew better.

Singleton was a politically adroit and ruthless self-promoter with a propensity to switch allegiances when it suited his purpose. The unsubstantiated rumor was that Singleton got canned after implying to the board that his CEO was involved in personally profitable misconduct. As the story went, Singleton even dared to offer himself as the interim CEO solution.

LaMantia chose to accent the positives with Ryman. "I've given your needs a lot of thought, and I think I've come up with the ideal candidate. He's technically proficient and street savvy, a combination rarely found in corporate CFOs."

Ryman saw the candidate as interim fodder. Somebody to placate Scarborough until Melrose officially came on board and picked his own guy. "Great; can't wait to meet him," said Ryman.

Singleton was a bald man in his early fifties. He wore Calvin Klein mini-glasses and dressed in a baggy suit and tie. He appeared to be charming, gracious, non-threatening, pleasant, and articulate. After a few introductory pleasantries, Ryman probed Singleton's technical prowess. "Jeremy, as you may be aware, we are mired in some complex income recognition issues with the SEC."

Singleton leaned back and smiled smugly. "Franklyn, I agree that Altman Bridges and his group at the SEC can be a contentious lot. In my prior dealings with them, I've found a successful outcome depends on how you frame the issue, rather than the issue itself. Under regulations guiding the income recognition of non-cash transactions, Sections 433B and 507A of the code, there is plenty of room to negotiate the intrinsic value of barter credit reserves and such."

Ryman was impressed, thinking maybe he had stumbled upon an experienced and flexible CFO. "Jeremy, after talking for an hour, it's obvious you know your shit. So why did you get canned?"

Singleton smiled and raised his eyes for punctuation. "Franklyn, as you can see, I'm a pretty damn good financial guy, but I'm not a politician. I figure, do the job, be loyal to your boss, and everything else will take care of itself. Right? Well, you know the story. A new guy comes in and wants his own man. I have no idea how to maneuver through the minefield. But it's okay. My exit package was fair. I think the new guy felt guilty. Follow me?"

Ryman decided he'd found the guy both he and Melrose could direct, so he launched into a dissertation about the Barter Bank, Marc Melrose, and the opportunity for founder's stock in the spinoff. Ryman was politically obligated to have Singleton meet Victor, but he wanted Singleton to know the ground rules. "Jeremy, assume I am going to make you an offer. But to keep peace in the family, you need to meet my junior partner. Understand?" Singleton loved the situation: two guys openly trying to screw each other, leaving him the chance for a big score.

Unlike Ryman, Victor had done his homework. He knew Singleton was a political animal that had probably charmed the pants off Ryman. After the usual questioning—work history, strengths and weakness, career interests—Victor made a political blunder. "So, I understand your exit from Rubbermaid was rather tumultuous?"

Singleton saw no reason to make nice to Victor. After all, Ryman was The Man. "Says who? That's a potentially libelous statement," said Singleton, mentally playing chess.

Victor moved his bishop into position. "Oh, you think it's unusual to check the background of someone applying for a high-profile job?" Checkmate! Game over! Singleton was pissed!

~

"So, what did you think?" Ryman asked Victor after Singleton left.

"I think we should interview a few more candidates. With his baggage, he's not going anywhere."

Ryman switched to steamroller mode. "I disagree. He's eminently qualified. Frankly, this is an area where I have scads more experience than you. I'm going to make him an offer."

"Didn't Phil ask to meet the finalists?" Victor had made another faux pas. Ryman had never had a conversation with Phil about the subject in Victor's presence. *Another example of shit going on behind my back*, thought an infuriated Ryman.

"Victor, let's be clear about something. I'm the CEO. I make the final calls."

Victor moved on. He couldn't win that argument, not today. "Ryman, do what you've got to do. I want to update you on the first-quarter deal status and revenue flow. It looks pretty good."

Ryman had no interest in discussing anything with someone who had just challenged his authority. "Let's do it later. I've got a couple of telephone appointments with analysts."

Ryman closed his door and called Singleton's cell phone. "Jeremy, got a minute? I want to make you an offer." Five minutes later, the two struck a deal: base, bonus, stock options, expense account, and promises of founder stock in the Barter Bank. "Jeremy, I think you, Marc, and I will make a great team."

Jeremy went for the jugular. "Franklyn, does Victor agree with the offer? I'm not sure we hit it off."

"Don't worry about Victor. Just do your best to make your bones with him in the short term. I'm going to make some changes around here after we complete the Barter Bank financing."

Ryman next called Phil to announce the hiring of Singleton. "Phil, remember the resume I sent you? The CFO candidate recommended by Croft Rockman, Jeremy Singleton. He's terrific. Victor and I interviewed him. We both loved him, so I made him an offer."

"Jesus, Franklyn, I thought we had an understanding."

"I know Phil, but the guy had two other offers. Victor said, 'Let's not lose him.'" Scarborough knew Ryman was lying, but there was no point in being acrimonious because Singleton came recommended by Crofts Rockman.

Big mistake!

51.

Manhattan Here We Come

Victor had convinced Sandra they were rich now, but she still harbored doubts about their new circle of friends.

"From what you've said and what I've seen with my own eyes," said Sandra, "I don't think you can trust any of them."

"Honey, your husband's a big boy. Thanks to A&J, I know my way around corporate power struggles."

"A&J," replied Sandra, "was like playing in the minor leagues compared to these guys."

"Now when did you become such a sports buff?"

"Since I talked to my father."

"Now that's somebody with boardroom experience," commented Victor sarcastically.

"I hate when you're such a condescending little shit," glared Sandra. "Unlike your new buddies, my father has only one interest —to make sure his daughter and her family are happy and well. I love him for it. I'll always love him for it."

"What was your father's advice?"

Sandra didn't want to get into a squabble. "He helped me complete a 213-page notebook filled with practical ideas about how to treat your soulmate better. I'd be happy to go over it point by point," teased Sandra.

~

Victor's 40th birthday was days away. Sandra wanted his present to be something special. With the ITI stock rising and splitting, and Scarborough's supportive endorsement of her husband, Sandra felt she could afford to splurge on something quasi-practical—a luxury two-bedroom Manhattan apartment. The logic? If Victor was going to spend so much time in the City, so was she. The boys were old enough to babysit themselves.

Unstated, but present in her subconscious, the apartment would also serve as an insurance policy. Her mere presence, or intent to be present, would keep gold-diggers away from the front door.

"Mrs. Martini," said Fredericka DuVoe of Douglas & Elliman, Manhattan's elite real estate agents who specialized exclusively in the East Side. "After listening to your requirements, I would recommend we look for a full two-bedroom, two-bath unit with a convertible den. You and your husband would have plenty of room during the week, and the place would be more than comfortable when the kids or friends visit on weekends."

"Sounds good to me," said Sandra.

"We happen to have a unique listing in The Horizons on East Thirty-Seventh Street. It was voted the number one condo in New York last year. Quite magnificent—a white glove building with all the amenities: pools, health club, full-time masseuse, and tennis courts. There's even a roof-top lounge with a wet bar and a full kitchen where you can entertain 150 to 200 people. Plus, the building is in a very quiet neighborhood, just a short cab ride to Grand Central and less than twenty minutes to LaGuardia, which would make it convenient for you and your husband."

Fredricka could smell new money a mile away, so she went for the upsell. "I'm thinking of unit 43B; it's on the top floor with panoramic views of the city and the river. The current owner-occupant is the Secretary-General of Thailand. It's tastefully decorated and furnished down to crystal, china, and artwork."

The apartment was as billed: spectacular, and then some. The comfortable, contemporary furnishings suited Sandra perfectly, including the art, mostly Michael Delacroix and Thomas McKnight signed and numbered serigraphs. There were even two original oils from her favorite contemporary artist, Thomas Pydinsky of the French realist school.

"Fredericka," said Sandra, "the place is beautiful, but I suspect a bit out of my price range.

"That's the good news. The Secretary-General has been recalled to Thailand because of some impending coup, and there is limited interest in fully furnished apartments of this size. I think we can steal the place for about three and a half million dollars, which is almost 40 percent under the appraised price." Sandra hesitated.

"Mrs. Martini," said Fredericka, who had done her homework, "why don't you talk to your financial advisor? I'm sure with your husband's stock position, something can be worked out."

Sandra called the only woman she knew in the ITI deal: Louisa Dothan. "Louisa, I'm not sure how this whole thing works. But can I sell some of the ITI stock to buy Victor an apartment for his birthday?"

"Dearie, the stock is fully vested, but the certificates are in his name. I don't know how you can sell any shares without him knowing," replied Louisa.

"Victor transferred all the shares into my name a while ago. He said it would be safer that way, whatever that means."

"Dearie, you have a gem there. John would not transfer squat into my name. Not in a million years."

Sandra did not want to go there. She just wanted to buy Victor a birthday present. "So, can I do it?"

~

"I've talked to my advisor," said Sandra to Fredricka. "There appears to be no issue with me selling some ITI shares."

"Excellent," said Fredericka, who had done her homework. "ITI's closing price today was twenty-five dollars and change, so your birthday present will cost less than seven hundred thousand shares."

"Maybe we should check with Victor first," said Sandra, never having done such a transaction.

"Don't be silly," replied Fredricka, "that's less than two percent of your total holdings. It's so minuscule Victor will never even know the shares have been sold. Where are the certificates held?"

"In our safe deposit box."

"Wonderful, so here's all you have to do. Get the certificates and messenger them to me. My firm will take care of breaking them up and getting new certificates issued. I'll place a sell order today. In three days, we can wire the money to the escrow agent and, presto, you are a Manhattanite!"

Six months ago, Sandra would have gagged, but she was now worth some $200 million; $3.5 million was chump change.

A week later, the offer was accepted and contracts were executed.

~

Sandra and Victor celebrated his birthday with a gourmet candlelight dinner at home, fittingly prepared and delivered by the Four Seasons in Manhattan.

As they finished, Sandra handed Victor an envelope with a $10,000 gift certificate for the restaurant and the deed of trust for the apartment, along with pictures of the building, the amenities, and the view. "Victor, I hope you enjoy your birthday presents."

"My God," said Victor. "I don't believe it! Fabulous, fabulous! What a great surprise." He gave her a big kiss.

Suddenly she pulled away. "Oh, I almost forgot, I have one more birthday present." She slowly opened her dress to reveal her scanty negligee.

The dinner portion of his birthday was officially over!

52.

Barter Bank Hits Rough Seas

Melrose had been around the block when it came to dealing with the SEC. He knew no news usually meant bad news.

"Tom, it's Marc. How is my favorite attorney? I just thought I would check on the status of the Barter Bank prospectus, since I haven't gotten a final draft yet. I assume you've been buried?"

Kugle realized Melrose knew nothing about the Ryman-Scarborough disagreement about the Barter Bank, ITI's credit line and cash flow issues, or the SEC's delay tactics.

"Marc, I think it's more appropriate for you to talk to the company. I'm happy to fill in the gaps later."

"What is that supposed to mean?" replied Melrose. "We may have a temporary hold on the Barter Bank."

"A temporary hold? What the hell is going on?"

~

"Franklyn, I've been speaking to Tom Kugle. He tells me the Barter Bank may be on hold."

Ryman went ballistic. "That stupid fuck! Why would he make such a dumb statement? It's patently untrue; you have my word. Let's get Kugle on a goddamn conference call right now!"

Ryman went right for the jugular. "Tom, this is Franklyn. I've got Marc on the other line. He thinks there's a hold on the Barter Bank."

"Victor and I discussed the matter yesterday," replied Kugle. "I believe he was going to talk to you about the ITI *material events* announcement that needs to be released."

"Fuck that bullshit! I'll tell you the same thing I told Victor. We are not issuing some ridiculous material events press release. We are moving full steam ahead on the Barter Bank, and we are going to file a new $75 million financing. I thought I made myself clear. I'm your client, not Victor, so get your ass in gear and deliver a current draft of the prospectus to Marc.""

Melrose was appalled at Ryman's rudeness to a fellow attorney.

He knew something was very wrong.

~

"Victor, this is Marc Melrose. Since we're going to be working closely together on the Barter Bank, I thought we should get to know each other. How about bringing Sandra over to the house for dinner on Friday evening? I'm sure Eleanor will enjoy her company. From what I gather, the four of us may have something in common."

"What's the commonality?" asked Victor bluntly.

Marc smiled. "We may be the only normal people in this whole deal."

~

Purchase, New York, was a very discreet enclave for the super-rich, just thirty minutes from Manhattan. The Melrose driveway was the length of a passenger jet runway and lined with enough shrubbery and flowerbeds to fill the Bronx Botanical Gardens.

The house, a Palace of Versailles knock-off, was vintage Melrose, elegant but not garish. The walls were adorned with exquisite art and artifacts. Eleanor Melrose, a graduate of Smith College, was a wealthier, more polished version of Sandra Martini — gracious, but heavily made-up and a bit pompous. The ladies quickly bonded. Eleanor was disarmingly blunt. During cocktails, she began asking the questions Marc had not or could not answer.

"Sandra, dear, this whole Barter Bank adventure is a bit of a mystery to me. My sweet darling Marc has been extremely tight-lipped. All I get are sweeping generalities. 'Don't worry, dear, this new bank will reap significantly greater rewards than the International Monetary Fund position.'"

Eleanor's comment had a familiar ring to Sandra.

"As the wife of one of the company founders, perhaps you would be kind enough to fill in some of the blanks."

Sandra answered with a question. "How long have you and Marc been married?"

"Thirty-three years. He robbed the cradle," joked Eleanor.

"We have been married virtually all our adult lives, too. Perhaps that explains why Victor and Marc are so dismissive. Eleanor, to tell you the truth, until you just mentioned the Barter Bank, I'd never even heard of it. All I know is the company has had two quarters in a row of positive earning since the financing closed, and the stock has risen to twenty-five dollars. I'm not complaining, but it seems a little crazy that we're already worth a fortune. Companies like Lucent have billions in revenues, and their stock is priced at five dollars. Somehow, it doesn't make sense."

~

"Do you mind if I'm a little nosy?" asked Eleanor.

"Not at all. We have ten million shares after the recent reverse split," said Sandra, turning toward Victor. "See, Victor? I'm learning the lingo. We have 9,925,000 shares plus something called warrants. I bought Victor an apartment on the East Side for his birthday," smiled Sandra.

Eleanor gasped, calculating that Sandra had spent around $3.5 million on Victor's birthday present. What else was there to know about the Barter Bank?

~

"So, what is this Barter Bank?" asked Sandra. "Eleanor and I are curious."

Ever the chameleon, Victor became humble. "Honey, I didn't realize you were that interested in the day-to-day machinations of ITI. How about if I get a copy of the latest business plan and a

first draft of the Barter Bank offering prospectus to your office at the hospital tomorrow for your review and approval? Shall I messenger a set to Eleanor as well?"

They all laughed. During dinner, Marc, determined to impress Victor, explained his vision and concerns and made numerous comments about how the prospectus could be improved to make it more SEC-friendly.

After dinner, Melrose changed his tactics. "Let's retire to the library for cognac and cigars. I've got a bottle of Louis Crystal that's been waiting for a special occasion.

"I had a disturbing telephone conference with Tom and Ryman on Wednesday," continued Melrose. "I think Ryman has intentionally withheld relevant company developments from me. I'm just looking for a little clarity. I'm a big boy with an enormous monthly overhead to satisfy Eleanor's appetite for the good life. I can't afford to get into a precarious financial situation. In your opinion, will the Barter Bank make it to the marketplace?"

~

Victor saw this as his opportunity to make Melrose go poof and disappear, thus ensuring his own ascension to the throne as Ryman was almost certainly on his way to self-destruction. "Marc, I understand your concerns, and to a certain extent, they may be justified. We've run into some unexpected short-term difficulties, but I'm optimistic that we'll work through the issues," said Victor as he planted seeds of doubt.

"Could you be a bit more specific?"

"Only if we can speak off the record," said Victor. "As you can appreciate, I have certain fiduciary responsibilities." Victor painted a grim picture. "We got carried away with our plans for rapid expansion. Opened offices, added staff, contracted more deals than we had credit lines to execute, all of which have forced us to make expensive third-party financing arrangements, which squeezes our margins and cash flow.

"In the meantime, Franklyn has continued full speed ahead on acquisitions and the Barter Bank like they are a magic panacea. He's ignored Whitlaw's and Delano Mondrain Hudson's repeated advice to focus on turning cash flow positive and showing a consistent profit, and to put new acquisitions and spin-off projects on hold."

~

The crafty Singleton befriended Astrid and soon knew all about Scarborough's frustrations with the Barter Bank. He concluded that the situation was ripe for exploitation. Quietly, he worked off-site to build a presentation that dramatized the company's dire straits and offered an attractive, pragmatic solution.

"Ryman, I think it would be smart to review my thoughts for restoring business momentum at your apartment, sans Victor if you know what I mean." While Ryman was uncomfortable with Singleton's modus operandi, he was curious—did the proposal contain any ideas that might save his ass?

Singleton's pitch was organized and well-documented. He recommended a series of initiatives. Postponing the Barter Bank. Eliminating sixty percent of the corporate staff. Reducing finder's fees. Slashing executive salaries. Closing the Chicago and LA offices. Dramatically slowing new acquisition activity.

"Jeremy, that's a pretty aggressive plan," said Ryman.

Singleton took that to mean Ryman was in total agreement. "I also have one other cost-cutting idea: eliminate executive redundancy. I'd be happy to do double duty as CFO *and* COO temporarily. I'm not sure a company of our size requires that many management layers."

Ryman concurred on corporate cuts, slowing down new acquisitions, closing offices, delaying others, and reducing his base fifty percent, but protested the cancellation of the Barter Bank.

"Jeremy, you guys just don't get it. The Barter Bank is more than a sexy spin-off; it's THE permanent cash flow solution for ITI corporately."

Ryman seemingly ignored Singleton's gracious suggestion to can Victor and crown himself COO. But unbeknownst to Singleton, Ryman privately bought Singleton's executive-redundancy recommendation. Unfortunately, Ryman also knew Victor was the one who had cultivated close relationships with Scarborough and the company management.

Ryman also decided Singleton was, in fact, a corporate sleazeball, and when the moment was right with Scarborough, he would declare Singleton redundant.

53.

Saint Valentine's Day Massacre

Two nights later, Scarborough cut right to the chase before the first course arrived.

"Victor, everybody at Whitlaw thinks highly of you. The family and I trust you. At the same time, we've become grossly disenchanted with Franklyn. He has delivered on his promise to avoid drugs, but his questionable versions of the truth, the indiscriminate leaks, and his unmanageable behavior have made him an embarrassment. He's consumed with regaining his former wealth and stature by whatever means necessary. Herb Whitlaw has told me to get his resignation at the next board meeting."

"Suppose he says no?"

"Between you, myself, and Kugle, we control the board. We can drag his ass into court if necessary. But this action is contingent on you accepting the title of Chairman and CEO."

Victor feigned surprise. "I feel awkward. After all, Franklyn was my mentor."

In reality, Victor had crossed his own Rubicon. His quest for riches now superseded his boss. As the two men shook hands, Victor said, "Phil, I think we need a symbolic gesture to set a new company tone."

"Like what?"

"I take a forty percent pay cut." Victor knew the cut was like giving away snow in the winter. But it had to be done regardless.

Scarborough chuckled. "Excellent idea. Although this is the first time I've ever offered somebody a promotion and a salary cut at the same time!"

"Phil," said Victor with a smile, "you know me. Nothing comes without a price. Once we right the ship, the board can vote me a bonus and some stock options."

"At a multiple of twenty times, I presume," joked Scarborough. "I was thinking more like forty," said Victor.

~

The Whitlaw emergency meeting started promptly at 10:00 a.m. in the main trading room. Every investment banker stood by their stock terminal so they could hear Scarborough's update without missing a market tick. ITI's roller-coaster ride had given everybody more than just a mild case of indigestion.

"Gentleman, we've been family for a long time," said Scarborough, "so there is no point in sugar-coating. ITI is in significant financial trouble because of poor cash management, faulty initial acquisition agreements, and non-cooperative key employees."

Scarborough explained there was zero chance of a turn-around without significant surgery. And Ryman was about to be ousted and replaced by Victor. The group also suggested the firm's lead attorney, Clive Davis, attend all board meetings. "For the record," Scarborough assured everybody present, "you have my word that I will make all of you whole should ITI tank."

An embarrassed Scarborough knew there was also the issue of Whitlaw's own damage control. If ITI imploded, Whitlaw would have to inform long-time investors there was a high probability of losing their entire $75 million private placement, since ITI had no hard assets to liquidate. That was far more important than the family's loss of a few million dollars.

~

Later in the day, a flustered Scarborough lashed out at Dothan in his office, admonishing him for recommending the deal to him in the first place. "Goddamn it, John, I'm going to be the first failure at Whitlaw in almost twenty years."

"Easy, Phil. I understand you're frustrated, but we've got our own problems. Some of Louisa's clients, like Otis Weinstein and his orthodox Jewish group, have lost millions on ITI and are threatening a class-action suit, which could destroy us financially."

Scarborough was unsympathetic, preferring to wallow in his self-pity. "I can't believe how I allowed myself to get duped. I..."

Dothan exploded. "Phil, cut the crap! We all jumped on the bandwagon for the same reason—we smelled a big score. We gambled that Ryman wouldn't self-destruct again."

~

Unaware of the Whitlaw ruminations, Ryman decided his corporate survival depended upon establishing a new détente with his politically savvy former student. "Victor," said Ryman, exuding honesty. "This thing's a mess because of my lack of focus." Victor waited for the inevitable curveball, but Ryman crossed him up with a fastball right down the middle of the plate.

"I've decided to take a fifty percent salary cut to show Scarborough, Nachman, and Toothson that I care about the company's success. My accountant also found a clever way to collateralize my remaining assets to personally guarantee a five-million-dollar line of credit. That should help us close some of the existing deals and relieve our immediate cash flow problem."

Victor was concerned that Ryman's plan might work, which would royally screw his impending coup d'état. "Are you sure you want to expose yourself to that level of risk?" he asked.

"Victor, I'll do what I have to do to protect my credibility. Nothing is more important in business than your credibility. I've got to salvage that at all costs. Besides, we can still turn the company around. The deal flow is there. We need a few damn breaks. I didn't come this far to throw it all away! Are you still with me?"

Victor nodded yes—like the Apostle Judas at the Last Supper. "I need you to do some stuff," said Ryman. "We've got to slash our general overheads. For starters, how about we share Astrid?

"You mean fire Janet?"

"Yes."

"But she's a much better administrative assistant than Astrid."

If Ryman weren't banging Astrid, his rationale would have been plausible. "I know, but Astrid's like a bomb waiting to go off. She knows too much. We've got to keep an eye on her." Reluctantly, Victor agreed, figuring he would hire Janet back after Ryman was out.

"You also need to take a symbolic salary cut," Ryman continued.

Victor started to poor mouth. "Sandra will go ballistic."

Ryman knew better. Louisa had told him about Victor's birthday present. "Come on, give me a break; you've already bought yourself a seven-figure apartment. Besides, when we get out of this mess, I'll make you whole, plus some." Ryman wanted to seal the détente. "There's one last thing. It's about Jerry. At his request, he and I had this private meeting about cut plans. The son-of-a-bitch recommended I fire you and make him COO *and* CFO. So tomorrow, his ass flies."

~

The ITI Saint Valentine's Day Massacre took place the next morning.

Victor fired administrative staff, closed down corporate flower and limo accounts, and called the primary acquisition finders to inform them of a 50 percent reduction in finder's fees.

While Victor was dealing with his project list, Ryman talked to Singleton. "Jerry, I've been thinking about your redundancy recommendation." Singleton smiled like a Cheshire cat. His moment had arrived; he would be the new ITI Chief Executive Officer. "I've decided to give both jobs to Victor. He knows operations, is well-respected by everybody, and has a pretty solid grasp of finances. Plus, he's loyal."

"Are you crazy?" gasped Singleton. "You don't know how to build shit! And Victor's a fucking amateur. You're a pair of fucking frauds!"

"Get your things and leave, unless you want an escort to the door!" said an irate Ryman.

"You haven't seen the last of me!" shouted Singleton as he stomped out of Ryman's office and grabbed his laptop, knocking over a vase on the way out.

~

About 5:00 p.m., Janet Waters walked into Victor's office, sat, and put her feet up on his desk. "We had one hell of a day, didn't we? Thank Christ, it's over."

A lump formed in Victor's throat as the beads of perspiration rolled down his forehead. "Well, not quite."

Nothing more needed to be said. Janet looked into Victor's eyes. "You can't be serious… not after ten years."

"We need to temporarily consolidate to one administrative assistant."

"Astrid? Christ, she's no admin. She's just an easy lay for Ryman. I can't believe it. After all we've been through." She fled the office in tears.

An hour later, Victor's phone rang. "Victor, this is Janet's husband, Jack. She told me you just fired her. I want you to know you're the ultimate piece of shit! How you can keep a tramp who's been stealing your confidential files for months to feed her coke habit, instead of my wife?! I hope you rot in hell!"

~

Victor recognized Sandra knew very little about what had transpired and was owed an update. After dinner, as she sat reading the newspaper, Victor poured himself a massive shot of his favorite turpentine-flavored Grappa di Nebbiolo.

"I have an announcement," said Sandra excitedly. "The hospital chairman, Frank Barnes, called me to his office today to tell me I've been promoted to Assistant Hospital Administrator and given a seat on the board! He said the promotion was a unanimous opinion because 'cream always rises to the top.'"

Sandra's good news made Victor's bad news even more difficult to share.

"Sandra, a lot of weird stuff has been going down at the office. We've got cash-flow issues, we had to let some employees go, and we're struggling with the SEC about the Barter Bank and future financings."

"Look," said Sandra remaining positive "I'm sure you and Franklyn will get things sorted out. You're my rock, always have been and always will be."

"Suppose I told you Phil and I met privately? He told me Whitlaw & Company was committed to forcing Ryman's resignation at the next board meeting. They want me to replace him, and take a temporary salary cut until things get back to normal."

"Does Ryman know?"

"He knows he's in big trouble."

"Has he said anything?"

"In his own way. He apologized for being such a horse's ass. Then told me about Jerry Singleton."

"That creepy guy with the scary bug eyes and permanent sneer pasted on his face?"

"The same," smiled Victor. "Apparently, he lobbied Franklyn to fire me as a cost-saving measure, and told Ryman he was willing to be the CFO and CEO. According to Ryman, he fired Jerry because of his disloyalty, which is pure bullshit. He simply needs me more than he does Jerry because of my relationships with the companies and Phil."

"I don't know if I want to be part of all this anymore," said Sandra.

Victor laid out his twisted plan. "I figure I'll lull Ryman to sleep with a dose of his own bullshit. Tomorrow, I'll tell him that you and I talked, and you agreed to take a temporary pay cut as a show of management unity. Then we'll just sit back and let Phil and Ryman slug it out at the Board meeting."

"Can we afford to do that?" frowned Sandra.

"Sweetie, we've got almost 19 million shares priced around ten dollars a share, and a great apartment in the City. The cut is pocket change. Besides," said Victor with a Machiavellian smile, "I got Phil to agree that once he boots Ryman out the door, I get another million and a half options with a low strike price.

Sandra took Victor by surprise. "I vote we take the money and run before the board meeting. Louisa told me your two-year hold period is up. We can cash in the stock while it's still worth a ton and be comfortable for the rest of our lives. Call it what you want —woman's intuition, paranoia, fear. ITI feels like its careening towards a horrible, twisted ending, like one of those Alfred Hitchcock movies."

Victor was torn. Should he take Sandra's advice or play through? And what did Louisa have to do with all this?

54.

Bloodbath in the Boardroom

Scarborough didn't return Ryman's calls before the board meeting. Ryman sensed a coup coming, so, quietly, he had Allyn Tishman do a little housekeeping.

"Franklyn," said Tishman, "you were right. It never happened."

In the company's rush to close the Whitlaw investment banking agreement, the composition of the board had never been officially reconfigured. It was still comprised of Ryman, Victor, Tishman, Dawson, and Scarborough.

While Kugle had been slated to replace Dawson as a corporate secretary and had been operating as such for months, the resolution had never been formally drawn and adopted. As for Tishman, it was a simple oversight. Since he had not attended a board meeting in six months, everybody just assumed he had resigned.

"If we can get Marty on our side, we still control the board," concluded Tishman.

"You're the attorney. What would it take to entice another attorney?" said Ryman.

"The same thing that motivates you."

"I can't offer Marty a bribe; that's blatantly illegal."

"I'm not talking about money; I'm talking about *like-kind*. Suppose you offered Marty stock as compensation for his vote?"

"How can I increase the float without a shareholder vote?"

"Keep it simple. Just privately transfer a couple million of your founder shares to Marty."

"Why me?"

"Jesus, Franklyn, you've got fifty million shares. You can afford to lose a few."

Ryman agreed. "How about you make the overture? In case Marty says no, that still leaves me a shot to massage his ego."

~

Dawson and Tishman met in a quiet corner of the UN Plaza Hotel dining room. Tishman explained the ironic voting situation to Dawson. Stunned that he had never been removed as Board secretary, Dawson became hysterical. "Those smart-ass bozos were so anxious to kick me out that they forgot to do the paperwork!"

"With Victor defecting to the other side, we need your vote," said Tishman.

Dawson reveled in the moment. "So, what are you guys offering?"

"Two million founder shares."

The leverage was all Dawson's. "Allyn, I'd be delighted to cast my vote for Ryman, but I'm not sure two million shares is the right number. After all, the stock price has slipped noticeably in the last few weeks. Why not four million?"

Tishman realized he was sitting across from a ruthless pragmatist. The man who had advised Nachman and Toothson to screw Ryman was perfectly content to dig deep into Ryman's pocket to save Ryman's own ass. As lawyers do, they compromised. Ryman would be three million shares lighter.

"Email the signed agreement to my home. I'll countersign and get it right back to you," said Dawson. "And Allyn, please, no curveballs. No 144 legends, no vesting, no contingencies, no quid pro quos. Got it?"

~

"Mark your calendar. Tomorrow's the day!" crowed Victor as he poured Sandra a generous glass of wine at the dinner table. "By dinnertime, we'll be toasting the new Chairman and CEO of

Integrated Trading International."

"Where's Ryman going?"

"Out the goddamn door! Tom, Phil, and I have the controlling votes."

"Honey, I rarely get into the middle of your business. You've done pretty well by the kids and me, but it sounds like you're planning a covert coup d'état. Frankly, I've been thinking. The deeper we get into this thing, the more complicated it's become. Mona Toothson was right. This whole thing can be a snake pit. Let's walk away. Now. While we still can."

"You mean the drunken bisexual who lived secretly with another woman for ten years gave *you* morality lessons before she crashed her plane and left her kids without a mother?"

"Victor, don't be so damn condescending!"

"Here's the bottom line. I've broken my ass to get this far. I'm not turning back. So. You're either with me or you're not. I've tasted big money, and I'm not going back to A&J to worship at the altar of Gordon Naye and Rhoda Barbuto. That corporate bullshit is a long time past."

~

At precisely 9:55 a.m., Scarborough, Clive Davis, and Kugle walked into the ITT conference room. Victor and Ryman were already present and seated. The meeting began. Ryman wanted Scarborough to play his hand first. Dawson and Tishman waited in Ryman's office for the appropriate signal.

"Is there any new business?" asked Ryman, with the proper hint of arrogance.

Scarborough took the floor and made a motion to ask Ryman for his resignation, after providing a litany of reasons for the record. Michael seconded. As Kugle readied to take a board vote, Ryman interrupted. "Fellas, before we vote, I think *all* the current board members should participate," smiled Ryman. At that point, Astrid brought in Tishman and Dawson.

"Ryman, what the hell are you trying to pull?" contested Davis.

"Clive, my man," said a smirking Dawson, "whatever do you mean? Tishman and I are, and continue to be, members of the Board. Technically, our appointments are not up for another three months."

"That's impossible, Tom and I…"

Dawson glared. "You and Tom fucked up, big time!"

Kugle realized Marty was correct. Scarborough turned beet red, and Victor knew he was dead meat. The vote to oust Ryman was defeated three to two.

Scarborough lost it. "You goddamn piece of shit! You've embarrassed me and my firm to no end! You should have the common decency to step aside."

"Phil, I have two words for you: piss off!" said Ryman. He turned and glared at Victor, "As for you, you disloyal piece of shit, your pain has yet to begin!"

~

By noon the next day, news of the failed coup spread like wildfire. The stock tumbled sixty percent to four dollars. "Ryman, you have a phone call," said Astrid. "It's Mr. Weinstein."

"Tell him I'm in a meeting."

"Otis mentioned that if you used the 'I'm in a meeting' excuse, he was going to come over and knock the door down." The relish with which Astrid delivered Otis's demand told Ryman she had also defected.

"Ryman," said Weinstein, "what's going on? Did Whitlaw & Company try to bump you? Rumors are flying everywhere; the stock is getting bombed! The value of our ITI investment holdings is shrinking by the minute. I'm looking for the truth."

Ryman began to give Weinstein his version of the truth, still promoting and still optimistic as if nothing had ever happened. "Just a little hiccup. Happened to me in the hospital business, too."

Furious, Weinstein interrupted, "Ryman, stop with the bullshit! I mortgaged my assets and my home to buy more ITI stock at fourteen dollars a share. John and Louisa told me ITI was weeks away from a new $100 million offering and the completion of a $75 million Barter Bank offering, headed by Billingham's Marc Melrose."

"Well, Otis, you know how it is. We've had a bit of a setback."

"No, Ryman, I don't know how it is. You've misrepresented for the last time. After I sell my position, I'm telling everybody in my contact list to bail out. Then my investor friends and I are going to bring a class-action suit. You're going down!"

Ryman wigged out. "Listen here, you greedy little pig! You'll never make the suit stick. It's frivolous. Any fool knows you play in the stock market at your own risk. You're not buying CDs."

"Au contraire, according to my new best friend, Jerry Singleton. You remember him? We've got enough information to send you and Victor up the fucking river!"

55.

Everybody Wants a Piece of the Pie

The circumstances demanded Ryman and Victor become strange bedfellows. Neither would ever trust the other again, but each needed the other to survive.

Ryman was consumed with salvaging his reputation on The Street. For him, there would be other deals, so regaining his former wealth was now a secondary consideration. As for Victor, he still believed salvaging ITI was his chance to accumulate real wealth.

"Victor, I finally got it," said Ryman, leaning back in his chair. "Beneath that all-American organizational patina beats the heart of a fucked-up Machiavellian bastard. You'd sell your mother for thirty pieces of silver."

"You're not exactly Mary Poppins. You've lied so many times, you can't even remember the truth," replied Victor. "To you, there's no such thing as black and white; the world is just shades of gray. But guess what? I don't give a shit. Right now, I just care about getting out of this mess with enough money that I don't have to ever suck up to crap like you again."

"Likewise! Sounds like we understand each other perfectly," sneered Ryman.

~

Like a boxer's bell, the phone rang to end the round. It was Toothson, bringing manna from heaven. He and Nachman had found an inventory so large, so potentially profitable, that it could solve ITI's cash flow *and* credibility problems in one fell swoop.

Toothson waxed as Victor and Ryman were glued to the

conference speakerphone. "Sam's been talking to the entertainment giant TLP records. They have an inventory of almost one hundred fifty million units of old vinyl records, cassette tapes, and CDs they want to unload. They're willing to execute a receivable barter contract for the whole freaking amount if we can re-market the stuff outside the United States."

"Is that possible?"

"We've done some preliminary investigation. Sam thinks he has a wholesale distributor in Chile who'll take the entire inventory."

"How much?"

"Somewhere between ten and twelve million dollars. Since we wouldn't have to put up a dime to buy the stuff, I'm guessing that, after expenses, the deal has an eight-million-dollar profit."

"Jesus, *finally* a break," said Ryman.

"However, there are two small twists," said Toothson. "Our inside contact requires a 'referral fee' of $250,000 to guarantee a valid authorized contract. Ryman, Sam and I are so confident about this deal we'll advance the 250 grand personally. Remember, if you succeed, we succeed."

Ryman smelled a rat. "In exchange for what?"

"Twenty-five percent of the deal."

"In other words, 250,000 dollars for two million, a modest 800 percent return. Jesus fucking Christ!"

"Ryman, I'm just a businessman hustling to make a buck. Besides, we'll do all the work."

~

"What's the second 'small' thing?' asked Ryman.

"TLP requires four million dollars in escrow as a measure of good faith. When they're confident the stuff has been sold and distributed into the appropriate channels, they'll release the funds back to the company."

"Ed, give Victor and me a chance to huddle. Let us see if we can find the money in the coffers. You know the situation; ITI could benefit from all the earnings." Ryman hung up and began to rant. "Those miserable bastards. They are the scum of the earth. They'll sell their fucking kids for the right price!"

Victor could feel a curveball coming.

"We desperately need this deal to survive," said Ryman. "I'd put up the money myself, but I talked to my accountant last night. That miserable Aspen Club continues to be a money pit. I've even pledged my entire five-million-dollar line. I'm tapped out."

~

A light bulb went off in Victor's head. He knew how to get the whole deal for the company *and* fuck Ryman over, too! He just needed to bait the hook.

"Franklyn, let's think outside of the box," said Victor.

Ryman went for the bait. "Victor, I hate to ask but…"

"I don't have that kind of money," interrupted Victor.

"I wasn't going to ask you to take money out of your pocket," smiled Ryman. "I thought maybe we could use some of your stock as collateral, since it's legend-free and mine still has restrictions."

Victor knew he had control of the situation. "Jesus, Sandra will kill me if…"

"Don't tell her. You're the one with ten million shares at four bucks a share. You front the collateral loan, and when the profit comes in, we'll give you a five-hundred grand finder's fee off the top as an expense of the deal. The way I look at it, despite the Nachman-Toothson hold-up, your finder's fees, and any short-term loan interest, ITI still comes out way ahead."

Victor agreed.

"Let's keep these deal terms between us. All Phil needs to know is the bottom line," said Ryman.

~

The next morning, Victor sat with Marc behind closed doors to explain the deal, leaving out the $250,000 bribe and his $500,000 finder's fee.

Melrose was reluctant. "Victor, a personal four-million-dollar loan? Given all the rumors, I don't know."

"Mark, this one deal will fix the company's woes and accelerate the Barter Bank at the same time. To show my commitment to the ITI turnaround, I'll put up my ten million legend-free shares *plus* my house and apartment as collateral."

"That might give the loan committee the comfort it needs to issue the line. Can you live with a ninety-day irrevocable call?" said Melrose.

"If I have to."

"Let me see what I can do. I'll keep the ninety-day card in reserve, in case we have to beg," joked Marc.

~

The next morning, Melrose convened his loan committee to discuss the application. Melrose was purposely low-key. "Even though this is a somewhat atypical loan for Billingham, we can generate some significant above-market fees and still protect ourselves on the downside."

"What are you thinking?" asked the lone female, Mary Doherty, a superficially easygoing, gray-haired woman in her mid-fifties with big brass ones. "Let's charge him prime plus four instead of the usual prime plus one and hold the entire ten million shares plus his two houses as collateral. The houses alone appraise at more than $4 million, so even if he defaults, and the stock value tumbles, the Bank's protected."

"Doesn't that seem a bit exorbitant?" asked Melrose.

~

"I'm confused," said senior vice-president David Barth, the committee's most conservative loan officer. "Are we talking a personal loan, or a business-to-business loan? Generally, we only do loans of this magnitude with corporations. Don't you think this one might raise eyebrows with our auditors?"

David knew something no one else on the committee knew, *including* Melrose. He had learned through internal connections that his recent promotion to EVP had been squelched by Melrose because he was "too risk averse for a growth-oriented bank like

Billingham."

To return the favor, Barth had accumulated a mountain of internal documents that indicated Melrose was guilty of expense account padding, bribes-for-loans approvals, and other felonies. An internal investigation had been opened. Barth knew it was only a matter of time before Melrose's own world came tumbling down.

"David," said Melrose smoothly, "good question. This one's a hybrid, a personally guaranteed loan that will be used exclusively for corporate purposes."

"Do you know Mr. Martini personally?" inquired Barth.

"No more than many of our other customers."

~

Melrose called Victor to tell him the loan had been approved; however, the terms were "slightly more onerous" then they had originally discussed. In addition to the Doherty loan structure, the loan committee also included a 30-day call provision if the stock fell below a dollar a share.

~

"Marc, time is of the essence. What are the next steps?"

"Just sign and notarize the documents. About two hours after I receive the papers, your line will be available." A short time later, the documents arrived at ITI offices by courier.

Victor ripped open the envelope as Ryman watched. "Shit, these documents need to be countersigned by Sandra. There isn't a chance in hell she'll do that."

"I think we're in luck," said Ryman. "Astrid just got her notary license." This was Ryman's way of saying, *Forge the documents; I'll make sure Astrid notarizes them.*

~

"Astrid," said Victor, "could you give us a few minutes?" He then closed the door. "You realize Billingham's terms are outrageous," said Victor.

"It doesn't matter," responded Ryman. "This is a quick in-and-out deal."

"It does matter! My name is on these loan documents, and my houses are part of the collateral."

Ryman paused. "I get it. You want more. How much?"

"First monies repay my loan, and then I get the first four million in profits. The rest gets distributed as you see fit to Sam, Eddie, and ITI."

Ryman was incensed. "You fucking greedy little pig!"

Victor stood calmly. "So, what do you want to do?"

Minutes later, the door to Ryman's office opened. "Astrid," said Ryman calmly, "we need you to notarize some loan documents. Sandra signed them before she rushed to work this morning. There was a medical emergency at her hospital."

Astrid knew Ryman was lying because Sandra had signed for the package, and the two signatures didn't match.

"Let me make each of you a copy for your records," said Astrid. "I'll get the originals back to Mr. Melrose." Astrid made three copies of the documents. She sent the originals to Melrose, gave a set each to Ryman and Victor, and put the third set in the bottom drawer of her desk and locked it.

~

While pissed at Victor's Machiavellian cleverness, Ryman was confident that once the deal was announced, the stock would reverse itself. He'd solidify his position as CEO and be able to deliver an expanded acquisition deal sheet to the Dothans, who could then do their research report magic. Once the stock rebounded, Ryman planned to kick Victor's ass out the door!

~

Victor called Toothson to say the loan was in place. "Excellent," said Toothson. "The next step is for *you* to deliver John Doe's fee in cash before he turns the contract over to ITI. An envelope addressed to you should arrive around 5:00 p.m."

"To me?" said Victor quizzically.

"We're too well known to make the connection," explained Toothson. "You're the logical candidate because nobody will recognize you. The meeting is scheduled for Madison Square Garden during tomorrow night's Knicks-Celtics game. Pick your ticket up at the will-call window."

Toothson described what the contract looked like and the password that had been established for each party. "We'll have 48 hours to sign the contract and escrow the four million."

~

Victor's ticket led him to a courtside seat next to a tanned, well-groomed man with dark wavy hair. During a time-out, the two men exchanged passwords. Victor handed the man the envelope, which he immediately locked in a handsome brown leather Coach legal portfolio case. He then handed Victor an envelope with the contracts and an inventory addendum, then left. Victor looked around. He imagined 20,000 pairs of eyes must all be staring directly at him. He burst from the arena, gasping for air.

The next morning, a pleased Toothson called Ryman. "We've reviewed the inventory attached to the contracts; it's bigger than we originally expected. It looks like it may have an original wholesale value of two hundred million dollars."

"What does that mean in plain English?" replied Ryman impatiently.

"It means we could be looking at $12 to maybe $14 million in profits, after expenses," replied Toothson. Ryman smiled and closed his door.

Magically, by the time the closing bell rang, the ITI stock had begun to reverse itself.

56.

One Lie Leads to Another, and Another

A week went by. The call finally came. "Fellas, I want to provide an update on the TPL deal," said Nachman to Victor and Ryman.

"I've got a little bad news. Our Chilean buyer, Jose Luis Boloco, inspected the TPL inventory. He reported it was shit. Old tapes, broken packages, the works. Nothing like the oral representations."

"You sure?" groaned Victor.

"That was my first instinct also. So, I put Albert on a plane to Santiago to personally check it out. He confirmed what Jose found. They worked together for a week or so on the deal. Our only option was to fire sale the stuff in some less-developed South American countries like Paraguay, Ecuador, and Bolivia. I just got the final numbers. After repacking, shipping, and other costs, there's absolutely no profit."

"Sam, are you fucking sure?" shouted Victor.

"Easy, Victor, this shit happens sometimes. I know you guys depended on this one to make up for some of our bad breaks. We'll nail the next one."

~

Victor lost it. "Nail the next one? I'm fucking bankrupt! I put everything on the line for this deal, including my houses! I'm forty years old, and I don't have a dime."

"Kid, that's what happens when you play with the big boys," replied Sam.

"You said this was a slam dunk," yelled Victor into the conference phone.

'So? *I lied*," laughed Sam.

"Sam, thanks for the update," said Ryman calmly as he shut off the conference phone. "Keep swinging. We'll talk soon."

Victor slammed his coffee cup against the wall and slumped down into a chair, sobbing like a child. A disgusted Ryman pulled him up and threw him to the floor. "Grow up. Shit like this happens. That's business!" Ryman headed back to his office, leaving Victor weeping pathetically.

Out of the corner of his eye, Ryman noticed Astrid on the phone down the hallway, speaking quietly. He slipped over to eavesdrop. "Otis, I think you better get out while you can. The record deal fell through. Victor's wigged out. I don't see how…"

Ryman grabbed the phone from her and said, "You little bitch!" He slapped her, then pushed her roughly. "Get out of here, you little cunt! I never want to see you again!" He struck her again and again. She started to bleed across the mouth. As she pulled herself up from the floor, she had fire in her eyes. She spit in Ryman's face, spattering blood over his white shirt, and then stumbled out the door.

Ryman rummaged through her desk drawers, finding nothing of importance until he got to the locked bottom drawer. He ripped it open and found a library of ITI documents, files, and notes of telephone conversations. "Son-of-a-bitch. If I ever see her again, I'll kill her."

~

A few hours later, Astrid called Bloomberg. She knew the release of her newfound insider information would make the stock tumble when the market opened. It was a chance for her and Bloomberg to make a killing by shorting the stock.

"Parker, buy a million shares, and I'll split the profits with you."

Bloomberg had two thoughts: do the deal, and then figure out what to do about Astrid, because she was becoming a significant liability. As soon as the bankruptcy rumor hit the markets, the stock tumbled to a dollar a share. Through a series of complicated electronic procedures, Bloomberg transferred $10 million in quick profits to a series of overseas accounts.

Interestingly, Astrid was never heard from again. When her landlord went to check her apartment two weeks later, things looked as if she'd simply left on an errand. Everything remained as it had been.

~

Broken and humiliated, Victor returned home to an impatient and angry Sandra waiting for him in the living room. "The bank called today to confirm a two-million-dollar transfer in and out of our joint account," she shouted. "What the hell is going on?"

Victor tried his best to lie. "It was a business transaction. It was just more convenient to use our account."

"Oh? And that's not all! I got an apologetic call from the Beverly Hills Hotel. They said they had done an audit and found that the last time you stayed in one of their private cottages, they had neglected to charge your wife Barbee's use of the spa. Since the charges were over two thousand dollars, they asked if I'd like to put it on your house account!"

"Yes babe, I did have dinner with a woman named Barbee, but it's not what you think."

"Don't you *babe* me, you goddamn liar!"

Victor headed for the bedroom.

"Where do you think you're going?" asked Sandra.

"To bed."

"Not in my room."

57.

From Bad to Unimaginable

The next day, the wheels fell off everything.

A hand-delivered lawsuit met Victor as he entered the ITI offices. Otis Weinstein and John and Louisa Dothan had filed a $50 million corporate class-action suit against ITI, and another $50 million damages suit against Ryman and Victor personally. The summons required their appearance for initial depositions in two weeks.

At 3:00 p.m. the same day, the Special Crimes Unit of the New York Police department paid a visit to Melrose's office. He was indicted and arrested on forty-nine counts of embezzlement, totaling some $5.5 million in kickbacks over the past four years.

An embarrassed Scarborough angrily called an emergency board meeting. He also summoned Melrose and Dothan, and Whitlaw's legal executioner, Clive Davis. "What the hell is going on?" shouted Scarborough, ignoring the usual 'Robert's Rules of Order' protocol.

~

Ryman decided the best defense was a strong offense. "Phil, I'm as disappointed as you are. Victor, Ed, and Sam talked me into a big record deal that supposedly required no cash up front and had a 'guaranteed fourteen-million-dollar profit.' After they had me salivating, Ed and Sam told me the deal had one little wrinkle. We had to give the TPL president a $250,000 kickback to be appointed the liquidation vendor. I said no. Victor insisted we go ahead. He said he could raise funds privately. Without telling me, he obtained a short-term loan from Billingham and made me agree to give *him* a $500,000 kickback."

"Marc, is that true?".

"I thought it was a personal loan… that Victor was in financial difficulty," said Melrose, trying to save face.

"With all due respect Marc, today's indictment doesn't exactly make you a pillar of credibility," replied Scarborough.

~

"Phil, it gets worse," said Ryman. "At the eleventh hour, TPL demanded four million dollars in escrow. I went to Moshe Selman to finance the deal. He said yes; Victor said no. He convinced me that a Selman loan document could take weeks. Time was running out, and we needed the deal. Victor insisted on putting up the money. He forced me to agree to give him four million in profits off the top, after loan repayment."

"Victor, where the hell did you get the four million dollars?" bellowed a livid Scarborough.

"Marc helped me; I put my houses and stock up as collateral."

"Marc, did you really?" interrupted Phil.

"I was led to believe the deal had an enormous profit that would solve the company's immediate cash flow crunch. I didn't know about any side deals between Victor and Franklyn."

"Jesus Christ, you're the chairman of a major bank and you authorized loans for a bribe on an ill-conceived business deal. What were you thinking? You should be ashamed of yourself!"

Scarborough wasn't finished. "And Victor, did you really plan to skim $4 million off the top? What about conflict of interest? What about your speech about integrity? You've become a two-faced crook! And to think, I trusted you! You were a guest in my house!" Scarborough pounded the table again and again. "Why? Why?"

~

Ryman gloated. He kept pouring it on. "Phil, the situation is embarrassing for all of us," he continued, trying to ingratiate himself. "Why don't I come over to Whitlaw & Company and try to explain the whole thing to the partners? I'm sure there's a solution."

"Franklyn, please! What do you take me for, a fool? I've got everything. Everything! Including a sworn statement about your Norwest shenanigans from Otis Weinstein. Astrid, before she mysteriously disappeared, was kind enough to give me a copy of her diary. It's all there. The illegal meetings, the fake research reports, the telephone calls. And what Astrid couldn't supply, Singleton generously gave me. After we kick Victor the hell out of here, I want your immediate resignation, or Whitlaw & Company will file a grievance with the SEC and sue you to the moon. I plan to make sure you never do another deal on The Street, ever again."

~

Minutes after he was physically escorted to the door, Victor called Louisa Dothan to dump as much of his stock position as possible to salvage something. Unfortunately for Victor, Louisa's husband, John, had already gotten to her. She dragged her feet, knowing full well a press release was about to be issued by about ITI's illegal business affairs.

"What the fuck did you stupid morons do?" she yelled. "Never in all my years..." was the last thing Victor heard as Louisa slammed the phone in his ear.

The stock plummeted to ten cents, and trading was officially halted.

Victor had nowhere to go but home. As he sat on the commuter train he wondered, *How did I stray so far? How do I explain all this to Sandra?* His greatest fear at that moment was that he would lose her and his family, leaving him totally and utterly alone.

~

By the time Victor arrived home, the gravity of the situation was suffocating. His stock was worthless, leaving him had no way of ever repaying the Billingham loan. His family could soon be homeless. His immediate cash flow, personal benefits, and any future severance had completely dissipated. He was about to be embroiled in a class-action suit with a bunch of angry, irrational investors led by Otis Weinstein, who himself had lost millions. Worst of all, he had to tell Sandra he had forged her signature, making her party to an illegal activity she knew nothing about.

~

"I don't know what the hell you're up to now," said a glaring Sandra, "but a registered letter arrived a few hours ago. For dramatic effect, the damn thing was hand-delivered." The envelope contained a thirty-day demand request from Billingham for four million dollars plus accrued interest of almost $100,000, and a real estate foreclosure penalty for non-payment.

Victor spent the next hour providing Sandra with all the painful details—the compromises, the shortcuts, the bribes. He cried. She cried. How could she have been so trusting?

"I can understand if you want out," said Victor.

Sandra was torn and confused. Yes, she still loved the man. But she was repulsed by Victor's business activities and embarrassed by his antics.

"I'm not sure," she replied. "I have to think about it." She then turned practical. "In the meantime, why don't you go do something productive? You've got your family entangled in such a financial mess; maybe you should go back to A&J and beg for your old job back."

~

"Hi, Elizabeth. This is Victor Martini. Long time, no talk."

"My goodness, so nice to hear your voice! Mr. Naye tells me you're the toast of Wall Street. Everybody at A&J is talking about that piece on your company in *Fortune* magazine."

Little did she know. "I had a few minutes and thought I'd call to say hello. Is Gordon available?"

"He's just finishing up a meeting with the investment bankers.

I'm sure he'll want to talk to you. Can you hold a minute?"

The next sixty seconds of phone silence felt like a lifetime. "My goodness," said Naye, "you must have been listening. I was just talking about you. Don't know if you heard; we've decided to take A&J public. Imagine that, after sixty years."

"Why would you do that now?"

"Why not? Our financial performance and client successes speak for themselves. I thought before I retired, I'd make sure that the senior management team is taken care of for the next decade or so. Going public will require a few changes, but it doesn't sound onerous. But who am I to tell you about going public? You've been there and done that. For gosh sakes, you know more about it than me! I don't pretend to be a student of The Street. But it sounds like you're having a good time."

Naye chuckled. "Victor, as I'm sure you sensed, I was skeptical when you told me about your decision to leave. It was like a favorite son leaving the family. But I was wrong. You did it and thrived. Congratulations! Now, I can't imagine you ever returning to the advertising business."

Victor swallowed.

"And how's Rhoda treating the old gang?"

Naye's tone changed. "Terrible, just terrible. I usually don't make mistakes like that. She's been gone six months, and we're *still* mending relationships with some of our most important clients."

58.

Easy Money

Victor was lost. His world was no more.

He decided to call Tom Kugle, the one person he was sure he could trust.

"Tom, as you know, I've got an impending financial disaster on my hands with all kinds of liability exposure. And Sandra decided to file for divorce. I'm trying to find a reasonable solution for Sandra and the kids; they deserve better. At one time, I was a terrific father and husband."

Kugle interrupted with a surprising admonition, "You sound like me with my wife, Joy."

"I beg your pardon?"

"The other night, she dropped a little bombshell. After sixteen years, she decided to leave; she said I was a terrific father and husband, but she was tired of playing second fiddle to my career."

"Jesus, I'm so sorry."

"It gets better. Joy told me she began feeling emotionally marginalized about ten years ago and had found another partner, a woman she met at a book club."

"Sandra and I thought of you as the perfect couple."

"Just goes to show you," said Kugle, "not every storybook marriage has a fairytale ending."

"Isn't that the truth," said Victor, feeling sorry for himself. "Maybe this is the wrong time to talk about my stupidity."

"Naah, trying to help you might help me, too."

~

"I've been looking at few ideas to make partial amends by leaving Sandra and the kids solvent. I figure you'd give me some advice on plausibility."

"Such as?"

"Suppose I sued Nachman for damages because he misrepresented the record deal? The way I look at it, if I hadn't bought his recommendation, I would have never invested $250,000 of my own money in the record deal."

"Oh, you mean the money you borrowed from the bank by making illegal personal representations?" smiled Kugle.

Victor started to protest.

"You would have to wait in line on that one."

"Why?"

"According to Marty, Nachman fathered a child with a black chick named Rita. I guess he was supposed to support her, but changed his mind. Somehow, she found out about him selling the company at an LA Lakers game. So, she went knocking on Sam's door in Beverly Hills. Sam wasn't home, but his wife, Erica, was. The bottom line? Rita is suing for palimony and has a good case. And Erica was so embarrassed; she is counter-suing Nachman for divorce and half of their estate. So, even if you could develop a plausible case—which I doubt— there might be nothing left after the ladies get their just due."

"That brings me to another idea," said Victor. "Do I have a shot at a defamation of character suit against Ryman?"

"On what possible basis?" asked Kugle.

"He lied about the bribe, which positioned me as a crook to Phil, which led to my dismissal, which in turn led to my lack of severance and a negative press release, which then made the stock worthless."

Tom smiled. "What judge in his right mind would believe your version of the truth? The fact is, you forged a signature on multi-million-dollar loan documents with a major commercial bank, and only to give yourself the chance to earn share of profits that rightfully belonged to the company."

~

Victor switched topics. "What about the statute of limitations on life insurance policies?"

Kugle did not like the question. "The statute of limitations concerning what? That question is pretty broad."

"Boilerplate clauses, like the non-payment of premiums and policy lapses," said Victor trying to be specific, yet still vague.

"How old are the policies?"

"About three years."

"I see," said Kugle, trying to craft a discouraging response. "Victor, an unusual number of litigations have taken place between companies and policy owners and their families, and that has forced the insurance companies to close or reframe certain boilerplate clauses. Why don't you stop by the office tomorrow and bring the policies, and we'll take a look."

~

The next morning Victor put three life insurance policies with a total face value of $15 million into plain manila envelope and headed to Kugle's office.

"Why don't we start at the beginning," said Tom. "What are you trying to achieve?"

"I'm trying to say I'm sorry by providing Sandra and the kids with a measure of financial independence."

Victor slid the manila envelope across the table.

Kugle glanced at the policies. "I know what you're asking. Can death benefits be withheld from the beneficiaries in the event of suicide? The answer is no, not if the policies are more than two years old."

"And the proceeds are tax-free to the beneficiaries?"

"Yes."

"And the proceeds can be placed in a creditor-proof trust?"

"Yes."

"And my policies meet all those guidelines?"

"Yes." Kugle paused. "Victor, I understand you've lost Sandra's trust and are hurting financially, but people have come back from worse."

"To what end?"

"Do you still love Sandra?" said Kugle.

"Perhaps more than ever, if that's possible," replied Victor.

"And the kids?"

"I couldn't be a prouder father."

"Then here's my advice," Kugle said. "Get on your hands and knees and beg Sandra's forgiveness. Promise you'll do anything to regain her trust, even if it takes years. Do the same thing with your kids."

Victor was filled with insecurities.

"One more thing. Put these policies back into your safe deposit box."

~

After the men shook hands and he left the office, a conflicted Victor decided to walk to the lake in Central Park.

He sat on a bench adjacent to the Loeb Boathouse on Seventy-Second Street, surrounded by New York skyscrapers. Smiling families rowed little wooden boats around the lake, just as they had for more than 150 years.

Victor reminisced about doing the same with Sandra, Mark, and Matt. Close by, a row boat docked, and a little boy sporting an Afro filled with brown curls got out. Holding a big green sailboat, he smiled and waved. Victor waved back. The boy walked over to Victor and handed him the boat, "This is for you." The boat had the name *Easy Money* painted on its bow. Victor looked up; the boy and his family were gone.

THE WORLD OF
M.G. Crisci

Stories that entertain. People you'll remember. Literature that matters.
mgcrisci.com

Dear Reader,

I wanted to thank you for taking the time to read this book, and I hope you enjoyed the experience. I know life is hectic, and you have many choices.

I was wondering if you might be kind enough to do me one more favor? Post a short review on Amazon.com and goodreads.com.

As you know, reader reviews are more important than ever before. They are how many readers discover and decide to read new books.

My library now includes 16 or so titles, and I've learned many readers make selections after going to those two sites or my website.

Again, thanks for any help you might be willing to provide.

Cordially,

M. G. Crisci

The M.G. Crisci Library

PROSPECTUS

60,000,000 Units

INTEGRATED BARTER INTERNATIONAL, INC.

Each Unit consists of one share of Common Stock ($.000166666 par value) and one warrant ("Warrant"). Each Warrant entitles the holder to purchase one share of Common Stock at $.20 per share until 210 days from the date of this Prospectus, except until 90 days from such date the Warrant is not exercisable and may not be detached or transferred separately from the Unit unless an earlier date is agreed to by the Company and Southeast Securities of Florida, Inc. (the "Underwriter") (see "DESCRIPTION OF SECURITIES.")

Prior to this offering, there has been no public market for the Units, Common Stock or Warrants of the Company and there can be no assurance that such a market will exist after the offering. The public offering price was determined by negotiations between the Underwriter and the Company and bears no relationship to the Company's assets, earnings, book value or other generally accepted criteria of value. See "RISK FACTORS," "Arbitrary Offering Price." The Underwriter has agreed to make available at the public offering price up to 10,000,000 Units for employees and friends of Management of the Company.

THE SECURITIES OFFERED HEREBY INVOLVE A HIGH DEGREE OF RISK AND SUBSTANTIAL IMMEDIATE DILUTION. SEE "RISK FACTORS" AND "DILUTION."

THESE SECURITIES HAVE NOT BEEN APPROVED OR DISAPPROVED BY THE SECURITIES AND EXCHANGE COMMISSION, NOR HAS THE COMMISSION PASSED UPON THE ACCURACY OR ADEQUACY OF THIS PROSPECTUS. ANY REPRESENTATION TO THE CONTRARY IS A CRIMINAL OFFENSE.

	Price to Public	Underwriting Discounts(1)	Proceeds to Company(2)(3)
Per Unit	$.10	$.01	$.09
Total Minimum(4)	$3,000,000	$300,000	$2,700,000
Total Maximum	$6,000,000	$600,000	$5,400,000

(1) Does not include additional compensation to the Underwriter in the form of (a) an unaccountable expense allowance up to $126,000 if all Units offered are sold ($63,000 if minimum Units are sold) and (b) five-year warrants to be sold to the Underwriter at the rate of one warrant per 10 Units sold up to a maximum of 6,000,000 warrants, at a price of $.00002 per warrant, to purchase Common Stock of the Company at a price of $.13 per share, subject to adjustment under applicable anti-dilution provisions. In addition, the Company has agreed to indemnify the Underwriter against certain liabilities, including liabilities under the Securities Act of 1933. (See "UNDERWRITING.")

(2) Before deducting estimated expenses of $312,000 payable by the Company (approximately $.005 per Unit) if all the Units are sold and estimated expenses of $249,000 payable by the Company (approximately $.008 per Unit) if the minimum Units are sold, each of which figures includes the unaccountable expense allowance described above.

(3) To the extent any of the Warrants included in the Units are exercised, as to which there can be no assurance, the Company will receive additional proceeds none of which are taken account of in any assumptions or calculations included in this Prospectus.

(4) This offering is being made on a "best efforts" basis. A minimum of 30,000,000 Units must be sold if any are to be sold. If 30,000,000 Units are not sold within 90 days from the date of this Prospectus (which period can be extended for an additional 30 days), all funds received will be refunded to subscribers in full, without interest, in accordance with an escrow agreement with J. Henry Schroder Bank & Trust Company, One State Street, New York, N. Y. 10015. If 30,000,000 Units are sold, the offering will continue, without any provision for escrow or refund, until all the Units offered hereby are sold, or until 150 days from the date of this Prospectus, whichever occurs first. See "UNDERWRITING."

The Units are being offered by the Underwriter when, as and if received and accepted by it, subject to prior sale, allotment and withdrawal, cancellation or modification of the offer without notice and subject further to approval of certain legal matters by counsel and to the right to reject any order, in whole or in part, and to certain further conditions.

SOUTHEAST SECURITIES OF FLORIDA, INC.

5 MARINE VIEW PLAZA, HOBOKEN, NEW JERSEY 07030
(201) 963-4470   (212) 233-2772   (800) 526-6057

The Date of this Prospectus is December 2,

References

Books

Little, Jeffrey B. *Understanding Wall Street*. McGraw Hill, 2006.

Bond, Richard. *The Pink Sheets: The Ultimate Guide to Making Money with Pink Sheets*. Red Rabbit Company, 2016.

Malkiel, Burton G. *A Random Walk Down Wall Street*. W.W. Norton & Company, Inc. 2015.

Shiller, Robert J. *Irrational Exuberance*. Princeton University Press, 2015.

Holtzclaw, Dan. *The Little Black Book of Microcap Investing: Beat the Market with NASDAQ/AMEX Microcap Stocks, OTCBB Penny Stocks, and Pink Sheet Stocks*. Greek Financial Services, 2006.

Leeds, Peter. *Penny Stocks for Dummies*. John Wiley & Sons, Inc, 2013.

Crisci, M.G. *The Salad Oil King. An American Tale of Greed Gone Mad*. Orca Publishing USA, 2016.

Sama, David E.Y. History of Greed: *Financial Greed from Tulip Mania to Bernie Madoff*. John Wiley & Sons, Inc. 2010.

Graham, Benjamin. *The Intelligent Investor*. Harper Collins, 2015.

King, John Lafayette. *Human Behavior and Wall Street*. Swallow Press, 1973.

Weatherall, James Owen. *The Physics of Wall Street: A Brief History of Predicting the Unpredictable.* Houghton Mifflin Harcourt, 2013.

Articles

Devcic, John. *The Over-The-Counter Market: An Introduction to Pink Sheets.* January 2018, https://www.investopedia.com/articles/fundamental- analysis/08/pink-sheets-ottcb.asp

Duff, Victoria. *How to Purchase Stock on the Pink Sheets Exchange.* January 2107.https://budgeting.thenest.com/purchase-stock-pink-sheets-exchange-23596.html

"What are the Pinks Sheets?" Motley Fool, 2016. https://www.fool.com/knowledge-center/what-are-the-pink-sheets.aspx

Baldwin, William. *O-T-C Trading for Experienced Investors,* December 2012, https://www.forbes.com/sites/baldwin/2012/12/10/o-t-c-trading-for-experienced-investors/#423b5e23254f

Is Microsoft Among the Best Penny Stocks in History? Penny Stocks Buying Guide, 2014, http://pennystocksbuyersguide.com/is-microsoft-among-the-best-penny-stocks-in-history/

Leeds, Peter. *7 New Penny Stock Scams.* The Balance, October 2016, https://www.thebalance.com/new-penny-stock-scams-that-look-different-4100358

National Public Radio. *Beyond and Bulls and Bears: A Quick Guide to the Wall Street Circus.* August 2011. https://www.scpr.org/news/2011/08/12/28208/beyond-bulls-and-bears-a-wall-street-bestiary